MURDER IN MONACO

THE MAGGIE NEWBERRY MYSTERIES
BOOK 23

SUSAN KIERNAN-LEWIS

SAN MARCO PRESS

Murder in Monaco. Book 23 of the Maggie Newberry Mysteries.

Copyright © 2023 by Susan Kiernan-Lewis

All rights reserved.

Books by Susan Kiernan-Lewis
The Maggie Newberry Mysteries
Murder in the South of France
Murder à la Carte
Murder in Provence
Murder in Paris
Murder in Aix
Murder in Nice
Murder in the Latin Quarter
Murder in the Abbey
Murder in the Bistro
Murder in Cannes
Murder in Grenoble
Murder in the Vineyard
Murder in Arles
Murder in Marseille
Murder in St-Rémy
Murder à la Mode
Murder in Avignon
Murder in the Lavender
Murder in Mont St-Michel
Murder in the Village
Murder in St-Tropez
Murder in Grasse
Murder in Monaco
Murder in Montmartre
A Provençal Christmas: A Short Story
A Thanksgiving in Provence
Laurent's Kitchen

The Claire Baskerville Mysteries
Déjà Dead
Death by Cliché

Dying to be French
Ménage à Murder
Killing it in Paris
Murder Flambé
Deadly Faux Pas
Toujours Dead
Murder in the Christmas Market
Deadly Adieu
Murdering Madeleine
Murder Carte Blanche
Death à la Drumstick

The Savannah Time Travel Mysteries
Killing Time in Georgia
Scarlett Must Die

~

The Stranded in Provence Mysteries
Parlez-Vous Murder?
Crime and Croissants
Accent on Murder
A Bad Éclair Day
Croak, Monsieur!
Death du Jour
Murder Très Gauche
Wined and Died
Murder, Voila!
A French Country Christmas

The Irish End Games
Free Falling
Going Gone
Heading Home

Blind Sided
Rising Tides
Cold Comfort
Never Never
Wit's End
Dead On
White Out
Black Out
End Game

The Mia Kazmaroff Mysteries
Reckless
Shameless
Breathless
Heartless
Clueless
Ruthless

Ella Out of Time
Swept Away
Carried Away
Stolen Away

The French Women's Diet

1

Maggie stood on the terrace facing the driveway where her husband was packing up the Peugeot. The sun was just coming up. She squinted into the horizon past where Laurent stood. Even as early as it was, the weather was still and balmy, unusual for this early in spring.

She stepped down the broad slate pavers of their front porch steadying the two travel tumblers in her hands and went to the passenger side of the car where her best friend Grace sat.

"Thanks, darling," Grace said, taking the coffees and setting one in the drink's caddy. "I assume Laurent made the coffee this morning?"

Maggie smiled. It was well known that Laurent liked things just so, and the kitchen was one of his main areas of expertise. Before she'd met Laurent, Maggie didn't know that a cup of coffee could be actually transcendent.

"Are you sure you've got everything?" Maggie asked.

"I do as long as Laurent brings his checkbook," Grace said.

She and Laurent were headed to a small village in Italy just over the border to purchase a vintage secretary for one of the bedrooms in *Dormir*, the bed and breakfast Grace ran.

"How about a couple of croissants for the road?" Maggie asked.

"Heaven's no," Grace said. "We're going to Italy, remember? My lunch alone will use up my calorie allotment for the rest of the month."

"You hardly need to worry about your figure," Maggie scoffed.

"Cheers, darling," Grace said. "Is that because I'm so painfully single? Because even at forty-four I still have hope, you know."

Maggie gave her friend an admonishing look. While it was true that Grace was recently recovering from a devastating breakup with her ex-husband, it was also true that no matter how old she was, Grace would always be breathtakingly stunning, probably into her eighties, and still be attracting men to her like flies to honey.

Maggie and Grace were radically different people in almost every way. Maggie was the down-to-earth, practical one. She paid little attention to her wardrobe, often wearing the same clothes multiple days running. She barely noticed her hair, trusting it to do as it pleased. After living twenty-five years in a foreign country, she'd learned not to concern herself unduly with what other people thought of her.

Grace on the other hand was always perfectly coifed and generally obsessed with appearances—hers and anybody else's —which included her clothes, furnishings, hair, and without doubt what people thought of her.

And yet the things that did bind the two of them together— their love for their children, their mutual respect for each other, and their very differences—connected them to each other closer than sisters.

"Are you sure this nightstand is worth all this trouble?" Maggie asked. "It's three hours each way."

"Don't be silly, darling," Grace said. "It's a Louis XVI secretary. Laurent's nearly as excited to see it as I am. It will transform *Fraise* cottage."

Dormir comprised three cottages and the main house. Grace had named each of the cottages after fruit— *Mirabelle, Prune, Fraise*—to better guide her aging French handyman Gabriel who tended to struggle with understanding Grace's French. Maggie suspected it was also to help Grace keep the properties straight herself. Up until Laurent had given her this chance to run the business, she'd never worked a day in her life.

Laurent had bought the house and property from Danielle Alexandre, a dear friend of theirs who lived at *Dormir* with Grace, in order to turn the land back into a viable vineyard and the house into a working bed and breakfast.

At the time, Grace was recently divorced and had desperately needed the work and a stable place to raise her then ten-year-old daughter Zouzou.

It had been a lifesaver for her and also for Maggie—a lone expat living on a vineyard in the South of France. Maggie had moved to France with Laurent after he inherited a vineyard at Domaine St-Buvard which he'd since turned into a highly successful living. In the meantime, they'd raised three children, all gone now from the nest.

Maggie glanced over at her husband who held their granddaughter Amélie in his arms and was speaking to her in a low voice. He was a tall man, broad in the chest. His hair and eyes were dark and, much like his personality—hard to read. He'd had a mysterious past before Maggie knew him, one that often seeped into their present in strange and unforeseen ways.

He had been up for hours this morning prepping for the trip while Maggie had been busy keeping an eye on Amélie who had lately been pushing the boundaries with her behavior

—more so now that her beloved *Opa* was going on a trip without her.

Laurent set Amélie down and she stomped over to the porch and sat, scowling at the adults in the driveway. He turned to Maggie as she came around the car to hug him goodbye, a hint of a smile shadowing his face. In spite of that, Maggie saw the concern in his eyes. She knew he hated leaving her when Amélie was misbehaving.

"We will be back tonight," he said. "I have had a word with her and she promises to be on her best behavior."

Maggie nodded and glanced in Amélie's direction. She could handle whatever Amélie dished out. It wouldn't be pleasant, but Maggie could manage.

"Spend the night if you have to," she said. "I hate thinking of you driving those narrow twisty mountain roads after dark."

"You worry too much," he said. "We will be home for dinner."

He opened his arms and Maggie stepped into them, breathing in the smell of his cologne, citrusy yet musky too. He held her close, the embrace lasting a moment longer than it should have.

Finally, Laurent stepped back, his gaze lingering on Maggie's upturned face before kissing her quickly and turning to slide into the driver's seat. He backed out of the long drive.

"Enjoy your free day!" Grace called to Maggie with a laugh.

Maggie smiled and waved back. As she watched them disappear around the stand of holly trees at the end of the drive, she realized there was something odd in their goodbye.

She couldn't put her finger on exactly what, but it felt somehow ominous. Her grandmother in Atlanta would've said it felt like someone had just walked on her grave.

2

The produce market in Aix of nearly fifty stalls, tables and kiosks erected in Place Richelme sold everything from produce, fresh fish, olives, lavender sachets and clothing, leather goods and wooden bowls plus knockoff designer sunglasses. Maggie stood facing a long table lined with row upon row of shiny, polished lemons stacked in pyramids in front of a stair-stepped display of dozens of bottles filled with citrus-infused marinades and oils.

The fragrance of lavender and *herbes des Provence*, especially on a warm spring day, was every bit as intoxicating as the sight of the colorful wares themselves. The morning sunlight seemed to tease the leaves of plane trees that shaded the market, making a dappled pathway as she and Amélie walked down the wide aisles.

As they approached a table full of baskets and tins crowded with *calissons*, the popular and ubiquitous iced cookie of ground almonds and preserved melons for which Aix was famous, Maggie fully expected Amélie to beg her to buy a bag. But the child was looking elsewhere, a petulant frown on her face.

"Why do we have to do this?" Amélie said, crossing her arms. "*Opa* won't even be home for lunch."

Amélie squinted up at Maggie. The child had light brown hair and blue eyes like her mother Elodie and perhaps her father, although Maggie and Laurent had no idea who that was. Her grandfather Laurent had dark brown eyes.

"No, but we still have to eat," Maggie said. "And *Opa* will be home for dinner. Don't you want to make a nice welcome-home meal for him?"

"Why didn't he take me with him? He always takes me."

Maggie paused at a stand selling baskets of ruby red strawberries as well as plums and sweet figs which made her think about baking a fruit pie for tonight. It would be a good project to keep Amélie engaged too. She approached the stand and smiled at the proprietor. After twenty-five years living in France, she knew not to reach for the fruit herself but rather to point to what she wanted.

"Why don't we make a berry tart for *Opa* tonight?" Maggie said to Amélie.

"*Opa* says the tarts in the *boulangerie* are always better," Amélie said.

"Well, technically I'd agree with him, but there's something about knowing someone made you a tart with their own hands that's nice, don't you think?"

Amélie made a face and put her hand on a fat peach on the display shelf. Maggie saw the ever watchful proprietor scowl.

"Don't touch, Amélie," Maggie said lightly. "You know the rules."

"No, I don't," Amélie said as she pushed the peach until it rolled off the table and hit the ground with a soft splat.

Maggie clenched her jaw. She had long experience of feeling on the back foot while living in a foreign country. At first it was because she'd struggled to learn the language. She broke the rules accidentally a hundred times over and had apologized for mistakes she didn't know she was making.

For Amélie to *deliberately* put Maggie in this position exasperated her. She counted to ten.

"*Je suis désolée, Madame,*" Maggie said to the proprietor who now stood glaring at them as Maggie fished out a euro and handed it to her and then clamped a hand on Amélie's shoulder and steered her away from the market.

As they walked out of the crowd of shoppers, they passed a couple of children that Maggie recognized from Amélie's school. Immediately, the little girls put their heads together to whisper, looking guardedly at Amélie as they did.

Maggie glanced at Amélie, but she seemed oblivious to the girls, which only heightened Maggie's curiosity.

"Is everything okay at school?" Maggie asked.

"Of course."

"Weren't those girls we just passed friends of yours?"

"Who?"

"Never mind."

Maggie led Amélie to a favorite café where they sat to watch the shoppers and pedestrians while Maggie sipped a coffee and Amélie a hot chocolate. She had wanted a *Coca*, but Maggie knew there would be many battles fought today and she hoped to at least delay the start of losing them.

The little girls' reaction to Amélie worried Maggie. There was no doubt they were whispering about Amélie. It hadn't been the first sign that things were not as they should be at school. She and Laurent had gotten a call from Amélie's teacher two weeks ago saying that Amélie had had to be reprimanded for aggressive behavior.

Maggie eyed the child now. It was true that Amélie was more rambunctious than Maggie and Laurent's daughter Mila —now twenty-one and attending college in the States—had been. But then Mila hadn't been virtually abandoned by her mother for most of her life and then lost her mother to violent death.

Maggie's phone rang and when she pulled it out of her purse, she saw by the screen that it was the mother of one of Amélie's playmates.

"Bonjour, Brigitte," she said.

"Maggie, we have a problem," Brigitte said tightly.

Maggie knew how bad things had to be for a French person to skip the first few seconds of polite preamble to any conversation. She glanced at Amélie and had a feeling she knew what was coming.

"Chelsea says Amélie has been bullying her during recess," Brigitte said, her voice low and angry.

Maggie could almost feel the tension radiating through the phone.

"I am so sorry about that, Brigitte," Maggie said, still watching Amélie as the child swung her legs, oblivious to the uproar she had caused.

"Can you be more specific about the behavior?" Maggie asked.

"Is slapping Chelsea and pushing her down specific enough for you?" Brigitte said furiously. "I don't know what is going on at home with Amélie, but if Chelsea doesn't get an apology *and* a change in behavior immediately, I will report the incident to the school."

"I am so sorry this—"

"We insist on an apology!" Brigitte said. "From Amélie! My Chelsea has been in tears all last night!"

"Of course," Maggie said in a strained voice.

"And she isn't the only one," Brigitte went on. "Simone Guedin and Giselle Rousseau are also furious. Vivienne and Chantal are both being bullied by Amélie. You will fix this, Maggie. Or you can homeschool her like they do in America."

Brigitte disconnected. Maggie took a deep breath and

willed herself not to overreact to the emotion she'd heard in Brigitte's voice.

"Amélie," she began cautiously, "that was Chelsea's mother. She says you were mean to Chelsea. Can you tell me what happened?"

Amélie's face darkened, her chin trembling as she fought back tears.

"Chelsea wasn't playing nice and I only told her to be nice or we won't be friends anymore!"

"You didn't push her down? Or slap her?"

"She tripped! I didn't do anything! Are you going to tell *Opa*?"

Maggie sighed and pushed a lock of hair out of Amélie's eyes.

"You know you can't *make* other people be nice to you, right? You have to show them how it's done."

Amélie looked at Maggie, her blue eyes bright with anger.

"But why? when they are so mean?"

Maggie sighed. They'd never had any of this kind of trouble with Mila or Jem. Both children had been social and happy, integrating easily into their schools. But of course they hadn't had the start in life that Amélie had. Even now, Maggie grimaced at the memory of when she'd first met Amélie who was living in squalor, ignored, and often hungry and abused.

Something like that didn't erase itself no matter how many hugs and ice cream sundaes Maggie and Laurent tried to make sure she got now.

3

Later that afternoon Amélie fell asleep in the backseat of Maggie's car on the way home to Domaine St-Buvard. The quiet lack of tension was a respite for Maggie but she was worried. If there were problems at school, did that mean something at home was causing them? Or were the school issues the reason for Amélie's bad behavior lately at home? Perhaps a child psychologist would be helpful? *L'Aide Sociale à l'enfance* had suggested it last year when Amélie had first come to live with them, but Laurent had been resistant to the idea, believing that forcing Amélie to talk about her unhappy experiences might actually underscore them to her.

But now Maggie realized they were fast coming to the point where they would need to consider outside help. If Amélie was bullying children at school, whatever Maggie and Laurent were doing with her was not enough. Loving her wasn't enough. They needed to help her socialize with children her own age and to better integrate into society.

As Maggie drove, she saw she was getting a call from Danielle at *Dormir*. Danielle lived there and helped Grace run the bed and breakfast as well as raise Grace's nine-year-old grandson Philippe.

"Hey, Danielle," Maggie said.

"Are you already on your way back from Aix?" Danielle asked. "I was hoping to ask you to stop for bread."

"No worries. I'll stop at the *boulangerie* in Le Pechou. Everything okay there?"

She heard the sound of a dog barking on Danielle's end.

"Yes, everything is fine," Danielle said. "We only have one couple staying at the moment and they are very accommodating."

"So, not Americans?"

Danielle laughed. "No, they are German and very sweet."

"What's Philippe up to?"

"I think he is building something in the garden. Is everything okay on your end?"

"Yep. We saw Laurent and Grace off this morning and picked up a few things in Aix for tonight's dinner."

"Are you sure you don't want help with that?"

Maggie was making dinner at *Dormir* for Laurent and Grace's homecoming. If Amélie behaved, they'd leave her there for the night and collect her in the morning. Amélie adored Philippe and he could usually cajole her into behaving.

"It's just a simple roast chicken," Maggie said. "You can do the salad if you would."

"Will you pick up a *tarte* for dessert?"

Maggie laughed. "I was thinking of making something, but Amélie reminded me that Laurent actually prefers store-bought."

Maggie glanced in the rear-view window to confirm that Amélie was asleep.

"Well, it depends on the baker," Danielle pointed out.

Danielle's darling granddaughter Zouzou was a master

patisserie chef in Paris. Of course Zouzou's fruit tarts would always be sublime.

"True," Maggie said.

"How is Mademoiselle Amélie behaving today?" Danielle asked.

Maggie sighed. Of course everyone was aware that Amélie was going through a rough patch. Danielle had helped raise all three of Maggie and Laurent's children and Grace's two also.

"Well, I got a call from a parent today complaining that she's been bullying kids at school," Maggie said.

Danielle tsk, tsked.

"I know it is hard, *chérie*," she said. "And I know you would never give up on the child."

"Of course not," Maggie said, mildly flustered that Danielle would even suggest it.

"I think it is okay to imagine walking away from our problems," Danielle said.

"Seriously?"

"Yes. As long as it stays a fantasy. And then you may forgive yourself for being human before you pick up the flag again to continue the fight."

∽

That afternoon, Amélie amused herself by playing with Philippe and his dog Kip at *Dormir*. Maggie didn't push the suggestion of a nap, although Amélie was usually much better behaved after she'd had one. But her quick nap in the car had put the kibosh on that. Plus, Maggie was busy, and trying to get Amélie down for a nap was nearly as time-consuming as whatever time it would've bought Maggie in peace.

As she sliced the potatoes for the scalloped potato dish she would serve tonight with the roast chicken, she thought of the fact that Laurent never used a mandolin for slicing because he liked the irregular look of hand-cut potatoes. She'd often heard him ask where one drew the line at time-saving kitchen devices.

"Why not just grab take out if it's so much trouble to make dinner?"

She smiled thinking of him and his many opinions about food. As long as she'd known him, he'd made it clear that good food was as essential as air. In many ways that was a typical Frenchman's point of view, but Laurent also believed good food could cure a broken heart and ease the sadness caused by three beloved children leaving home to try their wings out in the world, leaving their mama to wonder if they were safe and happy.

As Maggie arranged the sliced potatoes in an interlapping style in the casserole pan, she glanced at her phone on the kitchen counter to see two text messages that had shown up an hour ago from people she knew at the school asking her to call them. Since Maggie was pretty sure she now knew what the phone calls were about, she decided to give herself the rest of the afternoon off and not deal with it. She texted them both back saying she was out of town and would get back with them tomorrow.

Dealing with all this would be a good deal easier with Laurent by her side, she noted, rather than trying to tackle it by herself. Not only was his French better than hers, but everyone wanted to please Laurent. Whatever vitriol these women were rightfully feeling—and expressing as only an irate mother can—it would be tempered by Laurent's even and genial affect.

Maggie looked in the direction of the vineyard directly behind *Dormir*. She always found it restful, not to mention picturesque, to live by a vineyard. It wasn't just beautiful but also gave her an opportunity to experience the seasons as reflected by what was growing or not, and to be affected by the rain and sun—to have her day affected by it, like in times past.

After years of living here, Maggie had only just begun to love the farmer's way of living.

At this time of the year, the fields at Domaine St-Buvard were poised to enter that stage of growth that would precede Laurent's busiest time of the year. The vines were awakening and he was busy trimming, topping and debudding. And also planting the new vines for the coming year.

Maggie didn't fault Laurent for breaking away while he could, regardless of how much harder it made dealing with Amélie for her. The fact was, a farmer's window for travel or doing anything that didn't relate to his fields and the harvest was remarkably small.

This day trip with Grace was likely his last brief moment of freedom until after the harvest in August—five long months away.

4

The sound of the children's laughter and squeals came to Maggie through the open kitchen window where she stood in the kitchen of *Dormir* as she prepped the chicken. Philippe was laughing and chasing Kip, the family's large golden retriever, while Amélie was doing her best to keep up. It was a peaceful, almost idyllic scene.

The bones of *Dormir* were solid and substantial but Maggie definitely appreciated the renovations that Laurent had done to make it more comfortable . Like every old house in the region, *Dormir* had a history and a story. Some of those stories Maggie would never know—the French could be notoriously close-mouthed about things that an American would think nothing of revealing. At one time when she was still writing her expat newsletter Maggie had made a point to visit the surrounding areas and interview people for anything they knew about the homes they lived in—how old they were, who owned them before them, did anything interesting happen in them during the war? Surprisingly, very few people were interested in sharing what they knew.

What Maggie did know about *Dormir* was that it had once been a fine *mas* rising among a field of vineyards, the stately home for generations of *vignerons* that only a few in Le Pechou, the closest village, now remembered. After the last world war, the owner of the house never returned from the German prisoner of war camp where he'd spent the war. His wife and two children moved to Paris where she had family.

Eventually the son sold the house to Eduard Marceau who envisioned becoming a major winegrower in the area. Eduard was Danielle's first husband and not a man she often talked about.

When Eduard died just after being released from prison, Danielle sold the property to Laurent who added the land to his own holdings and renovated the property to create the three small cottages with updated plumbing, plus added a new kitchen in the main house and a small pool in the garden.

It was a second life for the old *mas*, and Maggie always enjoyed hearing the laughter and voices of all the many children who lived there over the years since Grace had taken it over.

Maggie stood now in the remodeled *Dormir* kitchen and placed the chicken in a metal roasting pan. She'd bought the chicken at the market this morning with Amélie. It was fresh, not frozen, and Maggie was surprised that the difference in taste was so noticeable. She'd once tried to fool Laurent with a frozen one and had been forced to respect the differences ever since.

She'd already slid a roasting pan of onions, carrots and fennel tossed with salt and thyme and olive oil into the oven. She seasoned the inside of the chicken and then popped the pan in the oven while keeping an ear out for Amélie and Philippe in the front yard. It didn't yet stay light out until nine in the evening, but the children would have a good hour still before she'd have them come in. She could see Philippe's dog

Kip racing around with Amélie. Maggie frowned. Amélie had a stick in her hand and Maggie didn't trust her not to go too far teasing the animal.

"What will you do for vegetables?" Danielle said as she entered the kitchen. "I have asparagus."

Maggie knew Amélie didn't care for asparagus, but she also knew that Laurent had a strong rule about picky eaters—a trait he seemed to think was a uniquely American one. There would be a battle if Maggie gave the green light to asparagus. She sighed. Sometimes life was a battle and that's just what you dealt with.

"Great," she said to Danielle. "Roasted or steamed?"

"Steamed with egg salad on top?" Danielle suggested, pulling the vegetable out of the refrigerator crisper.

Maggie felt hopeful that the egg salad might go a long way toward encouraging Amélie to eat the vegetable underneath. She didn't want her throwing a fit at dinner. She wanted dinner to be a pleasant and relaxing affair while they heard all about Grace and Laurent's day.

She frowned and glanced again at her phone. She hadn't heard from him since before lunch but had decided to hold off calling him.

Let the man have some air to breathe.

The sun was quickly dropping as Maggie brushed the outside of the chicken with butter and tied the legs together with kitchen string. Danielle pulled plates off the open shelves to set the table for dinner.

"I called Grace earlier to ask where the summer tablecloth was," she said. "But she didn't answer."

Maggie glanced at the time on her phone. It was nearly seven o'clock. Honestly, she'd expected them back before now.

"She probably figures she's going to see you in a few minutes," Maggie said. "Or maybe she's napping in the car."

"Dammit!" Philippe shouted.

Maggie turned to look out the window to see both children and the dog standing perfectly still on the driveway. Suddenly Philippe turned on his heel and walked into the house with Kip by his side.

"Uh oh," Danielle said.

Maggie dried her hands and intercepted Philippe as he came into the kitchen—with a quickly forming bruise under one eye.

"What happened, sweetie?" she asked.

But Philippe walked past her toward the living room where he sat with his arms crossed, a look of fury on his face.

"I'm not playing with Amélie anymore," he said. "She's too rough. And she hit Kip!"

Maggie was afraid of that. She sat down next to Philippe and put an arm around his shoulders.

"I'm sorry," she said softly. "Maybe we can talk to her and figure out a way for everyone to have fun without anyone getting hurt?"

"No, I'm done," he said, standing up. "I'm in my bedroom until dinner. Kip!"

Maggie couldn't blame him. She watched as he and his dog bounded upstairs. She could hear Amélie in the kitchen now talking with Danielle. There was a distinct whine in Amélie's voice and Maggie guessed she was asking for something that would spoil her appetite. Danielle was an indulgent grandmother to all the children. But she was French first and there would be no *goûter* this close to dinner.

With resignation for the battle sure to come, Maggie got up from the couch and went into the kitchen. For months now she had looked for a gentle, age-appropriate way to teach Amélie how to play without aggression. She'd earlier suggested a game of tag instead of roughhousing, reminding Philippe that he shouldn't hit back when Amélie got too physical.

She'd seen the indignation in his face and realized that he didn't need to be reminded not to play too rough. Maggie had lived with Amélie so long, she'd forgotten that not every child dealt with their frustrations with their fists.

5

Two hours later the roast chicken was cold and congealed in its pan, the potatoes had hardened and the asparagus was cold and limp. It was dark outside. And they hadn't heard a word from Laurent and Grace.

Danielle stood at the kitchen window staring out into the inky darkness watching for Laurent's car headlights. Maggie dried the last dish from supper and put it away.

Amélie's naughty behavior with Philippe—and then again at dinner—had made the idea of her spending the night nonnegotiable. On top of that, the child was tired and cranky—her brief nap in the car not near enough to give her the will to mind her manners.

She sat now in front of an hour-long marathon of cartoons on the television set in the living room having eaten cereal for dinner after refusing to eat the chicken or any of the vegetables.

"When was the last time you talked to Grace?" Maggie asked.

"Before lunch," Danielle said, not turning her gaze from the darkened driveway. "She didn't answer."

The tension in the room was thickly palpable as Maggie reached for her phone again, dialing first Laurent and then Grace, only to be met yet again with the same robotic recording telling her that no one was available to take her call. A chill ran down her spine as she thought of the various possibilities of what might have happened. She had been trying for the past hour to keep her worries at bay, but her anxiety nonetheless ratcheted up with every minute that went by. She looked past Danielle to the drive out front. The darkness outside seemed to literally shroud the house with a cold dread.

The silence was broken only by the occasional sound of the television that Amélie was watching with Philippe in the living room, and the relentlessly loud ticking of Danielle's rustic Provence-style clock on the kitchen wall.

What could have happened? Where could they be? Why weren't they answering their phones?

Maggie knew there were plenty of dead zones up and down the Côte d'Azur, especially on the twisting hill roads between Nice and Monaco. There were few adults who didn't know about that horrible year when Princess Grace of Monaco plunged off one of those very same twisting roads into a deadly ravine.

It didn't happen often. But it did happen.

Images of Grace and Laurent laying amid twisted wreckage of steel and glass came to Maggie before she could tamp them down.

There has to be a logical explanation of why they're not answering!

Danielle turned from the window and wrung her hands.

"Why haven't they called?" she asked anxiously.

"I don't know."

"They're in trouble," Danielle said. "That's why."

Maggie glanced in the living room. It was nearly ten o'clock and she could see that Amélie was asleep on the couch.

"Do you have the number of the antiques dealer in Italy?" Danielle asked.

Maggie jumped up to get her purse. Why hadn't she thought of that? She rooted around in her bag before pulling out a scrap of paper with a phone number on it. Laurent was adorably anti-tech and had jotted down the number for her. She quickly called the number on the paper.

"*Allo?*" A grumpy voice answered on the other line.

"*Allo*, Signore Tassoni?" Maggie said breathlessly as Danielle came to stand next to her and listen. "This is Madame Dernier, Laurent's wife?"

"Ah, yes, Madame Dernier," the voice said, instantly friendly once he realized who she was. "How can I help you?"

"I was just wondering if...what time did my husband and Madame Van Sant leave your shop?"

"What time?"

"Yes, it's just that they're late getting home and I'm trying to understand why."

"Ach! They are not back yet? But they left here just after thirteen hundred hours."

Maggie's heart sank. She wasn't sure what she'd been hoping, but hearing that they'd left Italy at one in the afternoon was not encouraging. Yes, it was a long drive back to Domaine St-Buvard, but it was nowhere near nine hours long.

"Okay," she said, shaking her head at Danielle who turned to go stand by the kitchen window again. "Well, thank you so much."

"I am sure they stopped for dinner, no?" Signore Tassoni suggested hopefully.

"Probably," Maggie said, although she knew that was not likely. At least not without calling first. "Thanks again."

"No problem, Madame Dernier."

Maggie disconnected.

"Well," she said, with a sigh, "at least we know they made it to Italy okay."

She joined Danielle at the window and they both stared out into the night.

"I'm sure they're fine," Maggie said softly, almost to herself.

"I will be so mad with Grace when she comes home!" Danielle burst out. "For not calling to say they were delayed!"

"I know," Maggie said.

Suddenly Maggie's phone rang in her hand and her heart jumped with hope up into her throat. That hope quickly turned to a sickening dread when she read the identification on the phone screen: *The Monaco Police Department.*

Swallowing the lump in her throat and steeling herself, Maggie left the window and pressed the answer button.

"Madame Dernier?" A businesslike voice said into the line.

"Yes, this is Maggie Dernier," Maggie said, her voice faltering.

Danielle turned from the window, her face suddenly white with horror as she gaped at Maggie.

The policewoman spoke just a few brief lines before disconnecting. Maggie stood for a moment unmoving, holding the phone to her ear and then turned and reached for a kitchen chair before her legs collapsed beneath her.

"*Chérie!*" Danielle said, her voice shrill with fear. "Who was that?"

Maggie's throat was dry. She glanced at her hand, still holding the phone. Her fingers were trembling.

"That was the Monaco police department," Maggie said, feeling as if her voice didn't belong to her. It sounded far away and mechanical, as if someone else was speaking for her.

"*Mon Dieu!*" Danielle said and sat down hard on the chair next to Maggie's. "Tell me, *chérie*. Are they...are they...?"

Maggie shook her head as if to clear it. Then she took a long breath and faced Danielle.

"They found Laurent's car," she said.

6

Danielle's gasp was enough to make both children jump up and come in from the living room, their eyes wide with worry. *Mamère* didn't usually panic at nothing.

"It's fine, it's fine," Maggie told them. "*Mamère* left a duvet cover out on the line and it's going to rain tonight."

"Want me to go get it?" Philippe asked.

"No, I'll do it, *chérie*," Danielle said to him with a tremulous smile. "Has Kip been out for last call?"

"I'm just taking him now," Philippe said moving through the kitchen to the door that opened onto the garden.

"Bedtime in fifteen minutes," Maggie said to Amélie.

"No!" Amélie said. "I'm not tired!"

Maggie felt her anger well up in her and she sputtered to get the words out without scarring the child for life. Amélie must have discerned from Maggie's face that this was not the moment to push her.

"Ok, fine!" she said. "After one more cartoon!"

Then she turned and ran back to the living room. Danielle grabbed Maggie's arm.

"What are you saying?" Danielle asked, her face tense with the effort to keep her worst thoughts at bay.

"They said they found Laurent's car in a ravine six kilometers outside Monte Carlo," Maggie said.

"But...but where...?"

"They said there was no sign of driver or passengers," Maggie said, barely able to get the words out without bursting into tears.

"But there you are!" Danielle said hopefully. "That must mean they are okay."

Maggie looked at her, her eyes imploring her to explain.

"If they are not in the Monte Carlo morgue," Danielle said firmly, "or in an area hospital, then they must be alive and well. They must have walked away from the car for some mechanical reason."

Maggie nodded, trying to join Danielle in her hope that this was somehow good news. Philippe came back in with the dog and gave his *Mamère* a kiss.

"Dinner was great," he said.

"Aunt Maggie did it all," Danielle murmured, her fingers going nervously to the hem of her *tablier*.

"It was delicious, Aunt Maggie," Philippe said. "Can I have a strawberry tart to bring upstairs?"

"Remember to brush your teeth after you eat it," Danielle said automatically.

"I will," he said, pulling the little tart out of the bread keeper on the counter. He slipped it inside his shirt.

Maggie was relieved he bothered to hide it. If Amélie saw him with it, she'd have another battle on her hands and at this point Maggie would probably let the girl eat a pound of chocolate rather than argue with her.

Once he was gone, Maggie turned back to Danielle.

"But the car was found in a ravine," she said. "That doesn't sound like car trouble, Danielle. That sounds like a serious wrong turn."

"Laurent would never do such a thing," Danielle said. "He is too capable."

Maggie put her head in her hands.

"What am I going to do? They're not answering their phones and they are not in their car."

"The police had no suggestions as to what might have happened?"

"They didn't share it with me if they did," Maggie said.

Suddenly, Maggie snatched up her phone.

"Who are you calling?"

"The Aix police," Maggie said, finding the private number in her contacts.

"But Aix has no jurisdiction in Monaco," Danielle said, fretfully. "They're not even in the same country!"

"That doesn't matter," Maggie said. "Hello? Detective LaBelle? This is Maggie Dernier. Laurent's wife?"

"I know who you are, Madame Dernier," LaBelle said in a cold voice. "What do you want?"

Maggie didn't care that the woman was shooting ice shards through the phone. It only mattered that she was competent and according to Laurent incorruptible.

And she was in love with Laurent.

"I need your help," Maggie said. "Laurent left this morning for an antique buying trip to Italy on the other side of Monaco and the police have just called to tell me his car was found abandoned in a ravine."

There was silence on the line.

Maggie knew that while LaBelle didn't like her, she would do anything for Laurent—an alarmingly common effect Laurent had on most women he met.

The likelihood of the Monaco police being helpful to Maggie would increase significantly with a fellow police officer leading the charge. Even one from a neighboring country.

"I'll call you back," LaBelle said before disconnecting.

"Do you think she can help?" Danielle asked as she rubbed her hands together over and over.

"I do," Maggie said. "She'll at least be able to get us information."

Maggie sat back in the kitchen chair and stared at her phone although she knew Labelle couldn't possibly call her back so soon.

"Stay the night, *chérie*," Danielle said.

"I can't," Maggie said. "The dogs."

"They will be fine on their own for one night."

∼

An hour later, Maggie tucked Amélie into bed, humming a lullaby that had been passed down to her from her Southern mother and grandmother. Despite the warm spring night, Maggie made sure to cover the child with a heavy duvet, as if to protect her from the danger she now felt lurked outside.

Amélie was too sleepy to demand a story or to engage in any more questions about where her beloved *Opa* was and for that Maggie was glad. Though she tried to control her thoughts, Her mind raced with fears for Laurent and Grace, her imagination conjuring up countless scenarios of where they might be. Were they being held somewhere against their will? Were they hurt and in need of help?

As Amélie snuggled deeper under the covers, Maggie brushed a curl from her face. It was true that Amélie had been acting out even before her beloved *Opa's* departure this morning, and with Maggie leaving in the morning to go look for him, things would only get worse. Maggie also knew it was likely beyond Danielle's ability to control the child.

But even with Amélie's outbursts of temper, Maggie couldn't help but feel a deep empathy for the little girl. She kissed the girl's forehead then tiptoed out of the room to head to her own room where she shrugged out of her clothes and slipped under the covers, the stress and anxiety of the day suddenly weighing heavily on her, filling her with exhaustion.

Tomorrow she would go to Monaco. Amélie would not be pleased at being left behind once more, but she had to go—and trust that Danielle could handle the unhappy child for at least one day. There was nothing else for it.

She closed her eyes and willed herself to sleep. Tomorrow was going to be a long day. Maybe the longest day of her life. But by the end of it she would have answers.

7

It wasn't yet light out when Maggie dressed for her trip. The sky outside her bedroom window was overcast and gray, with dark clouds hanging low in the sky promising a depressing day's drive. Maggie made sure her phone was fully charged, and she had a wallet full of credit cards. She would stop at Le Pechou to hit the ATM and pick up a thousand euros in cash. She had no idea what she was walking into or what she would find in Monaco, but in her experience, cash helped regardless of the problem.

She made her way downstairs to the kitchen and paused at Zouzou's bedroom where Amélie slept. She hated not talking to the child before she awakened—Amélie had had enough abandonment issues—but Maggie expected a long day to be able to talk to people in Monaco and Italy.

Danielle was making coffee. When Maggie stepped into the kitchen. Maggie could also detect the scent of something baking.

"You will call as soon as you know anything?" Danielle asked. She looked to Maggie as if she hadn't slept a wink.

"You know I will," Maggie said.

"Meanwhile you are not to worry about anything here. I will bring the children to Domaine St-Buvard and collect the dogs."

"You'll have your hands full. Amelia is a real pill these days."

"I know, *chérie*. Don't worry about us. Just find them."

Maggie took the thermos of coffee from Danielle and a small sack of just baked croissants stuffed with ham and cheese. She gave Danielle a quick hug and hurried out into the cool dawn.

By the time Maggie pulled out onto the A8, after a brief stop in Le Pechou for the cash, she set the odometer to zero for the trip. The MapQuest app on her phone indicated it would take two and a half hours to drive to the antiques dealer in Ventimiglia.

Amazingly, Maggie had never been to Italy before today, and was both excited at the prospect of finding Laurent and Grace and apprehensive about the journey ahead. As she drove on the A8 which would take her all the way to Italy, she kept a steady pace and focused on the winding roads that lay ahead.

She knew she needed to try to imagine Laurent and Grace's most likely movements and not the dire scenes that came spontaneously to mind of them crumpled at the bottom of cliffs or being held in dank medieval basements by torturing psychopaths.

Those thoughts didn't help.

Almost as soon as she was on the highway, her phone rang. She recognized Detective LaBelle's number.

"Hey," Maggie answered. "What did you find out?"

Detective LaBelle didn't seem at all perturbed by Maggie's lack of conversational civilities. Not all French were alike, Maggie noted. Some of them were just like Americans and wanted to get to the point. Then again, some Americans liked to take their time in a conversation.

"No footprints were found around the car in the ravine," Labelle said.

"Okay, that means they got out before it went into the ravine, right?" Maggie said.

"That is the assumption."

"Was there any blood or DNA in the car?"

"None."

"What about at the top of the ravine?"

"Hard to say. It's been raining on and off since yesterday."

"But it hadn't rained yesterday. Did they not check?"

"It appears not."

"Great. Police incompetence. Good to know. Anything else?"

"It seems the Monaco police believe there may be nothing sinister involved."

Maggie furrowed her brow in confusion as she drove.

"Explain please," she said. "Their car is found in a ditch, and they aren't answering their phones but there's nothing sinister happening?"

"The police are suggesting that they faked their disappearance in order to run off together."

Maggie tightened her hands on the steering wheel until her knuckles turned white.

"So they're closing the case?" she asked.

"Not officially, but yes. It seems this sort of thing has happened before."

"And the missing pair was found drinking Mai-Tai's in the Turks and Caicos?"

"I'm sure once they close the case, the police do not investigate further."

"Sounds corrupt to me."

"Everything sounds corrupt to you."

Maggie remembered butting heads with the detective a few years back. The woman was hot-tempered but usually—at least in the end—fair and practical.

"Don't take this personally, Margaux. Does their behavior sound proper to you?"

"No," Margaux admitted. "Laurent would never run off with that woman."

Maggie didn't have the emotional energy to defend Grace or to comment on how it was that Margaux felt qualified to say what Laurent would or wouldn't do. It wouldn't help to get bogged down in petty attacks. They needed to work together.

"Give me the coordinates of where the car was found," Maggie said.

"What for?" Margaux said with exasperation. "It will have been towed by now."

"I want to see the ravine for myself. I want to see if there's anything else that Monaco's Finest missed."

Margaux sighed. "I'll send you the coordinates."

After that, Maggie worked hard to keep her mind from going to a dark place. She focused on the fact that she was retracing their steps to Italy right now and that once she left Ventimiglia, she'd be that much closer to being able to envision what had happened.

Why the car ended up in the ravine.

And why Laurent and Grace had simply disappeared without a trace.

8

By the time Maggie pulled into the dirt lot of the Italian antique dealer, it was lightly raining with sparks of sunlight flickering through the clouds overhead. In spite of the rain, the drive had been an easy one and she was now virtually humming with hope and expectation as she pulled up to the antique shop on the side of the road. She didn't know what Signore Tassoni might tell her, but she did know he was possibly the last person to see Laurent and Grace before they disappeared.

She parked in the unpaved parking lot in front of his roadside shop and got out, stretching the stiffness out of her back. It hadn't been a particularly long drive—not even as far as Atlanta to Savannah which Maggie had driven many times before moving to France. She looked around. It was amazing to think that two and a half hours from her home in St-Buvard she was now in a different country.

She walked to the front of the shop and gazed through the display window at the array of antiquities, most fragile and steeped in history. She turned to gaze down the highway. Suddenly, a voice behind her startled her from her thoughts.

"*Buon giorno*, Signora."

Maggie turned to find Signore Tassoni, the elderly proprietor whom she'd spoken to last night, standing in his doorway. He looked at her with concern.

"Are you OK?" he asked, as they shook hands.

"Honestly, I've been better," Maggie said.

The old man motioned for her to come inside. She stepped into the shop and was instantly bombarded by the smell of old bindery and older relics, some of which looked like they had been displayed in the same spot for decades, the dust on them thick and undisturbed.

"How can I help, Signora?" Signore Tassoni asked as he pulled out a chair for her.

Maggie seated herself and glanced around at the myriad of heirlooms and ancient *objet d'arts* everywhere.

"You said that Laurent and Grace left at about one o'clock yesterday."

"Yes, that is so."

"And they found the antique secretary they were looking for?"

"Oh, yes! Monsieur Dernier was quite pleased with it, I believe."

For some reason, Maggie found herself making a note to ask the Monaco police about whether they'd found the secretary in the car. Not that it mattered. Regardless of the time and expense that Laurent and Grace had gone to in order to procure it, it wasn't a particularly valuable piece of furniture.

"Were they here long?"

"Perhaps thirty minutes?"

"So they left around lunch time," Maggie prompted.

He nodded enthusiastically.

"*Si, si*! I recommended a place to them not far from here. The freshest rigatoni and seafood in Italy."

"Close by?"

"Si, Signora." He reached for a scrap of paper and jotted down an address.

Maggie wasn't sure if Laurent and Grace had stopped off for lunch before coming home but it was worth a visit. In any case, it was one more piece to the puzzle that she hadn't had before.

"I am sorry not to help you more, Signora," Signore Tassoni said sadly. "I hope this becomes just a misunderstanding somehow."

"I know," Maggie said, shaking hands with him again as she stood up. "Me, too."

As she stepped outside, Maggie glanced around the parking yard, taking in the view that Grace and Laurent must have seen too. She examined the tire marks in the lot but, as Margaux had said, it had rained recently and the only ones visible were Maggie's.

The restaurant address Signore Tassoni had written down for her was less than a mile away on the same highway. Maggie drove there and parked in the unpaved lot out front. There were no other cars in the lot.

The building itself was a plain, one-story structure with a cracked front walkway and a broken screen door. It was painted an off-white shade of paint, which was chipping, and featured a set of low windows whose panes clouded with dust. A sign above the door read "*Chez Nous*" and showed a hand-painted mural depicting a sunset over a mountain range.

The sidewalk in front of the restaurant was worn and cracked and contrasted with what must have once been a vibrant blue paint on the restaurant front door but which had now faded to pale blue with age.

The sign in one of the lower windows read: *Fermé pour la saison.*

Closed for the season.

Maggie thought that odd. It was late spring. She would've thought the season for enjoying the Riviera had just started.

This place was only seventy-five kilometers from Cannes and all its spring and summer festivals. It seemed logical to her that *now* would be just about the last time any restaurant would be closed.

She peered through one of the cloudy windows. From the looks of the interior, the place had been closed for a while. Every surface was covered in a thin layer of dust, thick enough to show visible footprints. Tables and chairs were stacked against the wall. She wondered how long it had been since old Signore Tassoni had eaten here.

In any event, it was a dead end. She turned and climbed back into her car and pointed it east toward the coordinates that Margaux had sent her for where Laurent's car had been found.

She felt a sliver of discouragement. How many more blind alleys and dead ends would there be before she found a lead that would direct her to where they had been? As she drove, she told herself to keep in mind that at least it appeared that everything had been fine when Laurent and Grace left the antique dealer's place.

It was only afterwards that something had gone badly wrong.

9

Maggie stood at the side of the road and stared into the ravine. She saw the deep grooves carved into the side of the hill where the car had been dragged out by the police. She glanced around and tried to imagine Laurent and Grace here.

Did they watch the car go into the ravine? Why did it fall? Where were they when it fell?

She turned and walked across the top of the ravine, making a slow and thorough search, looking for broken branches or debris, a dropped lipstick tube—anything that might tell her what had happened.

She stared again down into the ravine. No way this happened while Laurent was conscious, she thought. Is that what happened? Had they been assaulted by people? That had to be it. There could be no other explanation. Why else would the car fall into a ravine? It had to have been pushed. Laurent wouldn't have allowed that willingly.

Maggie looked around helplessly at her surroundings and then up at the hills that loomed around her. She could see the roads there and the spacing of the trees that lined it. A light blinked intermittently from a house in the hills. Was there someone up there who might have seen something? Were they watching her now?

She continued to scan the hills and trees for any other sign of habitation. From what she could see on Google Maps, there were very few residences around here. Most people lived close to the coast if they could afford it or, if they couldn't, inland and far away from this coastal road.

Maggie walked back to her car where she kept a pair of rubber gardening boots. She sat in the driver's seat and pulled them on. The ravine was steep, but not so severe she couldn't make her way to the bottom and—by pulling on roots and saplings—manage to get herself back up to the top.

She was about to tuck her cellphone into her jacket pocket when she noticed she'd gotten a call from Danielle. She called her back.

"You are all right, *chérie*?" Danielle asked breathlessly.

Maggie winced when she heard the desperate hope in Danielle's voice. She knew that it was one thing to be running around talking to people and climbing ravines. It was a whole different thing to be sitting by the phone waiting for news—as Maggie knew well enough from past experience.

"I'm fine," Maggie said. "I met with Signore Tassoni and he gave me a lead which I followed up on."

"Yes?" Danielle said excitedly.

"It didn't pan out," Maggie said, "but now I'm at the ravine where they found the car and I'm having a look around."

"Is it raining?"

"Not really," Maggie said, glancing up at the gray skies. "Sprinkles, mostly. How is Amélie?"

"She is fine," Danielle said too quickly which told Maggie that Amélie was being very naughty. "I am handling it."

"I know you are, dear," Maggie said. "I'm honestly not sure whose job is harder, yours or mine."

"Just call when you can. We are here and all is well."

After that, Maggie turned her attention to the business of getting down the ravine without breaking a leg. She stood at the edge of the crevasse and gazed into its depths. The embankment was muddy, the foliage and debris so thick that it was impossible to make out the shape of the ground beneath it. Maggie chose a spot not near where the car had skidded, but it had a less sharp incline. She eased herself down the hill bit by bit, feeling the mud squish under her boots as she descended.

The ground seemed to become boggier as she went down. She fell twice and slid the last ten feet to the bottom. There she got to her feet and stepped into a small clearing. There, amidst the mud and leaves, was the deep impression of where the car had been. Any footprints had been obliterated by last night's rain.

Maggie moved carefully in a circle around the area of the depression trying to see anything out of the ordinary and looking specifically for a cellphone or Grace's handbag—anything that might confirm what she already suspected and which the police were refusing to consider—that whatever had happened here had been deliberately and evilly done.

Suddenly, something caught her eye across the clearing—a glint of metal amid the gloomy foliage. It had started to rain harder, and as she picked her way over to the bushes, Maggie had to squint to make out what it was she was seeing.

Excitement fluttered in her chest when the object became clearer, and she ran the last few yards. There in the mud and the dirt, barely discernible beneath the bushes, was something that should not be there.

She leaned over and picked it up, her thumb caressing the small leather medallion with the Peugeot crest on it.

Laurent's car keys.

10

The rain let loose full bore after that.

It took Maggie longer to get back up the ravine since there was no traction and the mud simply gathered beneath her boots, refusing to let her go. In the end, she resigned herself to crawling to the top, pulling on any plant or bush she could reach.

When she finally made it to the rim, she was tempted to lay there with the rain pouring down on her until she got her breath back, but she knew she didn't have time to lose.

Laurent and Grace didn't have time to lose.

She'd found his car keys where they should not have been. Whatever excuse or fantasy the police had for why Laurent's car was in a ravine on the side of the road between Monaco and Italy made no sense at all if his keys had been deliberately thrown away.

This was no accident. This was staged.

She needed to make them see that.

By the time she'd climbed back into her car for the drive to Monte Carlo, the shower had given away to a deluge as if the countryside was attempting to cleanse the crime from its surface. She'd taken the time to take her boots off only because they were so filled with water that she knew she wouldn't be able to drive with them. She ended up putting the heat on to try and stop her shivering as she drove.

The police station was six kilometers from the ravine. It was situated directly across the street from a Monte Carlo casino where a huge billboard informed the world that the Formula 1 Monaco Grand Prix was held there annually.

The police station itself was an ugly gray building—the color of ash after a fire that has burned itself out. It featured a set of graceless limestone arches and columns, wide in the front and narrow towards the back, as if to illustrate the strength of the police force.

Inside, the station was abuzz with activity. Patrol officers walked up and down the corridors, with a wide curving receptionist desk anchoring the center of the waiting room—looking more like a hotel concierge service than a police station, Maggie thought. Maybe that was appropriate, she reasoned. Monte Carlo was a very big tourist town. And very wealthy.

Two uniformed officers sat at the reception desk looking at a map spread out in front of them. Maggie went up to them and asked to speak to Detective Auguste Latour. Margaux had told her he was in charge of Laurent and Grace's missing persons case.

"He might be at lunch," one of the officers said, eyeing her critically up and down. Maggie knew she looked much the worse for wear after field-crawling up the side of a muddy ravine. She hadn't dressed up for the day nor put on makeup. She knew how she looked. But she was determined to hold her ground.

"It is imperative I see him," she said firmly. "I'll wait."

She turned and found a seat in one of the uncomfortable plastic chairs in the waiting room facing the reception desk. Around her were both slovenly tourists wearing baseball caps and Bermuda shorts as well as well-dressed people. None of them were covered in mud anyway.

Maggie had been careful to retrieve the car keys without touching them with her bare hands in case whoever had thrown them might have left their prints on them. She knew it was possible that Laurent had thrown them into the bushes himself—in order to keep someone else from using the car—but it was worth a shot to see if the Monte Carlo police could identify anyone else in order to shine a light on what had happened to Laurent and Grace.

Within moments of sitting down, Maggie found herself staring up at the imposing figure of Detective Auguste Latour—a stern and pompous man in his late forties wearing wore a crisp navy blue suit with a white shirt and a red and black paisley tie which he adjusted several times as he stood there.

"Madame Dernier?" he said, his lips twisted in a brief, insincere smile. "You will come with me."

Maggie hurried behind him as he led her past the front counter and down a long hall to a small, austere room. Maggie was instantly discouraged that Latour felt it necessary to talk to her in an interview room, but she did her best to chase away her misgivings. None of this was pleasant. There was no point in getting bogged down in the details of how awful it was.

She sat down at the metal table in the room and immediately presented the detective with the car keys that she'd wrapped in several layers of tissue she'd had in her car's glove box.

"What is this?" he asked as he sat down across from her but made no move to touch the keys.

"These are my husband's car keys. I found them a few yards from where the car was abandoned."

"Okay," he said, picking up the keys and placing them to one side of the table.

"I believe they might be helpful in piecing together the

events surrounding how my husband's car ended up in the ravine," Maggie said.

After that, every time Maggie asked a question, he gave a vague or roundabout answer, as to mollify her but making no real attempt to inform or reassure her. Or even pretend to take her seriously.

Maggie felt her patience slipping. She had a feeling the detective was intentionally stalling, but for reasons she couldn't imagine. One thing was certain—incredibly—he wasn't taking the case seriously.

"Detective Latour," Maggie said. "I need to know what you're doing about finding my husband and Madame Van Sant and please don't tell me they ran off together."

Latour gave Maggie an intensely patronizing look.

"I can imagine how difficult this must be for you, Madame Dernier," he said. "We all feel that we know our spouses and our dearest friends well only to be rudely disabused of that fairy tale. It is of course unsettling."

Maggie didn't have time to convince him that that wasn't the case. He probably heard that all the time.

"Can you at least tell me how long before the lab can process the prints on the car keys?" Maggie asked between gritted teeth. "I'm sure you can cross check any prints you find with whatever criminal data base you use."

"Our fingerprinting cases are backlogged, I'm afraid."

"How long?"

"Excuse me?"

"How long are they backlogged? Because we're dealing with a missing person's case which I assume takes priority over robberies."

Detective Latour fixed her with a cool, haughty look, his lips pursed in a thin line.

"Let me be clear, Madame Dernier. I am the detective in

charge of this case. In fact, I am the leading detective for the entire country, eh?"

Maggie bit her tongue to prevent herself from replying that the entire country had fewer than thirty-five thousand people.

"And so," he continued, "I will be the one who decides what information is necessary and what resources we will employ to solve it. Yes? May I suggest, for your own sake, that you go home and wait to hear from your husband? In cases like these, the wandering husband frequently reaches out before too long. Freedom often only looks good in fantasies, eh?"

Maggie clenched her fists tight, determined not to lose her temper.

"Or perhaps you might want to enjoy some of the many benefits that Monaco has to offer?" he continued, oblivious to Maggie's growing outrage. "We have world-class shopping, for example."

He gave Maggie a disparaging glance that took in her clothes and hair. Then he stood up, saying someone would be in shortly to escort her out, and left the room. Maggie was trembling with fury by the time, ten minutes later, another detective entered the room and looked around. He frowned and glanced at his clipboard and then at Maggie.

"Where is Detective Latour?" he asked.

When Maggie didn't respond, he spoke slowly as if he were speaking to a child. "Has he finished the interview?"

"You tell me," Maggie said.

The man huffed in aggravation.

"Are you or are you not the wife of the man who ran off with the blonde?"

It was all Maggie could do to grit her teeth and nod. The detective looked at his clip board again and then at Maggie.

"And Detective Latour didn't ask you about the body we found?"

11

Maggie had been about to stand up when she suddenly found her legs unable to support her. She sat down hard on the metal chair.

"What...what body?" she asked breathlessly, her skin prickling with fear.

She could hear her heart pounding in her ears as the sounds of the police station seemed to fade into the background.

"Madame?" the man said, frowning at her reaction. "You are not well?"

"A...body was found?" Maggie stuttered.

He looked at his clipboard.

"As of yet unidentified," he said. "It was located not far from where the car was found. Possibly it is the blackjack dealer who went missing last week."

"A woman?" Maggie asked, feeling some blood come back to her face.

"You do not look at all well," the man said. "Do you need assistance?"

"You're saying the body was found near the car that was abandoned in the ravine?"

Suddenly the man stiffened as if realizing he'd divulged too much.

"I'm afraid I cannot say more, Madame," he said, nodding abruptly and leaving the room.

Maggie followed him out into the hall and saw a policewoman walking toward her. The woman took a firm grip of Maggie's arm and began to bodily lead her down the hall toward the exit. As she walked, Maggie pulled her phone from her purse.

"No use of cellphones in the station," the woman said sternly.

Maggie waited until she'd been led outside the building and put a call in to Margaux Labelle. She moved down the steps to the sidewalk along rue Suffren Reymond. The sunlight seemed to pour onto Monte Carlo Avenue, sending waves of hot light onto the street. Maggie turned and saw a line of casinos, condos and hotels up and down the promenade in full view. It was a perfect sunny day in Monte Carlo with the whole world busy planning their activities for the beach, the casinos, or the yachts. For Maggie, it felt like the end of the world.

Her stomach hardened as her call to Margaux went to the detective's voicemail.

"Margaux, call me back," Maggie said. "The cops have discovered a woman's body near where Laurent's car was found. I need you to confirm it isn't Grace. Please call me back!"

She disconnected the call and stood on the sidewalk, shaken and sickened.

It can't be Grace.

If the blackjack dealer had been missing for a bit, the police would know straightaway that the body wasn't recent.

But what was it doing so near Laurent's car?

Did Laurent and Grace stumble onto something they shouldn't have seen?

Maggie felt frozen on the sidewalk, trying to gather her thoughts. The Monte Carlo police were no help. The ravine had told her virtually nothing, and now Margaux wasn't reachable. She walked down the sidewalk until she came to a bench and sat down. She opened up a map on her phone and located a nearby hotel that wasn't too expensive—unusual this close to the beach with all the casinos. She booked a room online and felt a little better. It wasn't much of a plan but it was a start.

Thirty minutes later, Maggie checked into Hotel Port Palace on Avenue J-F Kennedy. She washed her face and put a call in to Danielle.

"Any news, *chérie*?" Danielle asked breathlessly.

"Yes and no," Maggie said, not wanting to completely dash Danielle's hopes as her own had been. "I've just come from the police station where I dropped off Laurent's car keys which I found near where the car fell."

Danielle sucked in a breath. "Is...is that good news?"

Maggie had to admit it wasn't good news. Not even a little bit. Suddenly she heard a crash on Danielle's end.

"What was that?"

"Nothing," Danielle said.

"It sounded pretty loud for nothing. Can I speak to Amélie?"

"Not now, *chérie*," Danielle said. "I'm trying to get her to go down for a nap."

It sounded like the child was tearing the house apart.

"Okay," Maggie said. "Well, I'm just checking in. Speaking of which, I booked a room for tonight. I hate to stay longer but—"

"Do what you must do," Danielle said. "We are fine here. Do not worry about us."

"I'll find them, Danielle. I swear."

"I know you will."

After hanging up with Danielle, Maggie sat on the bed, vibrating with weariness and discouragement. Her eyes fell on her hand and the friendship ring Grace had given her years ago when they'd done a weekend trip to Nice. She rubbed it lightly. It was a small gold ring with a plain gemstone in the center. Elegant and classic, like Grace herself.

Tears sprang to Maggie's eyes as she thought of her friend. They had been through so much over the years. Divorce, betrayal, and heartbreak, but also as much joy and happiness as two friends could possibly share, arm in arm together.

Hang in there, Grace. You're tough. You can do this. I'm coming.

She stood up and wiped the tears from her eyes. She thought of the crash she'd heard on the phone with Danielle and knew that Amélie was giving Danielle a workout. Her heart squeezed at the thought of what Amélie must have felt when she woke up this morning and realized that Maggie had left too.

Amélie was so different from Mila, now twenty-one and attending the University of Florida in the States. Maggie felt a wave of guilt. As much as she loved Amélie, she was struggling with dealing with her.

Laurent on the other hand had a natural way with all children and always had. He was confident and firm, loving and intuitive with them. And totally natural. They sensed his strength and felt safe with him. He'd always been that way—the veritable Pied Piper of little ones. For someone so big and gruff, it always came as a surprise to Maggie when she saw them flock to him, which they always did. There was something in his affect that everyone— especially children and dogs—just instinctively knew to trust. The children flocked to him like he was their North Star.

Maggie called up an image of her husband in her mind—big and handsome and mysterious, a shock of brown hair usually in his eyes—the same eyes that never gave anything away, the ones that she could always lose herself in.

Dear God, what will I do if he's really gone?

The horror of that thought, not just for herself although that was devastating enough, but for the children, riffled through her, accompanied by a wave of nausea.

She stood up and shook off her morose thoughts.

Enough.

She straightened her shoulders as if to physically force the depressing thoughts from her brain.

I refuse to imagine the worst until I have to.

And in the meantime, she would just do whatever she could to find them and bring them home safely.

Bring them both home to the ones who loved and needed them.

12

Grace opened her eyes.

Every part of her ached. She moved without thought and instantly felt the throbbing pain in her hips and legs. Suddenly panicked, she strained to see her surroundings, but the thick gloom of the room prevented it from coming into focus. The air around her felt damp and thick. She was lying on her side. She shifted to take the weight off her hip.

But her legs wouldn't work.

A flutter of dread brought her fully awake. She realized with a shock that she was tied up.

She sat fully up, her fingers frantically exploring the plastic ropes. Her brain began to race.

Somewhere she heard the muffled weeping of a woman. Grace turned her head in the direction of the sound. Instantly a sharp ache ignited in her temple.

What has happened?

She wet her lips and took in a shaky breath to try to stay calm. How did she get here?

She remembered Italy. The funny old antique dealer. The car. Laurent was driving.

Laurent.

A flash of pain slammed into her memory—vague and wispy—of horrible, sickening sounds. Body thuds. One after the other.

Now it was the smell of gasoline and stale perfume that came rushing back to her. Panic felt as if it were building in her chest, growing and expanding until she couldn't breathe. She turned her head and vomited on the floor, bracing herself with her bound hands. Then she sagged back onto the thin mattress, the numbing cold stabbing into her bones as she lay shivering on the floor. Her mind recoiled in horror at the reality of where she was and what must have happened. The smell of the dank space and her own sick filled her nostrils.

Then another memory came flooding back to her, foul and vivid. She remembered the car not working. They'd pulled off the side of the road. Laurent got out to look under the hood. She swallowed hard at the thought of him.

And then. She squeezed her eyes shut tight, wanting to remember. Wanting desperately not to. She'd gotten out of the car too. And then the memory of the overwhelming fear that filled her when the strange car pulled up alongside them. She remembered the men emerging from the car. Her memory of it was silent, as if it came with no audio.

Like in horror movies.

They grabbed her, dragging her toward their car.

Laurent tried to fight them, but...

What had happened to Laurent?

Grace struggled to remember but all that came to her was the physical memory of being shoved into the car, trying to scream and feeling a rag clamped tightly over her mouth and nose. Tears streamed down her face as the memories came to her. And then there was a nauseating swirling in her brain like she was falling off a cliff or whirling away on a run-amok roller coaster. Until finally darkness.

She lay on the mattress and pulled uselessly on the plastic ties around her wrists before stopping in frustration. She couldn't break the plastic. Not even close. The darkness around her felt suffocating and oppressive.

What was beyond the darkness? Was she in a basement of a house? Was she alone? Where was the crying woman? Grace strained to hear her again when suddenly she heard a voice, low and caressing and soothing.

"*You must remember to breathe.*"

Grace held her breath, chilled by the voice, yet willing it to come again. Was she hearing it in her head? Was someone watching? Was it help?

"Hello?" she croaked. "Laurent?"

But then, like an ice pick to the heart, the elusive memory came to her, quick and unwanted. She remembered the brief helpless look between them and then he was gone. Dragged away into the bushes, limp and no longer moving.

It was the last thing Grace remembered before she lost consciousness. And a part of her wasn't even sure she'd truly seen it.

13

An hour after checking in to her hotel, Maggie sat at a coffee shop called Casino Café de Paris on Monte Carlo Avenue. From this perspective she could see down Place de Casino to the string of casinos, night clubs and tourist attractions that made this town so famous. A small sun-soaked European principality perched atop a rocky cliff overlooking the deep, sapphire waters of the Mediterranean Sea, Monaco itself was surrounded by endlessly stunning vistas of sea and cliff. And Monte Carlo was the jewel in its crown.

Renowned for its combination of superior French and Italian cuisine, exquisite wines, and extravagant designer shopping experiences—not to mention the glamorous casinos that dotted its coastline, Monte Carlo was a city made for the adventurous—whether that be car racing or paragliding from treacherous limestone cliffs—or risking a fortune at the roulette wheel.

Maggie signaled for the waiter to bring her the check. She'd been trying to get her bearings, hoping that a plan of action might present itself, but she seemed just as flummoxed as when she sat down thirty minutes ago.

It didn't make sense to her that Laurent and Grace would have stopped in Monte Carlo on their way home. But considering what the antique dealer said about how early they'd left him, it was remotely possible that they might have come here if they had a reason.

Laurent was a cook and while Monte Carlo was as good as anywhere on the Côte d'Azur for amazing food and food ingredients, Maggie couldn't imagine there was anything here to lure him. Grace, on the other hand, was an avid shopper. She might easily have discovered something on the Internet about fashion or a piece of furniture for *Dormir* that she might want to pursue.

Maggie could imagine Grace talking Laurent into coming to Monte Carlo for an hour or so on the way home? Yes, easily. But without their car? What sense did that make? And not to call her to say they'd be late getting home? No way.

She felt a flush of frustration as she went over and over these same thoughts yet still came up with no logical explanation for their disappearance. She checked her watch and saw it was already late afternoon. Everything she'd done today had ended in frustration. She looked at her phone. And Margaux still hadn't called her back.

It would be nice if she could at least confirm to me that the dead body isn't Grace!

Maggie knew that Margaux wasn't fond of Grace. How could she be? Grace was a willowy blonde, the very personification of beauty and style—a woman every man desired. And Margaux was a chunky, swarthy woman with mottled skin and bad hair.

Of course Margaux disdained Grace! But this wasn't about Grace. Or whoever it was that Margaux feared Laurent might prefer to be stranded on a deserted island with! This was about Maggie needing the security of knowing her best friend wasn't lying in a Monaco police morgue!

Agitated now, she paid her bill and stood up, her mind buzzing uncomfortably. She needed a plan of action! She needed steps. What was next? She was in Monte Carlo. Were Laurent and Grace here? Were they buried someplace out in the countryside?

She angrily admonished herself for the thought.

What good does it do to think like that?

She walked away from the café, heading back to her hotel for no other reason than it was something to do.

She ran over the facts again, hoping that thinking as she walked might jar something loose that sitting hadn't.

What about the car? Losing the car meant they must be on foot. Even if they *had* decided to call for a taxi or car service to take them into town—perhaps while they waited for the car to be repaired?—they would've called her! Maggie shook her head in frustration. The fact that they *never called* was the real sticking point. It had to mean they'd lost both their phones somehow.

Or had them taken from them.

In any case, since the police were going to be no help, Maggie's only hope was to go door to door, asking if anybody had seen them and looking for any leads or information from anyone who might have seen them. It was a long shot, but it was the only thing she could think to do. Both Laurent and Grace were physically distinctive. Laurent was six foot five and darkly handsome and Grace was a leggy blonde along the order of Princess Grace of Monaco, for whom she was named.

But where? I can't just walk down the street knocking on doors! Where's my best chance to find people who might have seen them?

By the time Maggie reached her hotel and was walking through the hotel lobby, she was already discouraged about her plan. She took the elevator to the second floor and dug out her room card as she stepped off the elevator and then stopped, frozen in the hallway.

A figure stood by her room door.

Maggie walked quickly toward it, her heart beating with expectancy the closer she got, and the clearer it became that it was Detective Margaux LaBelle herself standing there waiting for her.

14

Margaux settled onto the only chair in the hotel room. She crossed her legs and leaned back against the upholstered cushion—with more buttons than stuffing—and tried to relax. Maggie's hotel room was definitely more deluxe than Margaux would've chosen. She watched uneasily as Maggie put the toothbrush and tube of toothpaste she'd bought at the hotel gift shop in the bathroom. Or was it something else that was making her uncomfortable?

Was it Maggie? The woman was hardly what anyone would call formidable. Half the time you could read her thoughts before she spoke them. Margaux would never understand how a man like Laurent would prefer to be with someone like her—someone so predictable, *and an American!*—than anyone else he might have.

On the other hand, Maggie wasn't quite as stupid as Margaux remembered. She continued to observe her as she went about the room, adjusting the air conditioning, flipping through the hotel room service booklet. She was clearly restless. Agitated. Understandably.

While Margaux knew *why* Maggie had called her—who else would she call when she needed someone with brains and an intuitive grasp of clues and theories?—she found herself surprised and grateful that she had.

"The body they found was that of Juliette Dubois," Margaux said once Maggie finally sat down on the bed opposite her. "She was a blackjack dealer from the Casino de Monte-Carlo who went missing a week ago."

Maggie's face showed her relief that the body wasn't her friend Grace, but her expression quickly closed up as if ashamed of her reaction. After all, someone else's family was in mourning today.

"Do the cops see a pattern?" Maggie asked.

"A pattern?" Margaux wrinkled her nose in confusion.

"A pattern of people going missing!" Maggie said. "The police don't think a body showing up the same time two people go missing is strange?"

"Madame Dubois wasn't a tourist," Margaux said.

"What's that got to do with anything?"

"Monaco is dependent on its tourist business."

Maggie gave Margaux a gape of disbelief.

"So, let me understand this," Maggie said. "You're saying this blackjack dealer Juliette Somebody goes missing and then turns up dead and that's not a big deal?"

"Yes, of course it is," Margaux said, feeling herself becoming as frustrated as Maggie. "She was shot in the back of the head. That's murder, and murder will always negatively impact tourism."

"My God, you're cynical!"

Margaux laughed in surprise. "It's not me! It's the way they think in this town!"

"Well, Grace is an American national. So why doesn't that get them moving?"

Margaux was ready for the question. It was one she'd mulled over during the two-hour drive from Aix.

"Because she's lived in France for fifteen years. She's less American than she is someone attached to Laurent Dernier—a French national also unconnected to the casinos or tourism."

"Unbelievable," Maggie said, shaking her head. "Okay. Whatever. So, a dead body isn't a big deal to the Monaco police. Fine. Or a missing American or a Frenchman. But what about the fact that the body was found near Laurent's abandoned car? What do they make of that?"

"In what way?"

Maggie felt a headache forming. "They don't think it's related?"

"Do you?" Margaux asked. "What do you believe a body found near their car means?"

"I think it might mean that Laurent and Grace saw something they weren't supposed to see."

Margaux stared at her. She should have thought of this. Why hadn't she? Had she been too focused on the expression on Laurent's face when she rescued him? She needed to concentrate on the facts and not the fantasy running around in her head!

"You think they might have seen Juliette Dubois murdered?" Margaux said.

"It's possible, isn't it?"

Margaux frowned.

"Maybe," she said. "But it's pretty coincidental. One of the detectives on the case told me that Laurent's car was found to have a mechanical issue which they believe was the reason he pulled the car over. Are you suggesting he just happened to pull it over near the exact spot someone was being killed?"

Now it was Maggie's turn to frown. "You're right. That's pretty coincidental."

"And then there is the question of: how did the car end up in the ravine?"

"And why did they leave it in the first place?" Maggie added.

"They might have gone looking for help," Margaux suggested.

"But why not just call for a taxi?" Maggie said. "They were only four miles from Monaco."

"Why didn't they use their cellphones when the car failed?"

Maggie chewed on a nail. Margaux thought she seemed to be letting Margaux's comment about the cellphones sink in. For Margaux, the most damning point of the whole scenario was the fact that neither Laurent nor Grace had been reachable by phone after the car was found in the ravine.

Suddenly Maggie stood up. "I can't just sit here and do nothing."

"You know I cannot do anything here officially," Margaux reminded her.

"Just getting the information from the police is worth a lot. But now it's up to us."

"What do you have in mind?"

"I thought we might split up and canvass some of the casinos."

Margaux's eyebrows jumped in surprise.

"Seriously? You think Laurent decided to play the slots before he came home?"

"No," Maggie said, her face pinched with annoyance at Margaux's sarcasm. "But I know we're not going to find any leads by sitting in this hotel room."

Margaux felt a spasm of discomfort.

"Everyone will know I'm a cop as soon as I walk into a casino," she said.

"Dressed like that, sure," Maggie said, her eyes brightening at the same time Margaux felt her stomach plummeting in dread at what she was suggesting.

Maggie watched a range of emotions spill across Margaux's face. For someone who wore polyester slacks and a gun belt most days, she was hardly going to be thrilled with the idea of putting on heels and crinoline.

"I saw a couple of second-hand clothing shops on the streets around the hotel," Maggie said. "We can be dressed in an hour."

"I don't like it," Margaux said stubbornly, dragging a self-conscious hand through her short hair.

"Think of it as being undercover," Maggie said.

Margaux scowled at her.

"I'm not afraid of doing it," she said defensively. "But are we really that desperate?"

"One thing I know for sure," Maggie said, "is that shoe leather trumps eyewitness testimonies or half-ass leads every time. I have thought of every single possibility there is. I've traced their tracks to the ravine, I've found Laurent's keys which I'm now convinced someone threw in the bushes to prevent him and Grace from going anywhere in their car. You're right about the rain ruining any footprint or tire tracks. There was nothing there. And then when you add in the unlikely coincidence of all that happening within a few feet of the blackjack dealer's body being dumped, I mean, it's pretty clear that someone took them. Right?"

Maggie held her breath as she waited for Margaux to answer. She desperately wanted her to disagree with her.

"I guess so," Margaux said. "But Laurent is a big man. It would be hard to maneuver him into a car if he didn't want to go."

"He maneuvers just fine with a gun held to his head," Maggie said grimly. "Or one held to Grace's head."

Margaux stood up and glanced at her reflection in the

mirror. She put a hand to her hair as if thinking about trying to do something with it.

"I guess we have no other options," she said.

"No," Maggie said. "We're exactly as desperate as you think we are."

15

The walk to the Monte Carlo Bay Casino—the first on Maggie and Margaux's list of likely places to try to find people who might have seen Laurent or Grace—was a glittering pathway shaded by royal palms towering over an impressive procession of tourists dressed in gym clothes and flip flops and mingling with men in tuxedoes and women in full ball gowns glittering with sequins and semi-precious gems.

The shop near the hotel that Maggie had found was a hodge-podge of vintage and consignment clothing and had no lack of fancy dress clothing—complete with accompanying costume jewelry. Maggie considered renting a tiara but decided that blending in and calling attention to herself were two different goals and she needed the former more than the latter. She opted instead for a simple sheath dress edged in rhinestones with her hair twisted into a classic chignon. Her makeup was spare with the only real attention given to her lipstick since she knew her mouth was one of her best assets.

Detective Margaux LaBelle on the other hand was never going to fly under the radar on this undercover operation. She was a stocky woman with reddish skin and she chose a violet dress studded with rhinestones. Her hair was already short, which made her heavy-handed makeup appear garish like a lady of the evening. Maggie wondered if Margaux had ever worn makeup before today.

As they stepped into the interior of the casino, Maggie was struck by how cavernous it appeared, with bright almost harsh lighting reflecting off nearly every surface. Several colored spotlights pointed down from the ceiling and created mesmerizing patterns on the carpeting. A chandelier made out of crystal-colored beads swayed above the casino floor. The whole place felt to Maggie like a psychedelic bar or club in the eighties.

A waitress in a tight-fitting silver and black dress stood at the entrance, welcoming one and all into the casino with a friendly smile. Behind her, Maggie noticed two burly doormen whom she imagined served as bouncers or security. Glitz and glamour seemed to drip from every point of the room - from the crystal chandeliers to the velvet carpets and the shining surfaces of the tables and chairs.

The air was filled with conversation and laughter, punctuated by the ding of slot machines and the tinkling of ice cubes in glasses. From the minute they entered, Maggie felt the excitement in the room needling under her skin.

People are here to make money, to get rich, to make their dreams come true.

A bell sounded somewhere in the back of the room followed by cheers and exclamations.

"You ever been to a casino?" Margaux asked Maggie as she scanned the crowd.

"No. You?"

Margaux shook her head. From the entrance, they made their way through a thick maze of people, their eyes searching the crowd for any hint of Laurent or Grace. Maggie spotted a couple standing with drinks in hand surveying the crowd. She pulled her phone out of her purse and approached them.

"Excuse me," she said. "Do you speak English?"

The woman looked at her curiously, but the man smiled.

"A bit," he said.

Maggie showed them the photograph of Laurent on her phone.

"Have you seen this man?" she asked in French.

"He's handsome," the woman said. "But I've never seen him before."

"Nor me," the man said. "Sorry."

Maggie thanked them and turned away. There were at least two hundred people in the room and five more casinos down the street. She straightened her shoulders with a jolt of determination. She would hit every casino and question every person in Monte Carlo if she had to.

For the next hour, she and Margaux worked the room showing photographs of Laurent and Grace to any mildly curious gambler or attendant who would look up from their cards or slot machines. Maggie did multiple circuits around the huge room, sidling up to tables and slot machines, asking everyone she encountered—waiters and dealers too—if they had seen Laurent or Grace. No one had.

At one point in the evening, her feet aching in her ill-fitting new shoes she found a small table and sat for a moment, discouraged and frustrated. She looked around the casino. The bright lights of the room reflected off the polished marble floors. She wondered how many of these people were tourists and how many were professional gamblers. The ones dressed to the nines were in a whole different category that she couldn't decipher. Maybe just bored rich people on a Thursday night?

"You have made me curious, Madame," a silky voice said at Maggie's elbow.

She turned to see a handsome blond man in a tuxedo. He was smiling but his brows were drawn together as if she were an interesting puzzle he was trying to figure out. Maggie had noticed him earlier. He'd stood out because she could sense him watching her.

"I'm looking for someone," Maggie said.

"I think you have found him," he said smiling in a way she was sure was an attempt to charm her.

Maggie showed him her cellphone with a photo of Laurent. He frowned at the photo and then at her.

"He is your husband?"

"Have you seen him?"

"As a matter of fact, I have."

16

Maggie tried to quell the exuberant excitement bubbling up inside her at his words. Had he really seen him? It was true that Laurent was not like anyone else. It was rare enough to find a tall Frenchman, but he was foot five. His affect was unusual too. His dark brown eyes missed nothing. Plus, in a world of oversharing, he was a man of few words.

She changed the photo on her phone to one of Grace.

"How about her?"

The man took in an abrupt gasp of breath. Yes, Maggie thought, Grace was beautiful, but still, the reaction was unexpected.

"Yes, her too," he said.

"You've seen her?" Maggie asked, feeling a flutter of hope ripple through her body. She reminded herself that Grace's resemblance to Princess Grace of Monaco would have many people who'd studied the princess's image in fan magazines, china plates, souvenir flags and postcards ready to commit to having seen her—in spite of the fact that the woman died forty years ago.

Already Maggie had talked to two women who thought Grace looked familiar to them but hadn't seen her at the casino tonight. One woman thought she'd seen her buying groceries at the *Carrefour*.

"I saw her tonight," the man confirmed, nodding at Grace's picture. "I am sure of it."

"Here?" Maggie asked. "In this casino?"

Just then, a woman joined them. Maggie remembered seeing her with the man earlier. She was young with bleached blonde hair and too much makeup. But she was pretty in despite it. The woman gave Maggie the once-over, clearly telegraphing that she found Maggie's outfit lacking if not downright gauche.

"*Chérie*," she said to the man, "you promised we would go to the bar."

He ignored her and took Maggie's hand.

"Luc Legrand," he said as he kissed her hand. "At your service."

"My name is Maggie Dernier," Maggie said, retrieving her hand. "I am looking—"

"American, yes? You are a tourist in town?"

"No, I am looking for these two people," Maggie said patiently, holding up her phone. "My husband and a dear friend."

"Ah," Legrand said, clicking his teeth in disappointment. "That is not good, eh? Your husband and best friend are both missing?"

Maggie felt a flare of annoyance.

"When do you think you might have seen them, Monsieur Legrand?" Maggie asked. "And where? It is very important."

"Perhaps you will share a drink with us?" he asked. "This is my girlfriend, Joelle. It is possible she saw your husband as well. Yes, Joelle?"

Joelle looked at Legrand and then back at Maggie. Her face instantly softened.

"You are talking about the big man with the woman who looks like Princess Grace?" she said. "*Oui*. I saw them."

Maggie felt a surge of excitement. Her heart pounded in her chest. and she struggled between embracing hope and giving in to suspicion. She wanted to feel optimistic, but she couldn't shake the feeling that there was something not quite right here.

"Where? When? Here?" she asked.

"Yes, here," Joelle said. "Your husband is very handsome. He was at the poker table for a while. It's where I noticed him."

"Can you remember which way they went?" Maggie asked. She looked around the room. "They're not still here, are they?"

"No, Madame," Joelle said. "They left with two men. Two very ugly men."

That made no sense to Maggie. The idea that Laurent and Grace had been in the casino at all was hard enough to believe but who was it they were supposed to have left with?

"Can you describe them?" Maggie asked.

"They were dressed in expensive suits, carrying briefcases and speaking Italian," Joelle said. "And now, Luc, you have promised me champagne."

"Ah, yes, *désolé*," he said to Maggie. "I hope you find your runaway friends."

He turned and walked away but as Maggie watched him go, he turned to wink at her over his shoulder. Something about him was hard to trust. He acted as if everything was a game—even a despairing woman canvassing total strangers in a desperate bid to find her husband.

Maggie sat at her table and considered what the pair had told her. A part of her didn't believe them. Laurent playing cards instead of calling home? On the other hand, while Laurent had not gambled in many years, he had been quite a gambler at one time. In fact, it was the only weakness she knew in him and one that at one point had caused a problem in their marriage.

Still, the idea of Laurent at a poker table in Monte Carlo when he was supposed to be on his way home for dinner was a difficult one to believe.

But not impossible.

17

The main gaming floor of the casino at this point of the night was a nightmarish cacophony of light, color and sound to Maggie. The pings, dings and bells of the machines echoed in a symphony of discordant noise. She gazed listlessly at a huge banner over the entrance to a side room that displayed the giant red words "Machines à Sous" in a flowing font. *Slot machines.*

As she continued to sit at her table, she watched the steady stream of people entering the casino on the red carpet which ran from the entrance to the elevators, to the cashier's cage, the poker room, and the roulette tables.

The din of the slot machines was deafening—even from a full room away. The clanging bells and dinging soon turned into a background buzz until Maggie wondered how many vacations—long planned for and saved for—were being ruined tonight.

She noticed a man in leather slacks and jacket leaning against the side of a roulette table. He was tall and sweating fiercely in his outfit. Maggie watched him talking to two blondes—surely not even out of their teens—wearing elegant, short black dresses and impossibly high heels. Both were dark from the sun and Maggie wondered if they'd come to the casino from one of the many yachts moored in Port Hercules. The man said something that made one of them laugh out loud and slap his arm lightly.

For some reason, the gesture saddened Maggie and she turned away. Tonight was a bust. Had Laurent and Grace really been here today? Or was she just a bit of amusement for the pair who'd insisted they'd seen them? Meeting those two tonight had inexplicably made Maggie feel even more discouraged than before. She couldn't imagine how it could possibly benefit them to lie to her and she desperately wanted to believe them.

But her gut was holding out on her. Her gut said *it's a lie*. Maggie had rarely had her gut fail her. And unfortunately, she had to believe it wasn't going to fail her tonight.

As much as she wanted it to.

She scanned the crowd to find Margaux and spotted her at a small table with a watery drink in front of her. Maggie hurried over.

"Any luck?" Maggie asked as she reached Margaux's table.

"No. You?"

"I met two people who said they saw them."

"Where?"

"Here. In this casino."

Margaux frowned. "Is that likely?"

Maggie threw her hands up in frustration.

"It's the only lead we have. They said they saw them leave with two shifty looking Italians."

"That is unhelpful. Italy is only fifteen kilometers from here. And I would argue that all Italians are shifty looking."

Maggie felt a wave of frustration and defeat.

"I was thinking of going back to the ravine where Laurent's car was found," she said. "It seems obvious to me that he and

Grace must have been taken from there. I've got my car. How did you get to Monaco?"

"I cannot accompany you, if that's what you're suggesting. I need to get back to Aix tonight. I'm on duty first thing in the morning."

Maggie's face fell at Margaux's words. She was surprised to realize how much she'd been counting on the other woman going to the ravine with her.

"Look, don't go out there at night," Margaux said. "Wait until morning. You can't see anything in the dark anyway."

"I just feel so helpless. Tonight was a complete waste of time."

"I know. But going to the ravine at night is not smart."

"What else can I do?"

Margaux waved her hand at the casino.

"Things are just getting heated up here. More people are coming in. Why not continue to show the pictures around?"

"What sense does that make? If the people are just coming into the casino, they won't have seen them, will they?"

"I'm just saying don't go to the ravine. Not tonight."

"Fine, fine," Maggie said, feeling miserable and defeated.

"Look, I need to leave," Margaux said. "But I'll contact the Monte Carlo police on my drive back. If I hear anything new, I'll call you."

"Okay. Thanks."

Maggie watched Margaux make her way to the entrance, turning plenty of heads as she went, but Maggie couldn't help but note not in a good way.

∼

After Margaux left, Maggie couldn't bear the thought of going back to the hotel room. She checked her phone to see that Danielle hadn't called again and decided to take that as a good sign. She straightened her shoulders and resolved to do one more circuit of the room, noting that Legrand and his girlfriend were now nowhere to be seen. The activity in the casino seemed to have intensified, with more flashing lights, even louder music, and more people than before.

Maggie stopped at the roulette wheel and stood there, lost in thought, wondering if there was a single person in the casino to whom she had not shown her photographs. Then she heard someone call her name.

She turned to find a woman waving to her from across the room, a woman she vaguely recognized from somewhere. She was dressed in a skin-tight dress sparkling with sequins and daring cutouts. She wore spiky heels, and her lips were painted a bright red. Despite the outrageous attire, the woman's smile was warm, and surprisingly genuine.

She walked over to Maggie.

"Luc told me you were looking for your friends? The blonde? I saw her too. She was wearing a blue dress and pearl stud earrings."

Maggie was taken aback. How did this woman know about the earrings? Grace often wore pearl stud earrings—at least for everyday wear. While she knew Grace hadn't been wearing a dress when she left Domaine St-Buvard this morning, she did tend to favor blue, and it was easily believable—if she had decided to go to a casino—that she might have dressed for it.

Could it be that this woman really had seen her?

"When did you see her?" Maggie asked.

"It would have been hours ago. I do not think she is still here."

"Did you see her with a man? A big man?"

The woman frowned. "I'm afraid not, no. She was with another woman."

That made no sense at all. Grace was very social, so it was possible she'd made a friend. But why hadn't she come home like she was supposed to? And if she wasn't in any danger, why wasn't she answering her cellphone?

"You didn't see where she went?" Maggie asked helplessly.

The woman laughed.

"At first, I thought it was Princess Grace herself. I couldn't take my eyes off her. And neither could any man in the room. She left about ninety minutes ago with the other woman through the back door."

Maggie turned to look where the woman was pointing.

"Not through the main exit?" Maggie asked dubiously.

"It's not a back alley or anything," the woman said. "It's just another lane off Place du Casino. There are usually smaller games happening in places all along there."

"Okay, thanks," Maggie said. "You've been a big help."

Maggie turned and hurried toward the back exit of the casino, nodding to security as she went. Her hopes began to mount with every step she took.

Finally. A lead.

18

The woman had been right. The rear entrance did not lead to a back alley, but neither would Maggie have said it spilled out onto a well-travelled avenue either. Or a safe one.

The lane was dark, with little activity or light. The few streetlamps were dim and the cobblestones that lined the lane were covered in a thick layer of dirt and moss.

As soon as Maggie stepped out into the street, the night air felt heavy, like a weight pressing down on her. The casino backed up to the sea and the ever present density of the humidity seemed to add to Maggie's feeling of dread. Unsure of what exactly she was looking for, Maggie slowed her steps as she walked along the dark cobbled street.

She could hear the hum of Monte Carlo's nightlife around the corner on Avenue de Monte Carlo, but it seemed far away and almost dreamlike from this distance. As she continued down the lane, she felt the hairs on the back of her neck stand up as if an unseen presence were watching her. She quickened her pace, her eyes scanning every doorway and window she passed.

No, it wasn't a back alley, but neither was it some place Maggie could imagine anyone visiting if they didn't have to. The image of Grace in this lane—beautiful, always-polished Grace—was an image that just wouldn't gel.

Maggie slowed. Her heart pounding, a visceral message flashing into her brain.

This was wrong. Could the woman have been lying to her? She'd seemed so earnest, so *kind*.

Before she knew she was doing it, instinct seized Maggie by the throat. She slipped into the shadow of a nearby door. She stood there, trembling in the light sea breeze against her bare skin, her heart pounding in her ears.

Wait, her gut told her. *Just wait.*

There was something unidentifiable in the air. It fluttered about her, light and insubstantial. The longer Maggie stood there, the more the pounding in her heart softened. And the more the fluttering she'd heard before became soft words floating on the breeze.

"...told her she would be here."

"...didn't you bring her, yourself?" a woman's voice said sharply.

".....so obvious!. Bijoux knows what to say to her."

"Shut up, Luc! I know you want to sleep with her!"

Maggie recognized the woman's voice as Joelle's.

"Shut up!" Luc hissed.

"She's not coming, you fool! You blew it!"

"Will you be quiet?" Luc said angrily. "For once?"

Maggie pressed herself further back into the doorway. They might come looking for her, but then again, they probably wouldn't expect her to be lingering in a dark lane waiting and listening. What sane person would be?

Maggie felt a mix of emotions as the reality of what had happened sunk in. Shock, anger, and humiliation were all vying for her attention. Tears of simmering rage pooled in her eyes as she thought about how easily they had been able to deceive her.

Opportunists. Evil people taking advantage of someone else's misfortune. That's all they were.

She had been so desperate to find some shred of a lead to possibly tell her what had happened to Laurent and Grace that she'd nearly allowed herself to be attacked in the alley.

They'd seen her desperation and they'd used it against her. And she'd nearly fallen for it.

19

Maggie waited until she was sure Luc and Joelle had left. She felt a strong urge to confront them—especially that weasel Luc—but doing it in a darkened alley was not the place.

Her watch told her it was one in the morning. She felt a throb of exhaustion buffet her shoulders as she turned to make her way up the lane toward the bustling avenue of Avenue *Princesse* Grace.

As tired as she was, she still couldn't bear the thought of going back to the hotel with so little to show for her day. She decided instead to visit the Casino Le Café de Paris next door. If she saw Luc—or that horrible woman Bijou who'd lured her to the back lane behind the casino—she'd happily confront them both, although what good that would do, she had no idea.

But at least going to another casino made her feel like she was doing something, whereas going back to the hotel felt like giving up.

Inside the casino, there were even more people than at the Monte Carlo Bay Casino. She scanned the crowd for Luc or Joelle but didn't see them. She made her way to the bar and ordered a club soda. The bartender smiled at her and Maggie pulled out her cellphone.

"I wonder if you've seen this woman," Maggie asked, showing her the photo of Grace.

The woman was shaking her head before she even looked at the phone.

"I heard about you," the bartender said as she wiped down the bar in front of Maggie. "One of the other girls on the earlier shift said you were looking for your husband and his girlfriend down at the Monte Carlo Bay Casino. I would've told you to let the dirty rats go."

"Thanks," Maggie said, dejectedly, drinking down her soda. "Good advice."

"You know the people you should be talking to are the waitresses, right? They constantly make the rounds of all the tables."

Maggie looked around the room.

"Thanks," she said, paying for her drink before heading for the first waitress she saw. She showed her Grace's photo and then Laurent's. Next she stopped and spoke to two more waitresses before a young waitress with beautiful eyes caught her eye.

Young, probably just out of her teens, this young woman had long, dark curls cascading down her back. She wore a slinky, crimson dress that clung to her curves as she gracefully wove her way between the tables of the casino holding a tray of drinks.

She moved with an effortless grace, her presence hinting at a worldliness beyond her young years. And although her demeanor was professional, there was something tantalizingly mysterious about her—even to Maggie, even as weary and heartsick as she was.

Maggie approached her and put two euros on her tray, then

showed her the picture of Laurent. The girl wore a name tag on her red dress that read *Annabelle*. She shook her head.

"I am sorry, Madame," she said.

Maggie showed her Grace's photo and the girl instantly whitened.

"You've seen her?" Maggie asked, surprised at her reaction.

Annabelle looked around as if suddenly fearful that she was being watched.

"No, Madame," she said.

"I can tell you recognized her," Maggie said. "Please. She is my friend and the mother of two small children."

The lie seemed to work. Annabelle looked at the photo again. She licked her lips.

"I haven't seen her. I swear to you."

"But?"

Annabelle looked over her shoulder, her fear palpable in the air.

"I can't say more," she said. "I don't know anything."

Then she hurried away. Maggie stared after her. The girl was clearly terrified. All at once, it occurred to Maggie that she had been going about this all wrong. Instead of showing a photo of Grace, she should have been asking *Did you know the blackjack dealer found dead in the woods today*?

Maggie stayed another thirty minutes, but no one recognized Grace or Laurent's picture, or seemed to know who she was talking about when she asked about the blackjack dealer. Discouraged and heavy-hearted, Maggie found a table and ordered a French 75, hoping it might at least help her sleep later.

A young male waiter whom she'd questioned earlier dropped off her bill. When she picked up the bill a few moments later, she saw that someone had written on the bill in a feminine hand, *I think your friends are with Bruno.*

There was an address.

20

Adele stood in the center of the dimly lit room. She wore a simple Oscar de la Renta dress and matching jacket with pumps. Classic and just this short of dull. It was her power suit in more ways than one. When she wore it, she felt invincible, no matter who she was with or where she was.

She glanced around the room. Even here she felt empowered—in a dingy, filthy room with shredded curtains that smelled like a rat had died in the corner.

Her men stood in front of her, their hands behind their backs, their expressions largely respectful but definitely compliant. For what she paid them, she'd expect no less. Her green eyes were cold and calculating as she fixed them upon them. Even Adele could feel the underlying menace that reverberated throughout the room.

"I understand the police have recovered the car," she said.

"And the body? You told us not to hide it."

She turned to the man who had spoken and narrowed her eyes. Donato wore cheap linen trousers and a black tee shirt with a thick gold chain around his neck. His dark eyes darted from side to side, his posture coiled with tension. Adele always thought he seemed to be constantly scanning the surroundings for anyone who might disrupt his business or hers.

"I am not berating you, Donato," she said. "But because of today we will have to move a little quicker than we'd planned."

As she spoke, visions of the next stage of play flashed through her mind. She smiled in spite of herself.

"So, are we staying in Monaco?" Donato asked.

Before she could respond, the other man spoke up plaintively.

"Juliette was so pretty," he said forlornly. "That wasn't fair!"

Adele felt a flash of annoyance as she turned her gaze on him. Younger and better looking than his cousin Donato, Estefan had been nothing but trouble from the beginning. Donato had begged her to hire him. She'd agreed and had regretted it ever since.

"She would *still* be pretty if not for you," Adele snapped. "Because she knew more than she should have. And whose fault was that?" She gave him a searing look.

Estefan reddened. He had a closely shorn head which accentuated his full lips and beautiful eyes. He stared at his feet in a sulk.

Why are the pretty ones always so stupid?

"What about the woman we got today?" he asked petulantly.

Adele glared at him in exasperation.

"Absolutely not," she said.

"But Madame B!" He looked at her pleadingly. "She is a movie star! A princess."

"She is neither of those things," Adele said sharply. "You may not have her before *Le Jeu* is finished. If she survives after that, I don't care."

"May I keep her?"

"*Keep her?* You are an idiot, Estefan. You of all people should know what happens after *Le Jeu*."

"But what if she wins?" he asked, looking from Adele to Donato. "What if she survives?"

"The people who are paying us forty thousand euros in antes are not expecting her *to win*, Estefan. Do you understand?"

"Yes, Madame."

"You only have to remember what happened to René to know I will not abide mistakes." She glared at both of them before turning to focus on Donato.

"You, Donato, will see that all evidence of what happened today with the big man is erased."

"It is nearly done."

"And you know what to do next?"

Her voice was harsher than she'd intended. She realized that her frustration with these two idiots was taking its toll. She took in a breath and let it out slowly.

"I'm not blaming you for what happened today," she said, attempting to soften her voice. She needed them. At least for now.

"He shouldn't have tried to protect the woman!" Donato said and then looked at his hands.

Adele noticed that his fingernails were still dark with the man's dried blood underneath them. She looked away quickly. It had all gone sideways so fast. And after all her work! But she knew there had been a risk of that.

"I don't blame you," she said, although he'd spoiled the best part of her plan—one that had been in motion for months. "It was regrettable but unavoidable. I see that. But I need to make sure there will be no more mistakes. You understand?"

Both men nodded sullenly and she felt her stomach tighten in a flinch of premonition.

"I need you to do one more errand. Can you do that for me?"

"I can do it, Madame B," Estefan said eagerly.

Adele looked at him, glad to see he was trying to regain her good graces. Even so, he'd made too many mistakes lately. As soon as she recruited his replacement, he would be history. Truthfully, he'd signed his own death warrant with what happened today.

"Very well, Estefan," she said, smiling at him. "But no mistakes, you understand? I need you to get in and get out without anyone seeing you. Can you do that?"

He nodded vigorously. "Is she pretty?"

Adele felt herself flush with a building fury that she worked to contain.

"What about the one we got last week?" Donato asked quickly. Adele knew he was trying to distract her from his fool of a cousin.

They'd found a woman passed out drunk in front of her hotel a few days ago. Normally Adele wouldn't greenlight the taking of a tourist—their embassies tended to get involved to a troublesome degree—but this woman seemed to be traveling alone. A quick search of her purse had revealed she was British. That was always a plus. It was always worth the risk to get an English-speaking player. She would likely scream her entreaties as she played the game. And since so many of Adele's clients spoke English, it would add to the fun for them.

"Yes, get her ready to play, too," she said.

"But not the big man?" Estefan asked.

Adele turned to him, and she smiled sadly, once more revisiting her recent loss and struggling not to blame this idiot for it.

"Dearest Estefan," she said. "Is there a way that you know of to make a dead man play any game?"

21

It was past three in the morning by the time Maggie found the address that had been scrawled on the back of her bill at the casino. A quick check of her GPS told her she'd need to use her car to reach the address. After thirty minutes of navigating her way down a convoluted series of increasingly narrow streets she ended up on a stretch of road off Boulevard de Suisse.

She'd used Google Earth as soon as she got the address to see what buildings she might expect and was vaguely horrified to see that the area was a strip of abandoned warehouses on the outskirts of town.

Once she stopped and turned off her car, she could hear and smell the sea. Because of a partial moon the top of a cruise ship was just visible over the line of buildings in front of her.

She left her car on the street and switched her GPS to pedestrian mode and watched the trail on the screen draw a path deeper into Monte Carlo's back alleys.

She stared up at the building that now loomed over her like a giant malevolent toad, squatting in the line of dark, uninhabited buildings. It was half the size of an airplane hangar, with a roll-up garage door positioned beside an overgrown shrub and a black and rusted sign lit by a single, dingy streetlamp announcing, "*Entrée interdite*." *No Trespassing*.

Scanning the building façade, Maggie noticed that it featured a twisted roof which appeared nearly collapsed, and its windows were boarded. A single light shone inside through a broken window. She felt a pulse of excitement.

Somebody is home.

She stared at the light and imagined Laurent in that room. In her mind, she saw him injured and shackled.

She shook the unsettling image from her mind and slipped into the shadows to plan her next move. If Laurent and Grace were in that building, then she had to get in there too. But going in unarmed with no idea of their exact location was probably going to end badly.

While she didn't know who had taken Laurent and Grace, she was convinced that they were being held somewhere against their will. If not here in this warehouse, then somewhere. If they weren't here, perhaps there was someone here who could tell her more.

If not, she would go back to the casino to ask the waiter who had written on her bill. Because that person clearly knew *something*. She realized now that she probably should have done that before now. She'd been so excited to have a real lead that she hadn't thought of it at the time.

She pulled out her phone and texted Margaux. She imagined the detective was likely all the way to Nice by now if not back in Aix. But she was Maggie's only hope for support.

<*I think I've found them. Need back up.*>

She texted Margaux the address.

Then Maggie called the Monaco police. She knew better than to tell them what she was really up to, but if there was a way to get a police presence here, she needed to at least try.

"Hello?" she said to dispatch. "I'm looking at a man

attacking a woman on the street! Please hurry!" She gave them the same address and then disconnected.

She looked back at the warehouse. The night air was thick and oppressive, and the very darkness of the vacant street seemed to press in around her like a physical force. She could hear her heart thumping rapidly as she watched the building, trying to decide if she should attempt to get inside. Somehow, as she waited, she felt almost preternaturally alert to every sound, every movement in the darkness. She strained to hear sounds of the police on their way—sirens, car engines, anything—but all was quiet.

Suddenly the light in the window blinked out. The image of Laurent wounded and trapped came back to her as viscerally as if she was seeing him right in front of her.

She felt a sudden stab of urgency and realized she couldn't wait for help to arrive.

She slipped out of her high heel shoes and hurried across the street to the warehouse door.

22

The detectives bureau in the Monte Carlo police station was a large room housing a dozen workstations, all of them strategically positioned to catch the spillover noise and radio chatter from the watch commander's office down the hallway.

Detective August Latour sat drinking coffee with his junior partner Jean-Luc Chasseur in the center of the bureau; their two desks facing each other. Chasseur, a small man, was leaning dangerously back in his swivel chair cleaning his nails.

"Oh, I meant to tell you," he said to Latour. "A detective from Aix came in today asking about the car we found in the ravine off the A8."

"What the hell was he doing here from Aix?" Latour said with annoyance. "Typical French. They stick their big noses in everywhere."

"It was a woman."

"Even worse. What did you tell her?"

"I gave her the guts of what I knew. She wanted the report itself. Can you believe it?"

"Their arrogance is unbelievable. I hope you didn't give it to her."

"I did not. She gave me some spiel about international cooperation."

"They always do when it's France that wants something. Or Italy. Screw 'em both."

"You wouldn't have said that if you'd seen her," Chasseur said with a sneer.

Latour barked out a harsh laugh.

"All the more reason to keep them in their kennel across the border. Let's knock off early. What do you say? We have enough to do without pulling graveyard shifts."

"You're the boss."

Suddenly the phone rang on Latour's desk and Chasseur groaned.

Latour picked it up. "Yes?"

"We have a call for help in the warehouse district near Avenue du Marechal Foch," a voice from Dispatch said. "Uniforms aren't responding. Confirm if you can take the call."

Latour and Chasseur exchanged a glance.

"Seriously? We're beat police now?" Chasseur said in disgust. He was already standing with his jacket in his hand, ready to leave for the night.

"No uniforms are available?" Latour said into the phone.

"Does a general call for assistance trump aggravated assault?" the frazzled dispatcher asked. "Because we've got a mugging in Port Hercule with injuries."

"What are the details of the call?"

"It was made by a woman. Spoke good French but not native. Do you want to hear the recording?"

"No, I want you to make a damn assessment, so I don't have to do your job too."

"It appeared as if no crime had taken place at the time of the call."

"Disregard."

"Disregard?"

"Yes. Confirm. Disregard. If she calls back and needs an ambulance, I presume you can handle it."

Latour disconnected and then started scrolling on his phone. The warehouse district was notorious for illicit activities—mostly pickpockets and prostitution. Half the time tourists heard footsteps behind them and thought they were in New York City and panicked.

"*Jimmy's Monte-Carlo* is still open," he said, jamming his phone in his pocket and standing up. "Interested in a night cap?"

Chasseur laughed. "I thought you'd never ask."

∼

Grace lifted her head from the stained mattress and listened.

The sound that had roused her was more a murmur than anything else. There were words, yes. But indecipherable. She sat up slowly, awkwardly, propping herself on her bound hands. Unlike the last time she'd awakened, she now knew she was in a basement of some kind. She looked around the room, but it was still too dark to make out many features.

A plastic water bottle sat next to her mattress, and she recoiled at the thought that someone had been in the room while she slept. Her mouth was dry, and her head throbbed. She reached for the bottle. The cap had been loosened and she hesitated.

She was almost positive she'd been drugged before. But she was so thirsty. She licked her dried lips but made no moisture. She was also sure that if whoever was holding her really wanted to drug her again, they could do it and her abstaining from water would make no difference.

Sickened by her logic, she put the bottle to her lips

intending to just wet her lips but couldn't help herself and drank most of it down. Tears sprang to her eyes in self-loathing as she put the bottle down. She looked around the room, forcing herself to peer into the corners, trying to make her eyes adjust to the dark. She felt an increasing feeling of panic warring with urgency. She couldn't just sit and sleep and wait for whatever was going to happen!

Where was Laurent? Had she dreamed that they'd killed him? Or was that real?

She moved slowly to her knees and crawled a few feet in one direction. When she did, she felt abrasions on her hands and knees. What had happened to her?

The pain in her hands as she crawled ignited a memory of being dragged. She sat back on her heels and looked at the palms of her hands in the dim lighting. They'd bled but were dry now.

That same sound came again, and she froze. It *was* words! She crawled another couple of feet in what she thought was bringing her closer to the sound. She didn't dare call out. She held her breath to hear better.

"You must remember to breathe."

Who was it speaking? Who was he speaking to?

She felt a spasm of panic well up inside her and she forced down the desperate need to scream. She knew they hadn't forgotten about her—whoever her jailers were—but she didn't need to remind them she was here any sooner than she had to.

At least not until she had some idea of what she was going to do.

She took in a long breath and let it out slowly until she realized she was doing exactly what the voice had told her to do. She felt a wave of shame and tried to wave it away.

Just because the Devil tells you to do it, doesn't mean it's wrong.

She crawled back to the mattress, feeling suddenly weary

and even a little dizzy. The water was definitely drugged. She could taste the bitter aftertaste of the drug on her tongue.

What difference did it make? She lay down, not even caring about the cold now and realized she didn't even have the energy or inclination to weep.

When she heard the scream—shrill and hysterical—somewhere else in the building—she closed her eyes and drifted back to blissful oblivion.

23

The warehouse door had a broken padlock that hung loose from its latch.

Her hopes soaring, Maggie reached past it to grab the doorknob, and felt it turn. Holding her breath, she pulled the heavy door open. Warm, stale air flooded out. Silently, she crept inside and inched along the cement floor of broken glass, careful not to make a sound.

She could barely make out anything in the vast dark space. The walls inside the warehouse were rough and covered in graffiti. With each step forward, her heart raced faster.

Maggie reminded herself to pay attention to her footing to avoid tripping over the debris that littered the floor all around her. The darkness of the warehouse seemed to swallow her whole and it took everything in her to continue when instinctively it was the last thing she wanted to do. She shivered when a sensation of dread crawled up and down her bare arms.

Where would they be? She pulled out her phone to use the flashlight function, praying nobody would see it although she couldn't go forward without it. As soon as she turned it on, she was confronted with a gut-wrenching sight. She had been two steps away from a steep set of stairs plunging into a startling dark void.

She swallowed hard.

If Laurent and Grace *were* in this place, they would most likely be in the basement.

Gripping the flashlight tightly in her right hand, she used her left to guide herself along the wall down the stairs, careful not to step on anything that might make noise—broken glass, twigs, dead animal carcasses—and give her away.

The more steps she took, the more aware she became of the sound of voices. She stopped to listen. She could hear sounds of cards being shuffled, chips clanking together, and laughter echoing from nearby rooms.

Am I imagining the card shuffling? Am I so tired I'm hallucinating?

She crept down the stairs leaning heavily against the wall until she came to a landing.

Where would they be holding the hostages?

She moved down the landing to the final set of stairs to face a steel door directly across from the last step. She paused for a moment, but what was there to think about? She either went in or turned around and left. She reached out, but still hesitated, her hand hovering over the doorknob.

If she opened it and the card-playing men were there, she could be killed and no one the wiser. But if Laurent and Grace were somewhere in this building, she had to find them! Her fear of the moment warred with her desperate need to see Laurent again. For one mad moment she found herself thinking it might be worth dying just to see his face again. Just then, she heard what sounded like footsteps coming down the stairs behind her.

Adrenalin shot through her system. She snapped her flashlight off and panicked, looking around frantically for a place to hide.

The footsteps were getting closer when suddenly she heard a noise that sounded like metal clinking, like an unlocking mechanism being activated. Her breathing quickened and beads of sweat formed on her forehead. She wanted to move but her feet felt stuck to the ground. She was literally pinioned by her fear.

Suddenly, the sound of footsteps grating on the landing behind her made her spin around to see a figure standing on the stairs. He was shrouded in darkness, but Maggie could make out the outline of a man. She stared at the shadowy figure as panic welled up inside her like a cascade of icy water overwhelming a dam.

That was when she heard Laurent's voice.

24

Maggie felt elation surge inside her.

"Laurent!" she shouted. "Where are you?"

The moment she spoke, she saw the figure on the landing swivel toward her. Fear exploded in Maggie's chest as she turned and raced down the hall. As she ran, she spotted an open doorway and plunged through it, her heart thumping wildly. But she'd run into another hallway that ended with only a single door with the word *Messieurs* scrawled on it.

The men's restroom.

Maggie pushed open the door and braced herself against the far wall, praying her pursuer had not seen her enter. She stood in the darkness, her heart pounding, her breath ragged. Was she trapped? Should she hide in one of the stalls?

She heard the sound of feet outside the door. Her breath caught in her throat. Waiting and hoping he would go away was not an option. Her eyes darted around the room until she spotted the window over the far bank of sinks. She vaulted for them and scrambled up onto the sink rims at the same time she heard the restroom door open. She pushed against the rusting frame of the window, and it pitched outward.

She went with it, cutting her arm in the process, and tumbled a few feet to a thick patch of weeds below. She jumped to her feet to the sound of her pursuer struggling with the restroom window just over her head. She bolted for the street, fearing there was no way she would make it to her car in time.

The partial moonlight illuminated her path, but it was still difficult to navigate the unfamiliar street without the use of her flashlight which she'd jammed into her jacket pocket in order to run. She prayed the police would be waiting for her when she reached the street but when she got to the front of the building there were no flashing lights, no bull horns telling people to come out with their hands up.

She heard him hit the ground behind her.

Maggie's heart hammered in her chest as she raced down the dark street toward her car. She heard the sound of his boots behind her and risked a glance over her shoulder.

He was close and gaining.

She felt cold dread gripping her like ice water, clouding her thoughts and numbing her limbs. Her lungs were on fire, and she felt like the very darkness of the night was closing in around her. Suddenly three figures morphed out of the darkness in front of her. All three were dressed in black. All three were armed with assault rifles.

"Is that you, Maggie?" Margaux called.

Maggie felt a wave of relief wash over her. Before she could answer, she heard Margaux quickly instruct her men to clear the warehouse.

Maggie stumbled to a nearby curb where her legs finally gave out beneath her. She sat down hard on the street, flooded with relief. She clutched her knees to her heaving chest and tried to follow the sight of the men's strobe lights as they went from window to window inside the warehouse.

Finally, she saw Margaux emerge from the building and walk over to her. Maggie got to her feet.

"Did you find them?" Maggie asked. "Laurent's inside! I heard him!"

"They're clearing the place now," Margaux said. "If he's in there, they'll find him. *Mon Dieu*, you look a sight. You're not going to get your deposit back on that dress, I'll tell you that."

"Well, *you* are a sight for sore eyes," Maggie said, feeling an irrational laugh well up inside her as Margaux frowned at the unfamiliar idiom. "Who are those guys?"

"Just some off-duty friends of mine," Margaux said.

"You came back."

Maggie was overwhelmed that Margaux had come back *and* called in reinforcements. And she'd done it for *her*. Well, mostly for Laurent, but that didn't matter. The end result was the same.

Margaux must have seen the look of gratitude on Maggie's face.

"Don't make it a big deal," she said gruffly. "I got to thinking as I drove back to Aix that there was no way you could handle this. And besides, these guys needed the practice."

"Is it safe to go in?" Maggie asked. "I know they're in there, Margaux. Let me show you."

"Fine, come on," Margaux said and led the way back into the warehouse.

"I just can't believe you came," Maggie said. "The police didn't when I called them."

Margaux snorted derisively as they walked through the entrance of the warehouse, now with Margaux's powerful flashlight high beam showing the way.

One of her men met them. He shook his head.

"Nothing?" Margaux asked.

"Just a bum trying to make some money." He nodded at Maggie.

Maggie was stunned. The man chasing her was only some

homeless guy? What about the sounds of card playing? And people laughing?

What about Laurent's voice? I did not imagine that!

Twenty minutes later, Margaux and her people had cleared every room in the warehouse—all three floors and the basement.

Laurent and Grace were nowhere to be found.

25

Maggie stared at the basement room behind the one door that had been found locked. Once breached by Margaux's team, it was clear that the address given to Maggie earlier in the evening had been the real deal.

All four walls in the room were concrete, measuring just a few feet from one another, ancient pipes ran across the top of the stone walls to the ceiling like a medieval prison cell. It was cold, too. It seemed to Maggie that the cold was coming up from the floor itself, from the ground below.

The room was bare except for two mattresses on the floor. The adjacent wall was covered in graffiti, finger-painted in black fingernail polish and faded Chinese calligraphy. Food wrappers were scattered on the floor along with a dozen empty plastic water bottles. And plastic zip ties. There were bloodstains on the mattresses.

People had been kept here.

"When were they here?" Margaux murmured to one of her men.

A tall man with no expression on his face, merely shrugged and looked around. "Hard to tell."

"I heard Laurent's voice," Maggie said. "I'm telling you, they have to be near."

Margaux merely glanced at her. The evidence spoke for itself, and it trumped whatever Maggie thought she had heard. Yes, hostages had been here but not for at least a day, maybe longer.

"Chief?" one of the men said to Margaux. "Take a look at this."

Just then, Maggie's phone rang. She dug it out of her pocket with frantic fingers, hope blooming in her chest. But it was only Danielle. For one mad moment Maggie was tempted not to answer, but if Danielle was calling at five in the morning, it might be important.

"Yes, Danielle?" Maggie answered. "Is everything okay?" *Because I don't think I can handle one more crisis right now.*

"We are fine, *chérie*," Danielle said. "The children are asleep, but I cannot. I hoped you might have news."

Maggie's shoulders sagged with relief that there was nothing from *Dormir* to add to her burden.

"Nothing, I'm afraid," she said as she glanced at Margaux who was looking at what appeared to be an old-fashioned cassette tape recorder.

"Philippe was so unhappy tonight," Danielle said. "He kept asking about Grace. *When is she coming back? Why hasn't she called him?* It is breaking my heart."

Philippe had lived with Grace for the past seven years. Abandoned by his mother, Grace's eldest daughter Taylor, and left with whoever and wherever Taylor happened to be at the time, it had taken Philippe a long time to feel safe.

"I know how hard this is for you," Maggie said, as she watched Margaux turn to her with the tape recorder in her hand. "But can I call you back? I'm here with the detective from Aix and we might have a lead."

"Yes, you go, *chérie*," Danielle said. "I was just hoping."

"I know. We'll find them," Maggie said. "Kiss the children for me."

Then she disconnected and turned to Margaux.

"What did you find?"

Margaux held the recorder out to Maggie and pushed the play button. Instantly the sound of Laurent's voice filled the cement-walled basement room. Maggie's eyes filled with tears and she clapped a hand to her mouth.

"It's not him, Maggie," Margaux said. "Listen carefully."

As soon as Margaux said it, Maggie knew she was right. The voice didn't belong to Laurent. It was close, but it wasn't him.

"But who played it?" Maggie asked in frustration.

The disappointment of the discovery was devastating. "The bum chasing me was in the hallway behind me. He couldn't have activated this."

"But he did, Maggie," Margaux said with a sigh. "He'd picked it up earlier and had it on him. He must have pushed the button while he stalked you. Your ears play tricks on you in these old buildings. Everything echoes and distorts sound."

"So, it wasn't Laurent I heard," Maggie said dully, staring at the machine.

The disappointment solidified in her gut like a lump of undigested food.

"Look, we'll find him," Margaux said grimly.

Maggie nodded but she couldn't help but think Margaux's words were every bit as false as when Maggie had uttered them to Danielle just a few moments before.

26

Twenty minutes later, Maggie sat in her car outside the warehouse and played the recording over and over again while Margaux debriefed with her men. The only thing on the recording was the one line spoken by a deep-voiced man—much like Laurent's, but of course Margaux was right—not him.

"You must remember to breathe."

What did it mean? Why was it on the machine? Was it something the kidnappers told the hostages to keep them calm?

Maggie felt her heart sinking as she listened. She'd been up all night and exhaustion tugged at her eyelids, threatening to shut them for desperately needed sleep. She wanted to give up, but something kept pulling her forward—despite the despair that threatened to suffocate her. Tears ran down her face.

She watched Margaux thanking her men across the dark street, and she felt a flinch of envy at how the detective was holding up—so competent and practical with not a visible sign of emotion or hesitation in her movements. As she watched the detective, Maggie realized that as bad as it would be to lose

Laurent and Grace, it would be even worse if she left Amélie to be raised by someone else.

Should I give up the search and return to St-Buvard?

She ran her fingers over the tape player as if it were a connection with Laurent somehow. Had he heard these words? *You must remember to breathe?* Had Grace?

She looked up to see Margaux walking toward her. The detective looked tired, and Maggie reminded herself that she also hadn't slept yet tonight and was leaving to go back to Aix to begin her shift.

"Are you alright?" Margaux asked as she leaned on Maggie's car window.

"What did you do with the vagrant who was chasing me?"

"Scared the hell out of him and let him go," Margaux said with a shrug.

"Will you report your visit tonight?"

"To whom? The Monaco police? There doesn't seem much point, does there?"

Maggie closed her eyes feeling her discouragement wash over her.

"I can't believe they didn't show," she said.

"Can't you?"

Maggie narrowed her eyes at the French detective.

"Do you think they're complicit with the kidnappers?"

"I don't know, Maggie. Monte Carlo is a city of gamblers, risk and big money. Anyway, you should go back to the hotel and get some sleep."

"I will."

Margaux arched an eyebrow at her as if to say she knew Maggie wouldn't do that. Maggie appreciated that Margaux wouldn't argue with her about it.

"Thank you again for coming," she said.

Margaux snorted and patted the car door before turning and walking back to the black SUV she'd arrived in with her friends. Maggie watched them leave with a deep-seated dread filling her. She looked up at the warehouse remembering how it had been such a source of hope and expectation just a few hours earlier.

She sighed and looked away from the place that may or may not have been where Laurent and Grace had been held the last twelve hours. She glanced at the player knowing it would surely be wiped clean of prints. She wasn't sure exactly what she'd learned from tonight, but she knew she couldn't give up just yet.

She put her car into gear and set her GPS for a route back to the Casino Le Café de Paris.

∼

Maggie stepped through the front door of the casino, amazed that the place was still hopping. Not only was it open but the bars were still serving drinks, the slots were still running, the gaming tables were still jam-packed.

She made her way through the crowd of gamblers and tourists to wander the back of the casino. She scanned the reduced wait staff to see if she could find either the waiter who'd given her the bill with the warehouse address on it or the waitress named Annabelle who seemed to know what was going on but was afraid to tell.

Unfortunately, it appeared that a whole new legion of wait staff had taken over. In one section of the restaurant area, Maggie noticed a squad of cleaners wiping down tables and vacuuming up broken glass and even hauling away broken furniture. It was amazing for Maggie to imagine people coming here to try to get rich on the slots and not leaving when exhaustion or closing hours—since there clearly were none—might hint at them to stop.

Who were these people who gambled on vacation in lieu of

going to the beach or dining in one of Monaco's world-famous restaurants?

As Maggie passed a gilt-framed mirror on her way through the casino dining room she caught a glimpse of herself and was startled. Her dress had split up the side when she crawled through the men's bathroom window at the warehouse. What fabric was still there had probably saved her from getting tetanus from the rusty framework of the windowsill, but it had taken a beating in the process. Her makeup had smeared badly as if she'd wept the rest of the evening away.

Her hair, once pinned into a neat chignon, was now pulled back into a messy ponytail. She'd forgotten to look for her high heels after she'd kicked them off and now wore a pair of gardening sneakers she kept in the car trunk.

In spite of that, she elicited no strange looks from a single person she passed. She was reflecting yet again on that wonderful moment tonight when she thought she'd heard Laurent's voice and so she jumped when a friendly voice interrupted her thoughts.

Maggie turned to see a middle-aged woman dressed in a crisp outfit of white shirt, black slacks and tie standing behind the bar. She appeared to have been tallying the night's proceeds with a pencil and a clipboard. When the woman looked at Maggie, her face softened and she smiled, as if it was her duty to provide a moment of comfort to a weary traveler.

"May I help you?" the woman asked, her voice gentle and concerned.

Maggie blinked, taken aback for a moment. Her weariness made her vulnerable. She hadn't expected kindness from a stranger. Embarrassed, she glanced away, feeling suddenly foolish.

"I...I just..." she stammered, at a loss for words. "I'm not sure what I need."

The woman nodded knowingly, as if she had heard this

answer many times before. "Well," she said, softly. "Why don't we start with a cup of coffee? You look like you could use one."

Maggie walked over to her as the woman called a young waiter over and gave the order for two coffees. She gestured to a small table near them, and Maggie joined her at it.

"You look like you have had quite a night," the woman said. "I am Madame de la Roche."

"Maggie Dernier. And you have no idea."

"Winning or losing?" Madame de la Roche asked, her eyes twinkling.

"Mostly losing," Maggie said, her eyes misting.

"I'm sure it's not the end of the world," Madame de la Roche said kindly.

"I guarantee you wouldn't say that if you knew my story."

When the coffees came, Maggie inhaled their enticing aroma. Even the fragrance felt restorative to her.

"Why don't you try me?" Madame de la Roche said.

"Would you believe me," Maggie said wearily, "if I told you that my husband and best friend are missing, having abandoned their car on the road outside Monaco? Or would you be tempted to tell me—as the police have—that they have abandoned their children, their loved ones, a thriving vineyard and twenty-five years of marriage to run off with each other?"

Madame de la Roche's face hardened.

"Tell me more," she said softly.

Maggie studied her face, remembering the three people tonight who had brazenly lied to her—one to the point of nearly setting her up for an attack in a back alley And yet there was something about Madame de la Roche that made Maggie feel she could be trusted.

If I stop believing in the good in people, I might as well give up now.

Maggie told her everything.

She told this kind woman what she had gone through

tonight and what she knew and didn't know about her dear ones and their mysterious disappearance. And at the end she was completely ready for the well-meaning but basically useless words the woman would give her. She told herself that, useless or not, the words would at least be the balm that she needed before she picked up the flag and tried again.

Maggie finished her coffee and realized that there was a plate of bacon and egg sandwiches which Madame de la Roche must have ordered while Maggie was telling her tale. She realized with surprise that she was hungry.

"You seem to know what I need before I do," Maggie said as she picked up a sandwich.

"I know something else," Madame de la Roche said.

When she said that, Maggie looked up for the first time since she'd started talking to realize that the woman's countenance had changed. No longer was she the kind, anonymous stranger hoping to ease the burden of another of the world's travelers.

The woman's face was distorted with loathing. So much so that it made Maggie's blood run cold.

27

"His name was Romeo," Madame de la Roche said, her eyes wet but hard as flint as she spoke his name. "He was my first cousin and so full of life and love—for his wife, his children, his parents, everyone who knew him."

Maggie felt a coldness intensify in the room as if someone had opened the door to a nearby freezer.

"What happened?" she asked.

"The police say he ran off, perhaps with a croupier. It is true, he was a gambler."

Maggie glanced around the dining room. Even now, at past six in the morning, she could hear the sounds of the gambling section of the casino, still running at high throttle.

"He disappeared?"

"Without a trace."

"Why do you doubt what the police told you?"

"Because unlike them I have a job that uniquely places me to hear certain things."

She stared hard at Maggie.

"My cousin didn't run away. He was taken from us."

Maggie felt the excitement begin to bloom in her stomach. She wet her lips.

"By whom?" she asked eagerly.

"I am going to tell you, Madame Dernier, because I don't think either of us can be in any more danger than we already are."

Maggie frowned. "Danger?"

"Because we know a little bit more than we should. And for the ones who fear what we know, a little bit is as bad as knowing everything."

"Tell me what you know," Maggie said firmly.

Madame de la Roche nodded at Maggie's conviction.

"I know that there is a secret gambling organization of very wealthy, very powerful men and women. This group organizes games in ways that a civilized world would never allow."

De la Roche signaled to another waiter and spoke quietly to him. Maggie waited, although her stomach was beginning to sour from the coffee and the terrible truth of what Madame de la Roche was hinting at.

When the waiter left, Madame de la Roche turned to Maggie.

"You will need to be very brave," she said. "Whether to endure the loss of your loved ones with no answers as to what happened to them, or to look for answers—that may well result in your own death. Do you have children who depend on you?"

Maggie thought of Amélie.

"I see from your expression that you do," Madame de la Roche said.

"A granddaughter," Maggie said.

"And no one to take your place should...something happen to you?"

Maggie thought of Danielle, eighty-three years old. What would happen to Amélie if Danielle died? The state would take her. She felt her stomach churn with dread.

Did Maggie have the right to go looking for answers when she had so much at stake at home?

"There are people," Maggie said finally, praying that Mila and Jem and Luc would step up.

A waiter brought a bottle of cognac and poured two glasses before disappearing. Maggie didn't care what time in the morning it was. The brandy was needed. And she had a feeling that Madame de la Roche was telling her it would be needed more when she told her what she had to tell her.

"It is called *Le Jeu*," Madame de la Roche said. "The Game. It involves playing with people who have been abducted to participate in a high-stakes game—one which is protected by the Monte Carlo police."

Maggie's stomach hardened although she'd half guessed at something along these lines herself.

"Are you suggesting these people are hunted in some way?" she asked.

Madame de la Roche shook her head.

"Nothing so active as that," she said. "They are set loose in a wild environment with boars and trained attack dogs and venomous snakes. They are given a certain time to reach a specific destination."

"And the members of this gambling group bet on whether or not they will?" Maggie asked.

"*C'est ça.* A friend of mine who works in the police morgue said three bodies have shown up in the last month with fatal snake bites."

Maggie's eyes widened. "The blackjack dealer's body?" she asked.

Madame de la Roche's eyes filled.

"Sweet Juliette. A dear friend of mind. She was not bitten but killed by a bullet to the back of the head."

Maggie flinched at the news. The thought that Grace and

Laurent might be in the hands of these monsters was almost too much to take in.

"And the cops know about this?" Maggie asked.

Madame de la Roche shrugged.

"Perhaps not the specifics. But there is enough money in Monaco to encourage them not to see what is right before them."

"Do none of the...contestants of *Le Jeu* survive?" Maggie asked.

"Some do, I'm sure. That's what makes it a gamble for the ones who bet on them or against them. But their survival is irrelevant to their ultimate end since they cannot be allowed to live to tell their tale."

"And you think your cousin died in this way?"

"I know it."

Maggie sipped her brandy. It went down like battery acid. But it felt better than what she was feeling in her gut as she imagined what might be happening to Laurent and Grace.

"My husband and friend were stranded on foot in the countryside," she said. "They were on their way home from a day trip to Italy."

"Car trouble? Have you ever noticed how unlikely mechanical failures have become these days? With the technological improvements, cars hardly ever break down anymore."

"You think it was sabotaged?"

Madame de la Roche shrugged. "It is one of their ruses."

"The police have practically stopped investigating the disappearance of my husband and friend," Maggie said bitterly. "And they were only reported missing a few hours ago."

"I am sorry, Madame Dernier."

"Why are you telling me all this?"

"I don't mean to put you in any more danger than you are already," the woman said, her face creased with sorrow. "But every step forward—even if you are unsuccessful in stopping them or in finding your husband and friend—will hasten the day that the group is forced to move to another location. Dubai, perhaps? Or London? I have lost a cousin, but I have other people I care about. I have a son. I am terrified every time he leaves the house."

Maggie finished her drink and thanked Madame de la Roche. The full exhaustion of her day and night had finally worn her down and she needed to rest before she could do anything else.

"If I find out anything," Maggie said to her as they shook hands, "I'll get word to you."

"Just be careful."

Maggie made her way through the casino, wondering if anyone was watching her, wondering if the secret gaming group knew that she was looking for them. Her stomach was lurching with too little food and too much coffee and alcohol on top of already frayed nerves. She was sickened by what Madame de la Roche had told her—but also strangely encouraged.

At least she knew what she was dealing with now. As she got in her car, noting that dawn was breaking over the harbor, she thought about texting Margaux to tell her what she'd found out. But if what Madame de la Roche said was true, everybody who knew anything about the secret gambling organization was in danger.

As resourceful and competent as Margaux was, she was still only one person and one who was unsupported in Monaco.

No, Maggie couldn't involve Margaux in this. She couldn't be responsible for the woman getting killed because she knew something she could do little to stop anyway.

As she drove back to her hotel, Maggie found herself wondering if Laurent and Grace had stopped at a gas station or a luncheon spot on their way out of Italy. There were dozens of them sprinkled around that stretch of the highway along the

Mediterranean between Italy and Monaco. All it would take to disable the car was one moment when Laurent wasn't looking.

She parked her car in front of her hotel and put a call into Margaux. She hadn't expected her to answer. After all, her morning shift was due to start in thirty minutes. But the detective picked up within seconds.

"Disabled how?" Maggie asked her in lieu of a greeting.

28

Maggie sat on the grand steps of the Casino Le Café de Paris and watched the sun rise slowly above the heavy clouds. The street was quiet, almost too still, and the morning air was thick with anticipation.

In the end, she'd left her car in front of her hotel and walked the eight blocks back to the casinos. She needed the air and her emotions were tumbling over on top of each other. There was no way she could sleep. Not while she knew that Laurent and Grace might be breathing their last.

What Madame de la Roche had told her was devastating on so many different levels. In every way, it was the affirmation of Maggie's worst fears. But at least she now knew what she was dealing with. If Laurent and Grace *had* accidentally stumbled onto some sort of twisted gambling game—or witnessed the dumping of the blackjack dealer's body which was likely tied to the game—then rescuing them would take an entirely different kind of skillset.

And not the legal kind.

Maggie stepped off the curb and watched people on the street as they prepared for their day. Tourists were out early snapping photos of the opera house and the luxury yachts in the harbor. Joggers dodged around shopkeepers who were sweeping the detritus and trash from last night's partygoers from the sidewalks in front of their storefronts. Businessmen speed-walked to their various destinations with briefcases and coffee tumblers in hand.

Maggie had to assume that the secret gambling group was aware that at least a faction of the police had tried to raid their warehouse the night before. She worried that they would be prompted to either kill their hostages or fly them some place further away to finish their game.

Her stomach tightened at the thought that she may have unwittingly shortened whatever time Grace and Laurent had left. But she shook the thought from her mind.

I can't think like that. I have to go forward as if I know they're alive.

Maggie took a deep breath in an attempt to steady her nerves. She clenched her jaw and consciously worked to keep her breathing shallow. But her mind raced and a single tear, escaped down her cheek.

Just then her phone rang, and she brushed the tear away angrily. Now was not the time for weeping.

She saw on her phone screen that the caller was Margaux who'd already texted Maggie a few minutes earlier that she'd call back with information on the car.

"I'm here," Maggie said.

"Okay," Margaux said. "It turns out someone added water to the fuel tank."

Maggie quickly opened a browser window on her phone and typed in *water-in-fuel-tank*. In seconds, she was reading that this could be done to a car and yet the car would still drive—for a while.

"So, it was sabotaged," Maggie said.

"Basically," Margaux said grimly. "Sounds like I need to

revisit your friendly Italian antiques dealer. I was due for a few sick days anyway. Anything else I should know about?"

Maggie had debated telling her but decided in the end that Margaux could at least help consult with her. She quickly filled her in with what she'd learned from Madame de la Roche.

"Have you ever heard anything like this before?" Maggie asked.

Margaux sighed. "Not confirmed," she said. "But yes. Rumors."

"Well, I think this is what's going on with Laurent and Grace. And I'm not sure how much you can help me at this point."

"What are you talking about?" Margaux said defensively.

"Margaux, I'm talking about you, a police officer *from a foreign country,* attempting to investigate an illegal gambling enterprise that the Monaco police are clearly aware of and, if not actively supporting, at least turning a blind eye. You're just one woman."

"And you're more than that?"

"I have resources you don't."

"You're talking about breaking the law."

"Which I would never ask you to do."

"Thanks a lot. You have just revealed to an officer of the law that you intend to break the law."

"Look, talk to Signore Tassoni," Maggie said. "Text me anything you find out that could help me track down who these people are. If he disabled Laurent's car, he did it on somebody's orders. After that, just keep your line of communications open."

"You mean in case I need to tell your next of kin what happened to you?"

"I don't like this any better than you do!" Maggie said hotly, her eyes filling with tears. "But this is not a job for a by-the-book police officer and before you think I'm disrespecting you, I am totally impressed with the fact that you're not corrupt."

Maggie paused but before Margaux could come back with a retort, Maggie jumped back in.

"Laurent would never forgive me if I asked you to break the law," she said.

"Even though in his day," Margaux said, "he broke every law ever written?"

"That's different. That was who he was then. But it's not who you are and it's not what he'd want you to do."

"You don't think you need my help anymore."

"I need you in a certain capacity," Maggie said, feeling the woman begin to wear her down. "Can we please stop arguing about this? Any news or information you get from the Monaco police or Signore Tassoni, let me know. Okay?"

There was a pause on the line.

"Fine," Margaux said. "I have to get back to work. What about you? Have you had any sleep?"

"I'll sleep when I have my husband back," Maggie said. "Right now, I'm going to track down that lying little weasel who tried to set me up to get mugged. I think he knows more than he's saying."

29

Maggie turned and walked down the street to the next casino in line, the Casino de Monte-Carlo. It was jaw-droppingly grandiose. Even more so than the Monte Carlo Bay Casino. In the distance behind the casino she could still hear the ocean.

As she walked up the street, she caught glimpses of the tops of two cruise ships visible in the harbor. A ship's horn bellowed and echoed down the winding roads from the yacht basin.

The façade of the Monte Carlo Bay Casino appeared over a century old, an obvious mixture of stone and plaster. The front doors opened up automatically when Maggie stepped up to them, revealing the inside of the casino lit up with lights that showcased a series of gilded domes, balustrades and statues in the massive and ornate lobby.

Maggie knew she looked a sight. Her hair hung in a tangled mess past her shoulders and her ripped dress now had a section of hem hanging, exposing several scratches on her legs. But it was early morning, and she was hoping at this hour that half the people who were here looked similar or worse.

The casino seemed a less busy to her than the Monte Carlo

Casino, but still had plenty of people attempting to get rich at the slots. There didn't seem to be many dealers on shift. She dug out the thousand euros from her purse that she'd gotten at the ATM in Le Pechou and marched to the cashier's cage on the perimeter of the lobby.

"Yes, Madame?" the young man behind the cage said pleasantly to her.

Maggie placed her cash on the counter and gave him her best clueless American tourist look.

"My husband lost a rather sizable amount last night," Maggie said with a shaky smile. "Once I allow him back out on the streets, I'm afraid he will *not* be visiting your fine establishment again."

"I am sorry to hear that, Madame."

"I was wondering if you could help me find the perfectly horrible gentleman who this money now belongs to. He said his name was Luc LeGrand?"

Maggie had a pretty good idea that the sight of so much cash would make this man's mind up for him as to how serious she was.

"It's a pain, I know," Maggie said with a long-suffering sigh "But if I'm asking everyone in all the casinos up and down the Place de Casino where I can find Monsieur LeGrand. I would happily give half of what is owed to Monsieur LeGrand as a finder's fee to anyone who can help me find the correct address."

She also knew that if the cashier did know Luc and Luc heard that a woman was trying to find him to give him cash, he'd be furious if the cashier didn't help her track him down.

The cashier licked his lips and pulled a pad of paper over to him where he jotted down an address. Maggie smiled and handed the man five hundred euros.

"*Merci*, Monsieur," she said.

∼

Maggie stood in front of the towering condominium high rises, each featuring an unbroken line of balconies on every floor—most of which faced the street or another condominium rather than the Mediterranean. From that side of the building, lucky residents might see the many billionaire yachts bobbing in the harbor, sparkling in the sunshine.

She glanced at the address the cashier had written down for her and then back up at the towering block of glass and steel which reflected the sunlight on its many windows. Maggie couldn't help but think that these buildings—nestled between the azure water and white cliffs—were in perfect harmony with the surrounding orange tile roofs and swimming pools.

If LeGrand did own a condo here, Maggie reasoned that thieving in Monte Carlo was clearly providing a good living. If, on the other hand, he was renting a short stay apartment—and she'd already spotted several tourists who clearly didn't live here full time—he wasn't doing so well.

Parking was impossible and after circling the area for twenty minutes, she'd been forced to leave her car three blocks away in a public parking garage and walk to the address. She still looked as if she'd swum through the sewers of France so she got looks from people as she walked, but she'd decided that a shower and a shampoo wouldn't get her any closer to where she needed to be.

I'll have plenty of time to shower the rest of my life.

Inside, the condominium lobby was a splendor of marble and gold featuring a grand staircase that curved gracefully to the upper levels beside a bank of elevators hidden behind a series of handprinted screens. The walls were lined with oil paintings, and the polished wood floors gleamed beneath the bright lights. Everywhere she looked, Maggie saw an oasis of luxury and refinement. Maggie wasn't sure what to make of the fact that, like most of Monaco and Monte Carlo, everything appeared dipped in gold.

"May I help you, Madame?"

Maggie turned to see a concierge standing at a large round desk in the lobby. She realized she looked even shabbier than most tourists he was probably used to seeing. She walked over to him, already fishing for her wallet.

Ten minutes later, she was on the freight elevator headed to the fifteenth floor. When the doors opened, she followed the thickly plush carpeted hallway to a door that she realized with surprise must face the ocean.

Again, she wasn't sure if that meant anything. She rapped on the door, praying he was home. Praying he robbed people by night and slept during the day like a vampire.

Once more she found herself wishing she'd brought her Taser. It was just as well. She still needed to ask LeGrand for his help. If she had the Taser, the temptation to shoot him first would be too great.

The door opened slowly. LeGrand stood in the doorway wearing only jeans and an open dressing gown. He blinked at her in confusion as if he had no idea who she was. He stepped out to glance up and down the hallway, and before he could step back in, Maggie pushed past him and entered the condo.

"Excuse me, Madame!" he said, indignantly walking in after her.

"Close the door, Luc," Maggie said. "You don't want your neighbors hearing this."

She walked into the living room and was briefly stunned by the view. Before her was a full sweeping vista of the Mediterranean Sea, so brightly blue it hurt her eyes to look at it. She could see the land sweep away to the southwest in the direction of Saint-Jean Cap-Ferrat and then, as she pivoted in awe in the opposite direction, east to Italy.

"What is the meaning of this?" Luc said crossly. "I must ask you to leave at once!"

Maggie turned to him. "Do you seriously not remember me?"

He opened his mouth to speak and then thought better of it. Maggie watched his eyes dart around the room and a bead of sweat formed on the side of his face.

"Ah. So, you do remember me."

Maggie turned back to look at the ocean view. It was so dramatic as to be positively hypnotic. She almost couldn't not look at it.

"Nice digs, Luc. I guess mugging unsuspecting tourists is a good gig for you. Go to school for that, did you? Or is it an inherited skill?"

"I fear you have mistaken me for someone else," LeGrand said, tightening the belt on his robe and scowling at Maggie, having clearly decided on righteous indignation as the appropriate reaction to her surprise visit. "You will leave, or I will call the concierge."

Maggie went to the hall and opened one of the bedroom doors.

"Ivan and I got real friendly to the tune of five hundred euros a little bit ago," Maggie said. "So unless I need him to throw you off your own balcony, I'm afraid he won't be very accommodating if you call."

Legrand opened and closed his mouth like a guppy starving for air. His eyes were huge and bulging.

"Where's Joelle?" Maggie asked.

"How did you find out where I live?" he said.

Maggie walked over to him and slapped him hard across the face. She was sorry she hadn't done it as soon as she entered the apartment. As she watched his eyes water and the red mark form on his cheek, she realized it was the best she'd felt since the moment she'd heard that Laurent's car had been found in a ditch.

"I'm asking the questions and you, you degenerate little twerp, are answering them. And if you don't answer them honestly, I will tell the Monaco police you attempted to rape me."

He looked at her in horror.

"That's right. I may look like something the cat drug in, but I have two things that will make them take me very seriously."

She pulled out her American passport.

"This for starters," she said. "And then this." She pulled out a press pass.

Years ago, Maggie had created a false identification when she'd needed to get into certain places where people for whatever reason were resistant to allow her. It had come in handy on many occasions.

"I'm a member of the press and as such a veritable fount of destructive public relations for this town. Cross me, Luc, and after my American Embassy puts you in prison for twenty years, they'll hand you back to Monaco to let them finish with you."

"What do you want?"

"Where is Joelle?'

"I don't know."

His shoulders sagged when he spoke, and Maggie thought she detected the first authentic sign of emotion since she'd met him.

"Explain."

"She was supposed to meet me back here last night, but she never showed."

"Is that unusual?"

"Very! We're engaged and very much in love."

Maggie held up her hand to stop him from speaking. She turned back to the ocean view and stood staring at it for a moment. Then she turned around.

"Do you have any reason to believe that you might have upset someone to the degree that they might take Joelle?"

He licked his lips and hesitated.

"Remember what I said about answering me honestly?"

"I don't know for sure," he said.

Maggie decided he was telling the truth.

"Well, then it's possible you might be able to help yourself as well as me," she said. "Do you remember those photos I was showing you at the casino?"

"Yes."

"Do you have any idea where my husband and friend might be? I warn you, to please think before you speak."

"No, Madame. I have no idea where they might be."

"Let me rephrase that. Do you have any idea who might have taken them?"

Luc sank onto the nearby couch, his face in his hands.

"They were taken by the people running *Le Jeu*, weren't they?" Maggie asked.

Luc's eyes widened in shock. He shook his head slowly, as if he could not believe what he had just heard.

"How did you know about *Le Jeu*?" he asked hoarsely.

"Who runs it?"

"I have no idea! Truly! None!"

He stood up and became instantly agitated, his eyes on the phone that Maggie now held in her hand as if he were expecting her to call the police at any moment.

"But you know someone who does," she said.

He swallowed hard and glanced down the hall. For a moment Maggie thought he might be thinking of Joelle. Maybe he really did care for her. Maybe he was wondering where she was and if she truly had been taken by these people.

"I...I might," he said.

"Okay," Maggie said. "Why don't you start praying that you do? Meanwhile, get dressed."

30

The door of the small cell opened and two men stepped inside. Grace felt her heart jump as she realized that she recognized their smell from the previous day. She used the cold stone wall at her back to help push herself to her feet.

The two men were dragging a woman by her arms. Her head hung down, her face obscured by a nasty tangle of wild hair. She was sniveling and then yelped loudly when the men gave her a push into the cell. She collapsed at Grace's feet.

Grace's instinct was to reach out to the woman and tell her that everything would be all right. But as she looked at the trembling figure, Grace knew the woman was way past believing such obvious lies.

The woman crawled to her knees and looked around the room, her expression a mixture of fear and confusion. When her gaze fell on Grace, she seemed to be searching for words, but all that emerged was a broken sob. It was a cry so deep and primal that it made Grace's stomach hurt. The men turned to leave, and Grace called out to them.

"Can you not at least untie my legs?" she said. "You can see I'm not going anywhere!"

One of the men said something to her in Italian, which Grace didn't understand. His meaning was clear though. It was leering and predatory.

"Where is the man I came with?" she asked. "What have you done with him? He is wealthy. If he's alive, you could be rich."

One of the men stopped, clearly interested, but the other one snarled at her in Italian.

"Five hundred thousand euros," Grace persisted. "His wife can get it for you by morning."

That made both men stop. Grace wet her lips.

"*Cinque centomila euro,*" she said, hoping she got at least most of the Italian right.

The predatory man's eyebrows shot up and Grace thought he was interested. Then he glanced at his partner who definitely seemed interested, and he hit him hard on the shoulder before snarling something that prompted both of them to exit and slam the cell door hard behind them with an loud clang.

Grace listened to the sound of their footsteps retreating. Her heart was pounding in her throat. Did that mean Laurent was dead? Or were they just afraid to double-cross their boss?

"Help me," the woman on the floor said.

Grace looked at her and felt a wave of pity.

"What's your name?" she asked.

The woman lifted her head.

"Rebecca Green. I'm a British national. They broke my tooth!" Her face crumpled up and she began to cry.

"Where did they take you from?" Grace asked, settling down on the cold floor once more, as she felt the familiar feeling of the exhaustion of her ordeal once more begin to overtake her.

"In Monte Carlo. At my hotel!"

Grace frowned. Those two cretins were seriously repellent. Grace found it highly unlikely that they could be anywhere near a four-star hotel in the heart of the one of the biggest tourist Meccas in the world and not have about a hundred people on the phone reporting them to the police.

"Inside your hotel?" she asked.

"No, outside," Rebecca said, touching her mouth and whimpering.

"What time?"

"What difference does that make?" Rebecca looked up at her with a scowl on her face.

"No difference," Grace said, turning away. "No difference at all."

"You have to help me!" Rebecca said in a shrill voice.

Grace looked at her in astonishment.

"You see my hands and feet are bound?" she said. "What in the world do you think I can do for you?"

"You spoke their language! They talked to you! Get them to let me go!"

"When did they take you?" Grace asked.

"How should I know? I was passed out when they found me."

That probably means they weren't worried about anyone coming to look for her.

"Look at my hands! This thing is cutting into my skin! Help me!"

Rebecca's plea had an angry tinge to it now. It seemed to ricochet off the walls of the cell. She yanked hard at the plastic zip tie, as if trying to break it with sheer strength. Her jaw was clenched and her eyes wild with desperation.

Grace wondered if the woman had gone mad while being held or if she'd been crazy before. She wanted to tell her that she couldn't possibly break the tie. As she watched Rebecca's wrist become redder and angrier until droplets of blood formed on the cement floor, Grace found herself moving away.

She needed to think.

31

The house was a three-story brick monolith with a large front yard and manicured greenery on the well-kept lawn. White pillars stood out front flanking the double doors. To Maggie, the building's façade looked like a tapestry of artisanal precision, and its Mediterranean roof tiles were a dramatic presentation of burnished reds and green. She noted the mammoth windows on the front of the villa were framed in heavy wrought iron, finishing the look of the quintessential South of France villa.

Maggie wasn't surprised that the mansion was located outside the country of Monaco. Only five hundred acres total, Monaco's available real estate was in such high demand by wealthy tourists as to be largely unattainable. She remembered hearing Grace talk about the fact that most of the new villas and mansions were now located over the border in the commune of Cap Martin or Beausoleil. While it was true that Monaco was known as a tax shelter, Maggie couldn't imagine why a powerful underworld mobster—the owner of the villa she now viewed—might need to be concerned with keeping accurate books.

The man they were attempting to beard in his lair was one Vittorio Giordano—a powerful mobster who Luc was sure definitely knew of the secret group if anyone did. And how to contact them.

Throughout the thirty-minute drive through the countryside to the villa, she kept checking her phone to see if Margaux had texted her back. But there was nothing. She consoled herself with the thought that Margaux probably hadn't even gotten off her shift yet. After that, it was a two-and-a-half-hour drive to Italy and, unlike Maggie, Margaux probably needed to sleep at some point.

With luck, Margaux's interview with Signore Tassoni would lead them both to the same place—the identity of whoever was running the secret gambling ring. But in case of the likelihood that Signore Tassoni was more afraid of the head of the illegal gambling group than he was of the French police who had no jurisdiction in Italy, Maggie needed to hedge her bets.

She and Luc now sat in her car at the crest of a small hill which gave them a good view of the villa without alerting the mob leader's security forces which Luc assured Maggie would be on full display.

"So how do we do this?" Maggie asked.

Luc ran a hand through his thick, wavy hair and sighed.

"We can hardly just knock on the door," she said. "Will they shoot us on sight if we try to cruise up the driveway?"

"I've never seen him here," Luc admitted.

"Come on, Luc!" she said with growing impatience. "Tick tock! How do we make contact without getting shot?"

"We should drive up," he said tentatively. "They will at least give us a chance to talk."

"You're sure?"

"Almost completely."

Maggie studied him for a moment and then put the car into drive. They didn't have a choice really. It was either risk getting shot—or turned away, more likely—or drive off and give up the only decent lead she'd gotten for finding the elusive gambling group.

As they drove toward the massive villa gates, Maggie glanced around the surrounding hills, looking for a glint of telltale light off sniper rifles or any other indication that they were driving into a one-sided battle. But the countryside was peaceful and quiet. If, on the other hand, she had thought even for a moment that they might have taken the mobster by surprise, that idea vanished when they approached the villa gates which automatically opened for them.

"Do you think they're expecting us?" Maggie asked grimly.

"Hardly," Luc said. "He's probably got spies or cameras out for miles around his place."

"Do you think he saw us on the hill?"

"I have no idea," he said, his anxiety clearly beginning to ramp up the closer they got to the villa.

There was nothing Maggie could do about that. She wasn't exactly calm herself, but she honestly didn't see any other option. The fact was, if Giordano wouldn't help her, she went back to square one. And with the clock ticking on whatever fate awaited Laurent and Grace, that was something she preferred not to dwell upon.

On the other hand, if she could convince Giordano to help her—and she had been running the possibilities through her mind of what she could offer him in return for the whole drive up there—she had a chance that no one—not even all the police on the Côte d'Azur—could give her.

The imposing gates of the mansion opened with a loud mechanical buzz as they approached. Guards stood nearby, assault weapons slung from their shoulders. Security dogs patrolled the grounds with their handlers.

It was almost as if they're expecting us.

Once through the gates, the sprawling estate unfolded

before them. A fountain stood in the center of the drive, and the villa rose up beyond that. Maggie felt a chill inching down her spine as they drove down the drive and got her first close-up glimpse of the looming stone facade, its ornate carvings illuminated by spotlights mounted on the eaves and on either side of its massive double door.

She brought the car to a stop in front of the main entrance and turned off the engine.

"Well," she said. "So far so good."

She turned to Luc and felt the tension pinging off him in waves. Suddenly it occurred to her that he was terrified.

And that maybe he had good reason to be that she had no idea about.

32

Two young men with AK-47s sauntered up to the car. One of them aimed his rifle at Luc who instantly held his hands in the air.

"We are here to see Signore Giordano," Maggie said in a clear voice. "May I get out of the car?"

The two men looked at each other and one of them nodded at Maggie. The other one held his gun on Luc.

"Not him," he said.

Maggie got out of the car. She felt suddenly very vulnerable as the young men looked her over from head to toe. She was still wearing last night's sequined A-line dress although now with her garden sneakers. Her hair was pulled back into a ponytail.

"May I bring my phone?" she asked. "I'm expecting an important call."

Two more men came over then, one holding the leash of a very tense German Shepherd. Maggie was careful not to look the animal in the eye. Normally, she had a special way with animals, especially dogs. There were few who didn't take to her immediately. But she wasn't sure how that worked with an animal who had been trained as methodically as this one surely had been. She decided not to press her luck, and kept her eyes averted.

One of the guards spoke into a radio communication device affixed to his shirt.

"Bring her in," he said to his partner. "Boss wants to see her."

"What about the other one?"

The guard looked at Luc and frowned. "Do I know you?" he asked.

"I am Luc LeGrand," Luc said, his voice nearly a squeak of terror. "I work the Casino de Monte-Carlo."

The guard snickered.

"Yeah, we know you," he said in French. "Stay in the car. Bruno! Watch him!"

Maggie snapped her head around at the name *Bruno* and saw the German Shepherd had sat down on its haunches, giving its full attention to the car and its lone passenger.

One of the guards plucked her phone out of her hand. She decided not to protest. She was willing to lose a whole lot more than a cellphone if she could get Giordano to help her.

"Hands in the air," the guard said to her.

"Give me a break, Carmine," the other guard said. "You can see she's not carrying."

"You want to tell the boss that?"

Maggie felt the man's hands pat her down efficiently and not for longer than was necessary to convince him she wasn't hiding a weapon.

"This way," he said, giving her a nudge to indicate she was to walk in front of him.

Maggie was torn between elation about the fact that she'd gotten this close to talking to someone who might know someone involved with the illegal game, and fear that she would blow it by asking the wrong question or insulting the mob leader.

She knew only too well that people who were ruthless murderers came in all stripes and colors. Some could be reasoned with. Some could be made to feel sympathetic.

Some would murder you for an evening's entertainment.

She was also aware from what Luc had said that Vittorio Giordano likely knew of *Le Jeu* because he'd played it himself—a brutal game of watching innocent, terrified, and desperate people attempt to fight for their lives.

Someone like that didn't hand out favors for no reason. Worse, if he thought Maggie and Luc believed he was complicit in *Le Jeu*, he could easily decide that killing them was the most convenient way of eliminating any possible threat.

As Maggie walked into the grand mansion, the thought occurred to her that dying and never coming home to her loved ones was a very real possibility.

33

Maggie walked up the wide marble steps through the front door, which was opened from the inside by another man—this one thankfully unarmed. The foyer was a wide expanse of marble punctuated by a series of bronze statues. Oil paintings depicting men in top hats and waistcoats hung in giant gilt frames from the walls. The scent of rosewood polish lingered in the air.

Directly ahead she saw a seating arrangement with an immense crystal chandelier dangling overhead. A man in his late forties stood waiting, his hands behind his back, his head tilted in curiosity as she approached.

Two more men appeared from behind him, but Vittorio Giordano waved them away. Maggie walked to the man. He was her only hope to finding Laurent and Grace. She wouldn't beat around the bush. She didn't have that kind of time.

"*Buona giornata*, Signore Giordano," she said, holding out her hand.

He smiled as if amused but shook her hand and indicated one of the two velvet chairs next to him.

"I fear I've missed your name, Signora," he said as Maggie seated herself.

"My name is Maggie Dernier," Maggie said. "I'm here because you are literally the only person on earth who can help me save my husband."

"And why do you think that?"

He made a gesture to one of his men and then sat back in his chair, his leg crossed, his fingers steepled on his knee.

"I have been told that you know the people running *Le Jeu*," Maggie said, deciding to come right out with it. If he needed to kill her because she knew that much, best to get on with it.

He raised his eyebrows but said nothing.

"I have reason to believe that my husband and my best friend have been forcibly recruited to play in the game," Maggie said.

"They are American like yourself?"

"My friend is. My husband is French."

He nodded. "Does your husband live with you in America?"

"No, Signore Giordano, he and I live on a vineyard in the South of France with our children."

Maggie was well aware that in dealing with criminals it was often helpful to humanize yourself. Of course, with psychopaths that didn't always work.

"Where in America are you from?" he asked.

"I am from the American South," Maggie said. "Atlanta."

"Ah, *Gone with the Wind*."

Maggie tried to smile. Just then a man arrived with a tray of tea and cookies and set it down on the table between Maggie and Giordano.

"Fool!" Giordano snarled at him. "She is not English! She doesn't drink tea!"

Maggie was sure that Giordano had misjudged her himself and ordered the tea. She prayed he wasn't going to kill this poor boy because he couldn't own up to his own mistake.

"I love tea," she said quickly. "In the South, we drink iced tea all the time."

She watched his face as he struggled to decide how he felt about what she was saying, and for a moment she feared he would think she had corrected him. Dealing with sociopaths was like tiptoeing through a field of landmines.

Suddenly the sound of gunfire erupted outside. Maggie jumped to her feet.

Had they shot Luc?

The front door swung open and two men came inside at a trot. Giordano snarled something at them in Italian and they pointed to the front of the house and shrugged.

"Have...have they killed my....my companion?" Maggie stuttered. If they had a problem with Luc the last thing she needed to do was claim him as a friend.

Giordano stood up and shouted at his men who turned and ran back out the front door. Within seconds, they dragged Luc into the foyer and deposited him on the marble floor, quaking and terrified.

"You see? He is quite alive!" Giordano waved his hand at Luc and smiled as if he had conjured the man up for Maggie's pleasure. He barked something at his men, and they went to Luc and hauled him to his feet.

Luc's pant leg was ripped as if the dog had gone after him, Maggie thought.

"Please, Signore Giordano," she said trying to smother her frustration. "I want my husband back. I need your help. I am prepared to pay you any amount of money you ask."

"You think I am a blackmailer?" Giordano's voice rumbled like thunder, his lips pulled back in a snarl. "Or *poor*?"

Maggie wrung her hands in agitation as she watched the face of the crime boss go purple with rage. She had no idea what would get the man to decide not to kill her, let alone help her. At the very least she needed to get out of this villa alive for Amélie's sake.

"Can you help me or not?" she said, raising her voice. "If you can't, I need to keep looking for someone who can."

Giordano glared at her for a moment and then waved his henchmen away with an impatient gesture before coming to sit back down in his chair. He indicated for Maggie to sit, too.

"What did you say your name was?" he asked, picking up the teapot and pouring both cups.

Maggie glanced at Luc who was looking around as if unsure whether he should leave with the guards or come over to Giordano and Maggie. He stayed where he was.

"My name is Maggie Dernier," Maggie said as she took the teacup from him.

She saw the recognition register in his eyes.

"Do you think you know my husband, Signore Giordano?" Maggie asked tentatively. "He used to work the Côte d'Azur many years ago."

Giordano suddenly howled with laughter, the sound reverberating off the marble walls like a wounded hyena.

"What is it you Americans say, Signora?" he asked, still grinning as he turned to Maggie.

Maggie shook her head, her cup shaking slightly in her hand.

"Oh, come on! You know the saying!" Giordano said. "About the small size of our world? Yes?"

He threw back his head and laughed even louder than before.

34

Joelle awoke with a start, her fingers clawing at the thin blanket that covered her hips and sat up from the cold ground where she lay. She looked around, eyes wide. The light was dim, and she widened her eyes further hoping that would help her see better. The walls were bare and made of dark stone. Fear welled up inside her.

She pulled her knees under her and leaned against the cold granite wall. A prison cell? In a basement? Or a mausoleum? Dread spiked inside her at the thought of being buried alive and she gulped down breaths to try to steady herself.

There were no other sounds except the steady dripping noise coming from somewhere outside the cell.

Joelle struggled to make sense of what had happened. She looked down at her dress and saw the rips and tears. A line of crusted-on mud edged the hem. Panic threatened to overwhelm her as she tried to remember.

How did I get here?

She glanced around the room, her searching gaze settling on the heavy metal door. Its bars were too wide for anyone but a child to attempt to squeeze through.

Her heart pounded as she surveyed the rest of her dank cell. Except for the slow drip beyond her cell walls and her own heart pounding in her chest, only an eerie silence permeated the air. She felt a thickening in her throat and took in a deep breath.

I'm on my own. I have to do this myself. Calm down!

She looked around again, this time searching for anything that might help her escape. A window, a weapon, an air conditioning vent, a sewer grate. In the corner of the room, she spotted a stack of tattered rags. She moved toward it and then froze. It wasn't a pile of rags. It was a man. He was completely still. Possibly dead. She moved closer. He was big, like a giant. She saw his hands in the front of him were tied.

A prisoner like me.

She crawled over to him.

"Monsieur? Are you awake?"

There was no answer.

Are you alive? Would probably be a better question.

She touched his shoulder, but he didn't react. This close, she saw his face was covered in bruises and cuts. His lip had bled but dried down his chin. There was a deep cut across his forehead. But Joelle could still make out his features. Her heart racing, she shook him gently. He groaned.

So he is alive.

"Monsieur? Wake up."

He opened his eyes.

Instantly, she felt a flush of adrenaline. She recognized him. She sat back on her heels staring at him as he blinked groggily.

How do I know him?

He closed his eyes again and she sat there watching him, trying to rerun the memory tapes in her head of all the people she'd been with in the last couple of days.

Was he a mark? Had he tried to buy her a drink at the *Monte-Carlo*?

In a flash it came to her then. He was the man in the photograph the American mark had shown her and Luc two nights ago. The missing husband. Joelle leaned in to examine his face.

Guess he didn't run off with the girlfriend after all.

"Hey," she whispered. "Can you hear me?"

His eyes flicked open, and he looked at her in confusion.

"My name is Joelle," she said. "I know Maggie. She's looking for you."

A glimmer of recognition passed over his face. "Maggie?" he croaked.

"That's your wife, right? Maggie? She's in Monte Carlo."

For all the good that'll do you.

He tried to focus his eyes on her.

"Man, they really did a number on you. You probably put up a fight. Rule Number One—don't put up a fight."

He was handsome, even in spite of his battered face. Joelle found herself thinking of the American woman who had been so desperate to find him.

I would've turned Monte Carlo upside down for this one, too.

He began to close his eyes again. Joelle didn't know if it was for humane reasons or because she felt panic at the thought of being alone, but she reached over and shook his arm.

"Hey, don't go to sleep, okay? That's not good for your brain."

His eyes opened again.

"You and me are in trouble," she said softly. "You know that, right? We need to get out of here before those bastards come back and finish the job on you."

35

The sun shone harshly down on the villa's outdoor pool area. The dining table was positioned poolside on the terrace and draped in white linen. Silverware sparkled in the sun from each place setting. An array of delicate pastries and finger sandwiches were arranged on crystal platters. A variety of salads and breads accompanied the main course of roast lamb and grilled vegetables. An icy pitcher of rosé gave the scene a bizarrely festive air.

Gently trimmed bushes of rosemary and lavender lined the pool's perimeter, adding a gentle fragrance to the air.

It was astonishing to Maggie that something that showed so much taste and refinement could be appreciated by someone like Vittorio Giordano. Obviously, he'd hired the best landscape architects money could buy, but even so he must have *some* kind of eye himself to be able to appreciate it.

Only the three of them sat at the lavishly set table—herself, Giordano and Luc. Silent servers came and went, never giving eye contact or looking up beyond the plate they held in their hands. Maggie got the impression they were all terrified.

Ever since Giordano realized Maggie's connection to

Laurent, he kept up a steady patter of old stories about the Côte d'Azur and his own exploits. While he hadn't known Laurent personally, he'd heard the stories. And he was impressed.

The servers placed heaping plates of risotto and ossobuco on the table. Maggie was too worried about time ticking away to have any appetite. She noticed that Luc seemed to have the same problem. He pushed his food around his plate with a fork and took small nibbles so as not to offend their host, but he probably needn't have bothered. Giordano appeared blithely unaware of their discomfort.

"Where does your daughter go to school?" Giordano asked. "In the South?"

"Yes," Maggie said. "She's a Junior at the University of Florida."

"Ah! SEC football! I'm a fan. You are surprised?"

Before Maggie could comment one way or the other—and again, she wasn't sure what answer might set him off—he continued.

"My son is at Old Miss. Are you surprised?"

Maggie hoped her jaw didn't openly hit the table when he told her that since surprise was the understatement at hearing that news.

"That's...that's amazing," she said.

She racked her brain for anything to say about SEC football. After living in France for the past twenty-seven years, she'd lost track of who played whom and who was usually winning but this was clearly something important to Giordano. The fact that she was from the American South had been a tiny foothold of luck that she was clinging to.

"I was wondering if you thought you might be able to help me find Laurent and Grace," Maggie said.

"Oh? Didn't I say?" Giordano said looking from Maggie to Luc. "But of course I will help! If that bitch has taken Laurent Dernier, I will insist she release him. She has plenty of others to choose from. She doesn't need everyone she finds, you know? I honestly don't know what she does with them all. The game is only played four times a year, if that."

Maggie nodded.

"How do you think you can get her to release them?" she asked.

He shrugged.

"I will just call her up, okay? I will say 'Adele, you have something of mine.' She is very respectful of Vittorio Giordano. She will hand him straight over."

Maggie wanted to believe that more than anything.

"And my friend, Grace Van Sant, too?" she asked. "She was with Laurent at the time they were taken."

"I will ask for them both! No! I will demand she return them both! Alive, of course!"

Maggie felt a wave of nausea grip her. There was something about the way Giordano was talking that didn't sound like he knew what he was saying. Could he really just call this friend up and demand these latest two hostages from her?

Was she crazy to trust a mobster? An underworld criminal? Probably someone with multiple murders to his credit?

Maggie looked over at Luc who hadn't spoken since they sat down. *Three* hostages. They'd already told him that Joelle was also missing, and Giordano had agreed to release her too.

Perhaps this Adele person owed him, Maggie reasoned. She glanced around the opulent dining room. Surely Giordano was top dog in this area of the world.

Suddenly, her phone vibrated on the table—Giordano had very generously given it back to her—and she saw from the screen that Margaux was calling her. But now was not the time to excuse herself to take a private phone call from a police detective. Win or lose, Maggie realized she had put all her chips in this new basket—this new highly illegal and criminal basket —and could not now fall back on Margaux.

"I went to a place last night where I believe they were keeping them," Maggie said.

But Giordano waved away her words.

"I know where they are," he assured her. "Or if I don't know exactly where they are—it doesn't matter. Adele moves her pieces around the board quite a bit, yes? Needs must, eh?—I can find out where they are easily enough."

"What can I do?" Maggie asked.

Something about all of this felt suddenly too easy. Even with all the agony of getting here and getting past Giordano's security, something was too pat. Maggie didn't want to listen to that feeling. Instead, she wanted to believe every word coming out of Giordano's mouth.

"Do? Nothing, *caro mio*," Giordano said. "You will *sit tight* as they say in your country, yes? Sit tight?"

"Okay, but will you call Adele?" Maggie pressed. "Or will you just show up where you think they're holding the hostages?"

"Like you did today?" He threw back his head and laughed. "I'm afraid only an American could get away with barging in uninvited. No, we will go a different route. Have you had enough to eat? Both of you? I have swimsuits if you would like to swim?"

"Señor Giordano," Maggie said, rubbing the back of her neck in mounting anxiety. "I'm very afraid that this Adele is going to start her game and kill Laurent and Grace and Joelle before you can rescue them. Do you by any chance know *when* she plans to play *Le Jeu*? And where?"

"Yes, of course," he said. "I am to play too, *n'est-ce pas*?"

Maggie felt her stomach drop at his words, but she reminded herself that she'd already suspected he played the game too.

"When?" she asked. "When is the game to be played?"

"Please not to worry! I told you I would get them back, yes? I will. Of course, I will. Adele can be very reasonable for the right price."

"Have you...do you know this Adele very well, Signore Giordano? Can you tell me what kind of person she is?"

"You Americans! Always with the strange questions. I do not know how to answer such a question. I have known her many years."

Then his eyes lit up. "In fact, you have just reminded me. Your husband knows Adele too."

Maggie stared at him. And her stomach reacted before her brain did. At first her mind couldn't wrap itself around the information that was coming down the track straight at her at full speed.

Is it possible?

The only *Adele* Maggie had ever known was an evil fiend by the name of Adele Bontemps.

36

Maggie was stunned.

Adele Bontemps was an old business partner of Laurent's from St-Buvard. Their partnership had ended badly twenty years ago with intense acrimony on Adele's side after which Adele had disappeared.

If Adele Bontemps was the leader of *Le Jeu*, Laurent was as good as dead.

"You are not eating, Madame Dernier," Giordano said with a frown.

He looked around as if he was searching for a server and Maggie had this terrible feeling that some poor innocent was going to pay for the fact that she wasn't able to eat just now.

"Please, Signore Giordano," she said. "The food is wonderful, and I hope you'll understand that it's only my nerves and fear for my husband's safety that is preventing me from enjoying it."

Giordano frowned and then seemed to notice that Luc wasn't eating either. He tossed down his fork with a loud clang onto his plate, splattering bright red tomato sauce onto the pristine tablecloth.

"Of course," he said. "Forgive me. I have been insensitive."

"Not at all," Maggie said, although again she hated to disagree with him lest that spark a negative reaction.

"No, no, in fact while we have been sitting here, I have been busy thinking, yes?"

He wadded up his linen napkin and dropped it onto his plate. Maggie watched in helpless fascination as the spotless fabric soaked up the dark sauce. He reached into his shirt pocket and Maggie felt Luc flinch at the movement. But Giordano only pulled out a cellphone.

"Before I talk to Madame Bontemps," he said, "I will prepare the ground first, yes?"

He held up a finger to indicate that Maggie should watch and learn.

"*Allo*, Giovanni?" he said, winking at Maggie. "I wonder if you would like a little wager with me and Adele at her place? Ah, yes? How about two million euros?" He laughed heartily at something "Giovanni" had said on the other line.

"*Exactement*," Giordano said. "Information like this does not come cheap," he said, waggling his eyebrows at Maggie. "If you want to know where the playing field is, I suggest you ante up, *non*?" He listened for a moment, his smile never leaving his face.

"*Bon*," he said finally. "Because I trust you, I will tell you where it will be played even before your money clears the bank, eh? It will be played starting at dusk today at Les Trois Corniches. They will start at the top and we will see where they land, eh?" He laughed again.

"Spread the word, okay? Not everyone may play but that doesn't mean everyone can't watch, you know?" He laughed again and then disconnected.

Maggie must have looked as baffled as she felt because Giordano quickly explained.

"By raising the stakes on *Le Jeu*—up! Up! Up! into the

stratosphere, yes?—I have done two things. First, it will prevent Madame Bontemps from moving the game if she was thinking of doing that, okay?"

Maggie nodded slowly.

"And second it will keep her from killing the hostages," Giordano said, reaching down the table to spear an asparagus stalk. "At least not right away. With the chance of such a big payday, Adele will take the risk of keeping them alive, you see?"

"I do," Maggie said hoarsely.

The fact that it was Adele Bontemps controlling the game might mean that Laurent would have a little more grace time. True, she was a woman scorned, but she'd loved him once, in her way. Perhaps not as a normal human might, but Maggie had to believe Adele would be loath to erase Laurent totally from her world.

At least not until she'd had the chance to sufficiently torture him.

When that thought came to her, so did the realization that Adele already had the most obvious way to torture Laurent.

Grace.

37

Laurent lay on the cement floor. He knew he was hurt. Broken bones, concussion, and lacerations, although he was no longer bleeding.

He'd awakened a few times before. Once when the girl spoke to him—unless that was a dream. And once when a severe thirst had brought him crawling away from the brink of death. Both times he'd seriously regretted becoming conscious.

His eyes watched as the door to his cell swung slowly open, its black iron facings showing splintered wood and a crudely made lock, as if knocked together with a few spare pieces of scrap metal. He closed his eyes again. His mind was playing tricks on him. He didn't know what he was seeing any more or why it mattered.

He opened his eyes when he heard the door rattle in its frame, and the floor beneath him seemed to vibrate and quake. He heard the patter of a raindrop hitting the roof. He must be imagining that.

He knew he was bound with plastic zip ties. He must have noticed that another time he was awake. Funny that he remembered that. He was hallucinating. Had to be.

"I was afraid we'd lost you."

Laurent started at the sound of her voice. It was smooth. Velvety smooth. And so familiar. His brain hungered for the kindness it promised. He peered into the gloom of the room. Was it the girl again? The one with the china doll voice...

"You have a very hard head."

He turned his head in the direction of the voice. His body screamed in pain as he did. The silhouette of a figure stood in the doorway, illuminated by the dim light. It moved closer, almost floating. Laurent realized that was familiar too.

"I know you," he breathed, his voice hoarse from lack of use.

The figure stopped and looked down at him. She was truly beautiful. Laurent could admit that. Like he could admit that a Rembrandt was a masterpiece. Although he'd not want one in his house.

"Indeed, you do, *chérie*," she said. "Did you ever wonder where I'd gone? Did you try to find me?"

She knelt in front of him. He remembered her scent then, too. Musk and gardenias. His stomach roiled and he wet his lips. She reached over and he felt the tension on the zip ties that held his hands together. Suddenly the tension broke and his arms fell away from him. His body reacted in agony from the release and a moan of pain escaped his lips.

"I didn't realize you were alive until I heard my men talking to the girl. Honestly, you still surprise me, *chérie*." She laughed mirthlessly. "You always could."

Laurent struggled to remember her name. Why, it mattered, he wasn't sure. Surely nothing mattered any more. He listened as she spoke, unable to fully comprehend what she was saying. His head hurt, his vision was blurred. He couldn't think straight. She seemed to sense his confusion and gently put a hand on his shoulder.

"You don't need to worry any more, *chérie*," she said softly. "I've got you now."

She leaned in closer, and there in her eyes was an unmistakable glint of malice. As muddled as he was, as much as his head pounded to the point where he couldn't think straight, there was no doubt this woman meant him harm. Even as she professed her concern for him with every glance and movement of her body.

"I was afraid I'd lost you," she said.

Adele.

He nearly groaned with the realization. They'd owned a wine boutique operation together a long time ago when Laurent was first getting started in the business. She knew a lot of people had invested generously in the enterprise. But she'd wanted a favor from Laurent, or she would ruin his oldest friend, Danielle's husband Jean-Luc. If she'd known him at all back then, she'd have known it was just about the worst thing she could try. But people like Adele didn't look past their own desires.

He looked at her now and finally saw her. In her early forties, Adele had been a beautiful woman, lush and ripe. In Laurent's opinion, she was more beautiful then than she'd been at twenty. But he wouldn't have been interested then either.

Today, she was pushing sixty. Still striking, although the work she'd had done told the world what she feared most. Laurent was surprised that Adele would allow herself to reveal so much about what really scared her.

Growing old.

She held a bottle of water to his lips, and he drank gratefully, a tear escaping down his cheek in his ardent need. She touched the tear with a long finger and brought the finger to her mouth.

"You know I won't let anyone hurt you ever again," she whispered. "I'll always protect you."

Laurent felt a chill go through him. As he looked into her eyes, molten golden brown, melting into him with an intensity that he would never forget, he remembered it all. There were nights after he'd ripped up their contract that he'd thought of her, knowing she hadn't forgotten him, knowing she was still out there in the world somewhere, hating him, wanting him.

But that day—twenty years ago—on the day his whole harvest burned to ashes, and he had to tell Jean-Luc there was no contract for their wine for the coming year, he'd also walked away with a lilt in his step.

The dissolution of the partnership with Adele had freed him.

When you have the things you really need—love, family, friendship—the rest is just icing.

And I can live without icing.

He reached out as if to touch her hand and she slipped into his arms, embracing him tightly. Tears of joy cascaded down her cheeks.

Although Laurent could barely sit up straight, he managed to wrap his arms around her in a return embrace. Adele clung to him, as he moved his hands up to her face and then to her neck, where he slowly wrapped his hands.

And squeezed.

38

Giordano led Maggie and Luc into the formal library in the center of the villa and told them to wait while he went to put his plan into action to free Laurent and Grace and Joelle.

"I will make sure everything runs smoothly, yes?" he said, rubbing his hands together excitedly. "It is the first step of my plan, yes? You wait here and I will bring Laurent and the women to you. Okay?"

"I can't thank you enough, Signore Giordano," Maggie said as Giordano turned and, giving her a jaunty wave over his shoulder, shut the door behind him.

Maggie stared at the closed door for a moment, feeling not at all reassured. She went to sit in a large, overstuffed chair. A large picture window overlooked the side courtyard showing an explosion of colorful flowers, ivy covered walls, and a fountain that bubbled in the center.

The library walls were lined with bookshelves filled with leather-bound tomes. Paintings of unknown Italian noblemen hung on every available space on the walls. An enormous fireplace occupied the far wall and in the corner sat an ancient harp. The air was thick with the scent of old books. Off the center of the room was a large oak desk. Two chairs were arranged in front of it.

Everywhere Maggie looked, she could tell this room was a place dedicated to history—and secrets. She could almost feel the stories that its walls held. But in Maggie's mind, these walls also held screams. Of the innocent, the unlucky, the damned.

"How do you know Adele Bontemps?" Luc asked.

"Through my husband," Maggie said. "They were in business together. Briefly."

"They were lovers?"

"No, but actually I think that was part of the problem."

Maggie came to sit opposite Luc.

"We own a vineyard in Provence," she said. "About twenty years ago Laurent partnered with Adele. They owned a boutique operation with a few other vintners to share joint leasing of the equipment needed to crush and bottle their wine."

"What happened?"

"I don't know all the details. I only know that one day he was in business with her and the next he wasn't, and she was ever after his sworn enemy."

"So she means him harm," he said, probing. "If he is in her hands."

"Yes," Maggie said stiffly. "I'd say that's a fair statement."

Maggie didn't really know why the partnership had ended although she had her theories, most of which had been echoed by Grace who was pretty good at ferreting out these things. She'd heard gossip that Adele had finally made her big move on Laurent and been unceremoniously rejected.

Maggie had to smile at the thought. Laurent didn't waste time on fools. For children and the elderly, he was endlessly patient. For people attempting to manipulate him, he ran out of pat niceties very quickly. She was sure—if that was what had happened—that Laurent would have left no room for doubt about his feelings.

But that didn't help anything right now. A woman scorned—especially a woman like Adele—could hold a grudge a very long time. She shook off the image of Laurent caught in Adele's wicked talons.

"I'm sorry about trying to trick you," Luc said. "Earlier."

Maggie narrowed her eyes at him.

"The woman named Bijoux," she said, "she works for you?"

He looked at her, surprised that she knew the name of his confederate. Finally, he just sighed.

"Look, I'm sorry," he said weakly. "It's a living."

"A disgusting one. I came to you during the worst moment of my life, and you took advantage of it."

"I can only say I'm sorry," he said. "It wasn't personal. When you didn't respond to me and Joelle, I had Bijoux approach you. But what does it matter? You didn't believe her any more than you believed me and Joelle. You didn't bite."

But of course Maggie *had* gone for the bait. It was just sheer luck she hadn't walked right into their trap. Of all the people she'd talked to last night so many were unhelpful or, like Luc and Joelle and Bijoux, meant her harm. She thought of the waitress Annabelle. She still didn't know who had given her the warehouse address where the hostages had been held. Maggie didn't think it was Madame de la Roche. Maybe it was Annabelle?—who'd wanted to help but didn't want to get involved?

She sighed heavily. Luc was right about one thing at least. What difference did any of it make now?

"Where exactly are Les Trois Corniches?" she asked as Luc scrolled through his phone.

Maggie didn't know whether giving their phones back meant to them meant the mob boss trusted them or had no fear of the police. Or if he intended to kill them.

She tried not to think of what might be in his mind.

"It is just west of here," Luc said. "Beautiful coastal views."

"Why would Adele choose it as a place to release her hostages?"

"Some say it is the most dangerous road in the world. It's a series of switchback cliff roads. One wrong step, and it's a fifteen hundred-foot drop to the roads below."

"Will the hostages be in cars?"

"No, but the roads are still dangerous. The Grande Corniche was built by Napoleon. It is elegant and terrifying in equal parts."

"Isn't that where Princess Grace died?"

"It is. In some spots there is not room for two cars to pass. In the fog, it is a death trap." He looked up at her, his gaze unwavering. "At night, definitely so."

A light sheen of perspiration appeared on Maggie's forehead as she thought about the treacherous roads. She hated just sitting here and waiting—not to mention trusting someone who didn't appear at all trustworthy.

"Do you trust him?" Luc asked in a low voice, surprising her that he was tracking her own thoughts.

"Do we have a choice?"

But it wasn't a rhetorical question. If there *was* another way, she needed to find it. And fast.

"How is it *you* know Adele?" she asked.

He shook his head more in bewilderment than denial.

"I know her a bit. But you're right, it is possible I have upset her."

"How so?"

"I may have tried the wrong thing on someone she considered untouchable."

"You mean you tried to rob a friend of hers?"

He shrugged helplessly.

"It is difficult to understand why certain people do what

they do," he said. "I know she is angry at me because Joelle is missing."

"Would she kill Joelle to send a message to you?"

Luc stood up in agitation and clenched and unclenched his hands. A vein began to visibly throb in his neck. Maggie noted that his very body language was answering the question more clearly than any words could.

"Is there a reason why you do what you do?" she asked. "Is Joelle onboard with it?"

He frowned. "She knows we target wealthy tourists."

"Was I a wealthy tourist?"

"You are an American, so we knew you had money."

"You're an idiot, Luc. Seriously. It's a wonder you're still alive. Did *Joelle* know that by hanging with you she could be in this kind of danger?"

He stared at his hands, the picture of contrition and shame.

"I loved her," he said softly. "I did."

"She's not dead yet."

He shook his head angrily.

"As good as. I hope Signore Giordano helps you get your friends back, Madame. And because he seems to know and respect your husband, maybe he will. But there is no reason for him to bargain for Joelle. None."

"When Giordano and his men swoop in before the start of the game to collect Laurent and Grace, he'll collect Joelle too," Maggie said firmly. "That was the deal."

"Remind me again of what Giordano gets out of this deal? I only heard what you got."

Maggie frowned. That was a good point. Aside from Laurent's indebtedness to him—which wasn't totally nothing—why was Giordano helping her? He definitely wasn't doing it for magnanimous reasons.

"And what makes you think he'll swoop in *before* the game is played?" Luc said, throwing his hands up in frustration.

His words chilled Maggie. "What do you mean?" she asked.

"You heard him. He's ratcheted up the stakes for *Le Jeu* all across Monaco—maybe all of France! This is a very big game now with very big winnings to be had."

"You think he'll let the game start?"

"Start and finish. The only hope we have is that our loved ones survive the contest. And then, of course, that Giordano can convince Madame Bontemps to give the hostages to him."

"He said he'd pay her."

"He said a lot of things."

Maggie stared at him for a moment.

"I can't decide not to trust Giordano when he's the only chance I have of getting them back," she said finally.

"Logical," Luc said with a shrug.

"How is the game monitored?" she asked suddenly.

"I understand there are cameras set up at certain quadrants on the playing field."

"For what purpose? Isn't there a finish line?"

"Yes, of course. But Madame Bontemps will want to see how things are going. A lot of money is riding on the outcome."

"What can she do to affect the outcome?"

"Seriously? Did you not hear about the snakes and wild boars in the area?"

"I did. But it's possible the hostages won't run into any of those."

"That's not likely," Luc said wearily, "since I know for a fact that Adele's people will be releasing at least six wild boars into the field where the hostages are taken."

He paused dramatically.

"Along with nearly four dozen poisonous vipers," he said.

39

The man gripped Grace's arm tightly as he led her to the waiting van. She'd been so grateful to be outside that her relief had mitigated her fear. But now seeing that she was to be taken someplace else, her mind raced with mounting anxiety.

He opened the van door and Grace saw there were already two people inside. One was the woman Rebecca, whom she'd met before. Like Grace herself, Rebecca's hands were bound with plastic ties and she was gagged. Her eyes held an expression of terror that mirrored Grace's own feelings of dread as she climbed into the back seat.

The other woman was new. She was young, her hair a wild mess around her shoulders and her eyes above her gag were stricken with fear. She wore an evening dress that was ripped and stained with mud.

The man nudged Grace inside and she settled into a seat beside the other two women. The interior of the van felt suffocating after her brief walk from the house. She tried to calm herself by taking deep breaths through her nose, but the smell of sweat and body odor in the car made her nauseated. Where were they being taken? Was this human trafficking? Were they going to be forced into prostitution?

She turned to face their kidnapper. His expression was grim and businesslike as he leaned into the van and ripped off Rebecca's gag. Immediately, Rebecca coughed and then pleaded with him.

"Please, there's been a terrible mistake," she said. "I'm a British citizen! You've got the wrong person! Please!"

The man's face twisted into a visage of disgust. He roughly grabbed Rebecca's face and pressed the gag back onto her mouth.

"Which one of you is Grace?" he asked in French, his eyes scanning each woman in turn.

Grace cleared her throat. The man looked at her and then smiled, revealing a set of crooked teeth.

"Yeah, I knew it was you." He laughed harshly. "I just wanted to see if you would admit it."

Grace fought back tears. She swore that if she ever got out of this situation alive, she would never again feel pride about her resemblance to Princess Grace of Monaco. She would never again boast to acquaintances that that was the reason her mother named her Grace.

"Sorry, Princess," he said, breathing out a blast of garlic and onions into her face as he leaned in to adjust the gag around Grace's mouth. She shut her eyes so as not to see his face so close to her own.

Then he scanned all three women as if looking for something specific. Grace watched him and was surprised to see his gaze included the row of seats behind her.

Is there someone else back there?

She waited until the man slammed and locked the van door before turning to look in the backseat where she saw a man slumped in his seat. A ripple of anxiety shot through her. It made sense that they would position a guard inside the vehicle to ensure the prisoners didn't try to escape. But the man looked hungover and impaired. Grace turned in her seat to get a better look, and realized he wasn't moving. His head was down as if injured or sick. She wasn't sure he was even breathing.

She squinted to clear her vision and suddenly her heart jumped to her throat.

It was Laurent.

40

Maggie stared at Luc, her stomach twisting in nausea at what he'd just told her.

"How...how do you know that?" she asked.

"I hear things in the group I run with," Luc said. "A friend of a friend of mine made twenty grand to acquire a dozen European Vipers. He said they'd be released into the playing field to even the odds."

"But if the hostages are killed before they reach the finish line..." Maggie said, her thoughts tumbling on top of each other.

"Think about it. Most of the people betting are betting they don't survive. Signore Giordano will collect his winnings along with everyone else—unless he stupidly bets on their making it to the end alive, which I can assure you he did not. Then he'll come back to the villa to explain to you how sorry he is for their deaths and how he did everything he could. That is, if he decides not to just kill us—which of course is another option."

"I don't believe it," Maggie said.

Luc turned to her in frustration.

"Why would Giordano bet on the contestants making it to the finish line alive when he knows—as I do—that Adele will put her thumb on the scales to make sure they don't?"

Maggie got up out of her chair, a feeling of restless anxiety coursing through her body. She paced the length of the room, her eyes going through the French doors, where she could see Giordano's sprawling Italian garden. Wisteria vines climbed the towering arches of stone that surrounded the impressive pergola in the center of the garden which men with rifles patrolled throughout.

Giordano only wins if they all die.

Even if he does intend to put an end to *Le Jeu* for his own reasons after today, it won't be in time to help Laurent and Grace.

"They've turned off the Wi-Fi," Luc said morosely looking on his phone. "They don't want us contacting anyone."

Maggie glanced at the camera in the corner of the ceiling, its tell-tale red light revealing that they were being monitored. She sat down next to Luc in his chair and laid her head on his shoulder. He sat up straight in surprise.

"What's happening?" he asked.

"Pretend that you like it."

"Not the hardest thing I've had to do today," he said, relaxing back into his chair next to her.

"I don't want them to hear us conspiring," she said.

"Are we conspiring?"

"Giordano told us where the game is to be played," Maggie said, careful to keep her face turned from the camera.

"If you're suggesting what I think you are, we will be killed if we try anything."

Maggie reminded herself that Amélie was at home waiting for her. The child needed her. Laurent would be furious if Maggie risked not coming home to her. But she couldn't just sit and hope that an underworld mafia don would keep his word to save her husband and dearest friend!

"I'm going with or without you," she said.

"How in the world do you think we'd even get out of here? Forget the cameras, there are armed men—and an attack dog!—right outside the door. It's madness!"

"You said it yourself, we stay here and there's a chance we die anyway. Are you trusting Vittorio Giordano with your life?"

"At least there's some question about whether or not he'll kill us. If we try to escape, he'll definitely want us dead."

"With you or without you, Luc," she said. "What's it going to be?"

Luc let out a breath of frustration. "Why are American women always so pushy?"

"First thing we need to do is find where they put my car," Maggie said.

"How in hell do we do that?"

Maggie was silent for a moment, thinking.

"I'll tell one of Giordano's goons that I need something personal out of it," she said. "Surely they've already searched it, right?"

"Probably. But they'll just go get it for you."

"I'll say it's of a delicate female nature and I need to retrieve it myself. If they've already searched the car, they'll know there are no weapons in it."

Luc shook his head in disbelief or admiration—Maggie couldn't tell which.

"It's getting dark," she said. "When do you think the game will start?"

Luc squinted out the window at the fading light. "If not now then soon."

"That's probably where Giordano went," Maggie said, standing up. "Not to set up a plan to get them released. But to get a front row seat."

"You sound surprised."

She turned and smiled at him for the benefit of the camera blinking down on her.

"Just be ready to go when I get back," she said without moving her lips.

41

Grace's heart skipped a beat when she saw Laurent, his head slumped on his chest and his eyes closed. As soon as the van began to move, she climbed into the back seat and pressed her cheek against his. His skin was warm, so at least he was alive. He was bound but not gagged.

Because she was both bound and gagged, Grace could only make noises through the rag over her mouth in an attempt to rouse him. As she tried, she noticed the woman in the evening dress was watching her closely.

She leaned against Laurent as the car wound its way up a winding road. It was treacherous driving, she realized, and the van driver was driving slowly. Glancing out the van window, she saw that the road was wet with rain, and a haze of mist and fog was partially obscuring the road. There were no street lamps so Grace guessed they were in the countryside.

The wheels of the van occasionally hit loose gravel at the edge of the road. Grace could imagine how easy it might be to go pitching over the side of the road.

She tried to imagine why in the world they were all being driven up this narrow and winding mountain road at night.

Was it a ransom scheme? Or would they be dragged out to a remote part of the countryside and executed? Nothing made sense, but one thing was certain: wherever they were going, it wasn't going to be good.

She turned back to Laurent and leaned into him again, this time putting her face against his neck and screaming as loud as she could through her gag. He groaned and instinctively moved away from her. She moved closer, aware that the two women were now turned in their seats watching her.

Again, Grace put her face into Laurent's neck and screamed. This time, when he pushed away, he also opened his eyes. When he did, Grace saw something flicker in them. She drilled him with her own gaze, willing him to keep his eyes open.

That was when she saw it. Laurent blinked and then blinked again and then she saw him look at her with recognition. Tears welled up in her eyes.

"Grace?" he murmured.

She nodded vigorously. Laurent looked around the interior of the van, his lids growing heavy again. Grace made a loud humming noise, and he turned back to her. She nodded again, her eyes wide in an effort to encourage him to stay awake.

Suddenly, the van lurched to a stop. Grace looked out the window. In the darkness she could barely make out the dense foliage around them, the trees and brambles adding to the feeling of unease that surrounded the van. Overhead, the night sky was a starless void of inky blackness that seemed to stretch endlessly above and around them.

Something was about to happen.

∽

The man who opened the van door was not someone Grace had seen before. He was stout with a scarred face and a grinning mouth full of yellowed teeth. His eyes were small and beady.

Instantly Rebecca began to whimper and cower away from him. Grace didn't know what had happened to her with this man, but it was clear she had met him before.

The man cleared his throat and held up his hands.

"Everybody speak English, yes? I speak English."

Grace turned to glance at Laurent, but his eyes were closed.

"We let you out now, okay? Everything is fine now. Just a little game and then we drive you back to your hotels, okay? Safe and sound. Okay?"

His words were at odds with the ominous undertone in his affect that sent chills up Grace's spine. From where one hand gripped the van door, it was obvious from the grime encrusted under his broken fingernails that he had not seen soap or water in weeks.

"Madame B sorry not to be here to say goodbye, okay?" he said. "But she is having a little accident, okay?" He glanced at Laurent and his face went cold as if suddenly realizing that Grace was not sitting where he'd put her.

"Madame B will be at the finish line to award you your freedom, okay? Freedom?"

When they only stared at him, he seemed momentarily flustered and looked from one to the other before reaching over the middle seat to where Grace sat, and roughly pulling her gag out.

"Who are you?" she asked, her voice hoarse from disuse.

"Not a part of the game," he said with a smile as if he'd been asked this question before.

"What game?"

"Good question! Very good question! All will be explained."

He reached into his pocket and pulled out a packet of index cards.

"The man is number one, yes?" He held the card out to Grace and then realizing that she still had her hands tied, he leaned over her and jammed it into Laurent's shirt pocket.

"And you are two, okay?" he said to Grace, holding up the card with the numeral two written on it.

She stared at him as if he'd lost his mind. He turned and tucked the other cards into pockets of the other two women. To the one in the evening gown, he slipped it into the front of her dress.

"Why are we here?" Grace asked.

A flinch of annoyance passed his face.

"I will tell the rules in a minute," he said looking flustered as if trying to remember where he was in his spiel.

"There is a flag—" he started.

"What kind of flag?" Grace asked.

"Just a flag!" he said with aggravation. "A flag that waves in the air. There are four flags. You find the flags. When you find them all, we will pick you up and you will be..." He hesitated and then cursed and pulled his cell phone out of his jeans pocket. He read from something on his phone.

"Clues will lead you to the flags. If you find them all before morning, you will be well compensated for your inconvenience."

"And if we don't find them all?" Grace asked.

He nodded as if expecting this question and once more referred to his cellphone for the answer.

"Then you will have a story to tell your friends and your grandchildren for the rest of your life." He beamed at her as if expecting her to nod. "Okay? You won't be hurt. It is just a game."

"What if we don't want to play?" Grace asked.

He looked at his phone but clearly didn't find the answer to this question. He began to look agitated.

"You must play," he said in frustration.

"And what happens if we don't find any flags before morning?" Grace asked.

The man jammed his phone in his pocket and gave her a look that made her blood run cold.

"Well, then what happens is your own fault," he said coldly, no longer going by the script.

42

Maggie strode to the front door of the villa and pulled it open. Instantly, a young man with an AK-47 on his shoulder stepped in front of her.

"Boss says you're not to leave," he said in broken French.

"I don't intend to leave," she said imperiously, reminding herself that, gun or not, he was a boy no older than Jemmy. She put on what she hoped was her most serious, business-like affect.

"I have something I need to retrieve from the glovebox of my car," she said. "Something of a highly personal nature. Would you mind escorting me there?"

The boy hesitated for a moment. He looked around as if he'd prefer to have someone else make this decision but there was nobody near. Finally, he nodded.

"Follow me," he said.

Maggie walked behind him down the wide marble steps of the front entrance and across the roundabout drive, her heart pounding with each step. The car had been moved from where she'd parked it in front of the steps to the furthest arc of the roundabout where it was blocked from view by the large central fountain.

When they reached the car, the guard opened the door for her and then stood back and watched as Maggie retrieved a packet of tissues from the glovebox. She noticed the car keys were still in the ignition, probably to make it easier for the guards when they had to move it again.

Maggie smiled at the boy in gratitude, and he nodded in acknowledgement before they retraced their steps back across the roundabout drive and up the broad steps to the front of the villa. As she stepped back inside, she turned to the boy.

"Can you show me where the bathroom is?" she asked.

He looked briefly panicked and looked over his shoulder.

"I'm not allowed in the house," he said.

"No worries. I'll find it." She smiled and closed the door on him, forcing herself not to glance up at the camera that she knew was positioned on the foyer. She didn't want anyone watching to know she was aware she was being watched.

She turned to look at Luc who was standing stiffly by a sculpture of a cherub in the foyer with an odd look on his face. She didn't have time to decipher it. She knew where the car was and she knew that night was falling. Things needed to happen quickly if they were going to do this.

It occurred to her that if she was not at all sure about Giordano's promise to help her, that breaking out of his house and racing away in the night was probably not going to endear her to him. But she couldn't risk that he was not truly on her side.

"You ready?" she said to Luc, attempting not to move her mouth too much in case whoever was watching could lip read.

"As I'll ever be," he said.

Maggie turned her back on the camera and prayed the foyer wasn't miked for sound too.

"The car is past the fountain on the roundabout," she said under her breath. "The keys are in the ignition."

Luc didn't answer.

Maggie would have dearly loved to take the shortest route to the car—to just make a break out the front door and beeline it across the roundabout. But she knew they had to use stealth if they didn't want to bring the whole household down on them.

"Bathroom break!" she sang out and walked down the hall toward the kitchen.

As planned, Luc shrugged as if uninterested and turned to walk away until he was out of sight of the camera lens. He joined Maggie in the hallway where they both walked in single file to a set of stairs that they'd seen the servants use. Maggie didn't know exactly where the servants' entrance opened onto but it was already almost dark outside. Wherever it was, unless it opened right onto the main drive, they would have the cover of darkness to hide them.

Leading the way, she hurried down the stairs toward the sounds of the kitchen. Two people stood in the kitchen with their backs to her, scrubbing the large pots and pans from lunch. Neither of them turned around, either because they didn't hear Maggie and Luc or because they preferred not to know what was happening.

Maggie hesitated at the exterior kitchen door. She knew there was a chance it was connected to a sensor of some kind, but she had to believe that with the kitchen staff still here, it was less likely to be activated. She opened the door and slipped out, saying a silent prayer of gratitude when no alarm sounded.

The door opened onto a covered patio area with another smaller swimming pool, all surrounded by a high fence. There was no one in the pool area. The air that met her was crisp and dry with a slight tang of chlorine and freshly mown grass. The sky was already dark, but not dark enough that Maggie couldn't easily see the area around her.

She felt a burst of adrenalin as she quickened her step

around the pool, aiming for the side of the villa. Once there, she instantly went into a crouch until she felt Luc join her from behind. Together they crept around the side of the villa towards the front, staying low and silent. As they approached the entrance, Maggie saw a patrol of two men coming around the corner. Quickly, Luc dove into the bushes pulling Maggie with him and pressing his hand against her mouth. It was all Maggie could do not to gasp out loud in an attempt to breathe past his hand, but she forced herself to remain quiet.

"Did you hear anything?" one of the young guards asked as they strolled past.

"It's only the stupid dog."

"Why doesn't Tony just shoot him? He bit Benito last week!"

"Shut up. I'll relieve you in an hour. If I find you sitting down again, I'll shoot *you*."

The patrol moved on, and Luc and Maggie crawled out from under the bush and got to their feet. Maggie felt several cuts and abrasions on her elbows and knees. But right now she felt only exhilaration that they were so close to escape.

"Hey! What are you doing out here?" a surprised voice said.

Maggie froze. When she looked up she realized it was the young man who'd escorted her to the car. Luc came up behind her and snaked an arm around her waist. Maggie stared at the boy, her brain gone suddenly blank as to how to explain why they were there.

The boy seemed to take in the situation quickly. He began to lift his gun at the same time he turned his body to call to the others. Maggie froze in horror. She glanced past him to the fountain where the car was parked. They were so close! Suddenly she felt Luc's fingers pinch into her arm.

"Come on!" he whispered as he tugged her away.

Maggie snapped her head back in time to see the boy crumple to the ground, a long Chef's knife sticking out of his side.

Maggie turned and ran, running as fast as she could, ignoring the noise their footsteps made on the gravel as they raced across the driveway and past the fountain. Luc reached the car before she did and jumped into the driver's seat. Maggie scrambled around to the far side to pull the passenger's side door open. The car roared to life and peeled away before she was completely inside..

"Get your head down!" Luc shouted as he gunned the sharp turn of the roundabout and headed for the closed gates. The sound of multiple gunshots riddled the body of the car in a steady, staccato stream.

"Here we go!" Luc shouted.

And floored it.

43

Detective Latour sat in a high-backed leather chair in the empty conference room. The window behind him was framed by a pair of olive trees and showed a blue cloudless sky outside. He often stole in here on busy days, knowing it was one of the last places his associates would choose to spend time when they weren't required to. He found it immeasurably peaceful to be some place most others avoided. He sat in the room now and felt a rare sense of calm wash over him. He had no idea why the sensation had come, or how long it would last, but he knew he wouldn't waste it.

He closed his eyes and breathed in deeply, taking in the silence, the stillness, and the peace. He let his thoughts drift, allowing himself this moment, not knowing if it would come again, not expecting it to.

Not deserving it to.

Suddenly his phone rang. He glanced at his watch. He'd told Liza he'd meet her at *Pigalle's* for drinks before dinner and he didn't want anything getting in the way of that. But he had plenty of time. It wouldn't be Liza calling.

The number was listed on his phone screen as *Unknown*.

"August?" a sultry voice purred over the line.

His stomach muscles tightened.

"I need you," Madame Bontemps said. "I need you and all the people you can scrape together. As promised. As paid for."

Latour felt a burgeoning excitement well up inside of him at her words.

"I can promise a big bonus this time," she said. "One hundred thousand euros."

The idea of the money took his breath away. It was more than had been promised. Much more.

"What's happening?" he asked.

"You are," she said. "If you can help me."

"I can."

"I need at least a dozen of your people. Out of uniform. What kind of arms do you have?"

"Don't worry about that."

"Very good."

"When?"

"This evening. I'll text you the coordinates and the exact time."

"We'll be there."

"Good. I'm counting on you, August."

She hung up. The pounding of his heart drowned out everything else. He could no longer hear his own thoughts. He sat unmoving. He'd known this call was coming. All that remained was to send the word out, the word that would pull him out of Monaco. He thought with regret about Liza. He'd miss their date tonight—and every night after tonight. He was sorry about that. Liza had felt special.

But he'd waited for this too long to let anything stall it now. Everything else was nearly ready to go. He would find another Liza. Maybe in Lisbon. Or South America. He took in a breath and imagined himself already crossing over into his new life.

He picked up his cellphone to begin the series of calls that would set everything in motion. His life in Monaco was over as soon as he crossed that line. Well, he'd crossed it many times before now. But tonight would make it official. There was no coming back after tonight.

He'd thought about this day, planned for it down to the last detail. He was ready. Ready to walk away. Ready to retire to the Caymans. Or wherever.

Before he could make the first call, his cellphone rang in his hand. Madame Bontemps again with one last bit of crucial information? But no. He recognized this number. Although it was not one he had expected to hear from.

"Yes?"

Three minutes later, Latour was back on the phone, assembling his army, arranging the armaments. His face was hard with focus and determination. A team of mercenaries willing to fight for the right price—better yet, willing to fight for him. If one man faltered, Latour simply upped the price until he agreed to join.

He had been waiting months for this. For years. And now it was happening. Granted, it wasn't happening as he'd envisioned it, but he was soldier enough to know that surprises were always a part of any battle plan. All he had to do was accommodate them as he found them, and all the pieces would fall into place.

He paused for a moment between calls to consider. Things were happening quickly. His life was being reshuffled as he sat there. One thing was certain, this time the stakes were higher than ever. Higher than he'd even imagined.

That was just fine with him. A wave of anticipation washed over him. After the long wait, it was finally go time. No, not as he'd imagined, but even so. Win or lose, succeed or fail, one thing he knew—he would not let emotion weaken him.

Or under any circumstances let her down. Even if it meant his life.

44

The minute Grace was pulled from the van she found herself blinded by a sudden flood of light. The two other women were dragged out of the vehicle behind her, where they now stood next to her while the two men cut their zip ties and removed their gags.

They're no longer afraid of anyone hearing us scream.

One of the men Grace knew as her jailer—the one who'd escorted her to the van and vaguely threatened her. The other man she hadn't seen before tonight, but in many ways the two men resembled each other as if they were related in some way. Or perhaps they just shared the same genus of evil.

As soon as Rebecca had her gag off, she began to hyperventilate. The other woman stood stock still, massaging the red marks on her wrists and staring around at her surroundings. Laurent was dragged bodily from the van and tossed to the ground with his hands still zip-tied behind his back. The men turned to climb back in the car.

Grace felt a flair of desperation descend on her.

"Are you afraid that a man beaten senseless is still a threat to you if he has his hands free?" she called to the men.

The man who'd initially questioned her in the van stopped at her taunt. He turned to her and pulled out a knife. Grace braced herself but didn't move. He walked over to Laurent but kept his eyes on Grace.

"You and me have a date later," he said to her. "So I'll need this guy to keep you in one piece until then."

He cut Laurent's ties and then held up his finger to pretend to shoot her with a gun and then turned and walked back to the van.

Laurent groaned as he moved his just released shoulders. Grace watched the van disappear into the night, then hurried over to him, but the woman in the evening dress was there first.

"Take it slow," she said to him. "You'll pull a muscle if you go too fast."

Grace intervened between them. Laurent held an arm out to her, and she slipped under it, supporting him.

"I thought you were dead," she said as he brought her in for a hug and rested his chin on her head for a moment.

"I did too," he said, and then turned to the woman. "Remind me."

"We met in your cell," she said. "I'm Joelle. Your wife has been showing your picture all over Monte Carlo."

"Maggie?" Grace said with excitement and then dismay as she turned to Joelle. "You saw her?"

"What are you people talking about?" Rebecca said in a whiny voice. "We need to get moving! They said we'll be rewarded if we can find the flags. If not, we go home empty-handed."

Grace realized this idiot thought they had joined some kind of reality TV game show. She decided not to waste her breath talking to her. She turned back to Joelle.

"How do you know Maggie?" Grace asked.

"I met her at the Monte Carlo Bay Casino. She's looking for both of you."

Laurent took in a long breath.

"Never mind about that now," he said. "We need to move."

"Move where?" Grace asked in bewilderment. "Where are we going?"

"I told you!" Rebecca said plaintively. "We need to make it to the—"

"Please stop talking," Grace said to her tartly. "You're giving me a headache and I really need to *think*. Laurent, darling, do you think you're able to walk?"

He grimaced. "I'm fine."

"You're in better shape than the Queen B," Joelle said. "I heard the goons talking before they shoved me in the van." She turned to Grace. "He tried to strangle her."

Grace looked at Laurent. "Who did you try to strangle?"

"It doesn't matter," Laurent said, dragging a hand across his face before reaching for Grace's hand. "Let's go."

"I'm pretty sure it mattered to *her*," Joelle said. "They said they got to her just in time."

Laurent paused to look at Joelle and the memory came rushing back to him. *Adele*. Her neck in his hands. He'd wanted to kill her. If he hadn't been so weak after the beating the day before, he would've killed her.

No time for that now. He stepped off the path into the darkened woods. The rain had stopped but raindrops hung off the branches and leaves of the trees. Rolling clouds had gathered overhead obscuring the moonlit landscape from view and giving it an eerie glow. The night air was heavy with earthy smells. It was quiet, but not silent.

"We need to stay in the lighted areas," Rebecca protested. "This is a dangerous stretch of road. I read about it. You can fall to your death!"

Laurent kept moving. Grace hurried to catch up with him. She had a million questions. Where had he been? Did he remember the actual kidnapping? When was he beaten? Why were they here? Was he truly okay?

She paused as he stopped in front of her. He bent over and threw up. Grace felt a stab of fear. She thought about all the celebrities she'd read about who had sustained head injuries, affecting to be perfectly fine, before lying down for a nap and never waking up again.

"Laurent?"

"I'm fine, Grace."

"You were going to...to murder her?"

Laurent shifted his weight to lean against a nearby tree for a moment. His hip was throbbing and for a moment he didn't know if it would hold his weight.

"Apparently," he said.

He turned to look at her and his heart ached for how afraid she looked. He couldn't imagine what she'd been through since he'd last seen her. But whatever had happened since then, it would've been a thousand times worse if he'd been successful in strangling Adele. The two goons would likely have just shot them all and dumped their bodies. He hadn't really thought it out. He'd instinctively reacted. At the time, it had seemed the most natural thing to do.

He counted his head injury for why he hadn't been thinking properly. Suddenly his ears perked up and he turned his head. It was faint but was clearly the sound of dogs baying. He felt confused. Their kidnappers knew exactly where they were. They didn't need to track them. He glanced at the three women standing behind him on the trail looking at him for answers.

If they set the dogs on us, it's not to pick up our scent. It's to rip us apart.

"We need to split up," he said thickly, his tongue suddenly feeling too big for his mouth.

"No way!"

"I'm not leaving you again."

"No!"

Laurent turned back to the trail, too exhausted to argue with them. Should they run or hide? There was no way they could make a stand. In the end, he decided all they really could do was put one foot in front of the other.

In any case, he didn't have the energy for more.

45

Maggie fumbled for her phone as Luc sped down the A8, reversing their route of just a few hours ago. She put a call in to Margaux, knowing she was breaking any semblance of a deal with Giordano that there would be no police involved. On the other hand, it wasn't likely there was a ghost of a chance that Giordano would help them now—not after they'd killed one of his guys and blown a hole in his security gate.

Besides, she was tired of playing by everyone else's rules. The police, the bad guys, even Margaux. Her call ended with Margaux's voicemail. Maggie hesitated. She wasn't sure what in the world she could say in a message that wouldn't ultimately just serve to get Margaux killed, so she just said: "I'm checking in to see what Tassoni had to say" and disconnected.

"You have somebody else on our team?" Luc asked, glancing at her as he drove.

"Yes, but no one nearly as connected as Signore Giordano."

"Well, you can cross him off your list since he definitely isn't going to help us now."

"It doesn't matter," she said. "You were right. He wasn't going to help us before."

Luc nodded in acceptance of her semi-apology. Maggie watched him as he drove. She was surprised she ever thought he was handsome. Stress and fear had altered his features. He looked as if he'd aged twenty years since she'd met him at the casino last night.

"I take it we're heading for the Grande Corniche?" he asked.

The famous route ran between the sea and the mountains, curving around the contours of the land, and in daylight providing stunning panoramas of azure blue waters merging with the horizon.

"We are," Maggie said, punching in the coordinates for the road. Les Trois Corniches was twenty miles in length. Luc had suggested that the contestants would start *Le Jeu* at the top—which was the Grande Corniche—and Maggie didn't have time to rethink that. At fifteen hundred feet above sea level, the Grande Corniche was the highest of the three roads.

It was also the deadliest.

"Do you think Giordano will send his goons after us?" she asked.

"Hard to say. Not until after *Le Jeu* has finished playing anyway."

"How long does the game usually take?"

"Depends. Sometimes an hour. Sometimes all night."

"When we get there," she said, "we'll ditch the car and go the rest of the way on foot."

Luc nodded but kept his eyes focused on the road.

"Where did you get the knife?" she asked.

"In the kitchen."

Maggie hated to think that there might have been another way than killing the boy who'd helped her earlier. But she had seen in the boy's eyes that he was going to raise the alarm. She couldn't have done it herself. She found herself sickened and glad that Luc had been able to.

After that they drove in silence for the twenty minutes it took them to reach the area east of Menton where Les Trois Corniches began. There the road wound its way around the cliffs—the glittering Mediterranean barely visible in the moonlight stretched out before it, while craggy hills and mountains rose behind it, their jagged peaks forming a perfect backdrop.

Luc turned onto the Grande Corniche and the road rose up, twisting and turning along its path, its surface slippery with the mist that clung to the rocks. Despite its beauty, it was clear that Les Corniches was not for the faint of heart.

Maggie saw glimpses of the Mediterranean far below glittering in the moonlight—visible in nauseating snatches around each hairpin turn. She could see how misjudging the angle of any of the sharp corners could easily mean a fall off the edge of the sheer cliffs to the rocks below.

As she watched the sweat pour down Luc's face, Maggie realized it was even worse to be driving this road at night when you were already petrified with fear.

46

The path ahead was only shadows.

Grace couldn't see where she was putting a single step. She just had to trust that the ground littered with leaves and twigs would hold. In the rain, the trees dripped all around her and the fog clung to her knees as she walked.

She glanced at Joelle and felt buoyed and heartsick at the same time at Joelle's news.

God bless Maggie. She was trying to find them!

Surely she would have contacted the police? Grace frowned. But it had been nearly two days! Why was nothing being done? She glanced at Laurent and was surprised that he didn't seem affected about the news that Maggie was looking for them.

As usual, he was a Sphinx. She could only imagine what was going on underneath that taciturn facade.

She took in a lungful of air inhaling the scent of freshly mown hay and woodsmoke. Somewhere out in the dark, a cow's lowing sounded and Grace wondered why it wasn't in a barn for the night. Above her, the overhanging trees were blotting out the moon and stars. The evening breeze seemed to breathe life into the pine branches, which creaked and moaned.

Joelle was in the lead as they walked and when she stopped, Grace did too. She peered around Joelle to see that a tree had come down blocking the way forward. Before Grace could turn to ask Laurent what they should do, they hear the sound of a vehicle on the winding road directly beneath them.

Instantly Rebecca ran to the edge of the road and grabbed onto the branch of a leaning tree to get a better view of the road below. Grace was tempted to pull her back to the trail, but she knew she didn't have the strength. She noticed that Laurent didn't even stop walking.

"It's a farmer!" Rebecca shouted back to them. She waved her arms. "Hello! Up here! Hello!"

Laurent stopped walking then but didn't turn around.

"Do you think...?" Grace asked him tentatively.

"That there's a farmer on a switchback coastal road in the middle of the night?" he asked wearily.

"You think it's a trick?"

"I don't know what to think."

That comment was so unlike Laurent that hearing it come from him made Grace uneasy. He turned away and began trudging toward the fallen tree.

"He's stopping! He's stopping!" Rebecca crowed.

"It could be the real thing," Grace called to Laurent, her heart pounding in her chest like thunder. "Shouldn't we at least talk to him?"

Laurent kept walking. He didn't have the energy to argue with her. He knew that the farmer—if he was a real farmer and not a part of *Le Jeu*—would not be able to help them. If he did, he would likely only get himself killed.

"With me, Grace," he said, breathing heavily.

"He's signaling that I can jump into the back of his truck!"

Rebecca shouted to them. "There's room for us all! He's waving to me to do it!"

That made all of them stop and turn. Suddenly, even without seeing the farmer or his wagon, Grace knew this was a bad idea.

"Rebecca, don't!" she shouted turning and running back to where Rebecca stood on the rim overhanging the road. When Grace reached her, she saw Rebecca's face was lit up with excitement.

Grace peered over the edge and saw the man below. He did have a truck and its lights were on. There was something about that that big empty truck bed filled with hay that looked so inviting. The man stood in the center of the road waving for them to jump into the back of his truck.

Grace felt a stab of unease.

What is he doing here in the middle of the night?

Rebecca eased herself down the embankment over the road, gripping another tree limb tightly with both hands to steady herself.

Grace turned back to the man below. Did he look like a farmer? Why would he encourage her to jump? Is that something a normal person would do?

Is any of this normal?

Joelle came up beside Grace and peered over the side.

"I don't like this, Rebecca," Grace said.

"Later, losers!" Rebecca cried out almost hysterically as she let go of the tree limb just as Grace reached out in desperation to try to grab her.

It was too late; Rebecca was airborne, flying over the low stone abutment, and disappeared into the dark until the only thing left of her was the horrified scream she left in her wake.

47

It was a strange and surreal scene in the woods, Adele thought as she viewed the three large SUVs, their headlights illuminating the trees behind her in the clearing. A dozen armed men were milling around the SUVs. A picnic table had been set up by her men and an array of food and drinks laid out. Large umbrellas were erected to protect them from the lightly falling rain.

The air felt cool on her skin, but the woods around her reeked of rotting leaves and mildew. The ocean's salted tang floated up to her on the sea mist.

She was sitting at one of the tables, a glass of champagne in her hand, her gaze resting on the TV screen set up on a tripod in front of her. It was almost a festive atmosphere, she noted, with people talking and laughing. Combined with the eerie darkness of the night, it was like a festival—only without music. She wondered if she should add music next time. Would that add something to the proceedings?

Estefan had barely gotten the monitor set up in time to see the British tourist fall to her death. Donato had played his part of the helpful farmer perfectly. Except for the bit where he neglected to bring the body back to dispose of it.

Adele sighed and took a sip of her champagne. Losing a contestant this early was desirable in that it ramped up the bets for the remaining survivors. It provided an edge to the stakes as it showed how easily they could all die. But still, it had happened so fast that Adele had nearly missed it. That was sloppy.

She turned to look at Vittorio Giordano who sat beside her glued to the television monitor. She'd been surprised at his participation; he hadn't seemed that interested before. She wasn't sure how she felt about how he'd taken the initiative to increase the online bets. She glanced at her phone where she could see them still coming in.

People were willing to pay a premium for being able to come into the game after it had started.

She closed her eyes for a moment and allowed herself to be transported to a world far away from this clearing in the woods. She allowed herself to go to that special moment twenty years ago when she'd crawled onto Laurent Dernier's lap, straddled him, and watched the surprise in his eyes—and the desire.

She touched the silk scarf around her neck.

And today he'd tried to murder her.

She licked her lips as she remembered how sensual and personal the moment had been.

How intimate.

"Won't the contestants stay away from the lights?"

She forced herself to break away from her thoughts and look at Giordano. He was focused on the monitor. There was no volume, just a picture of an empty clearing, the lights highlighting every blade of grass and every shrub. Laughter found its way across the campsite. Estefan was getting chummy with Giordano's men. She wasn't sure how she felt about that.

"Why would they?" she said, turning to Giordano. "They

don't know what they're for. When people are afraid, they go toward the lights."

She'd installed multiple cameras along the route, most with lighting since it was dark but not all. The system hadn't failed her yet. The fools invariably sought out the light. She looked back at the screen, her jaw clenching as her thoughts once more drifted back to Laurent, the man who had wronged her. The man who needed to pay.

She turned and snapped her fingers at Estefan. He saw her but decided to finish his conversation with one of Giordano's thugs before acknowledging her. Adele felt a pulse of fury at his hesitation. She would remember that.

And before Estefan died, so would he.

But for now, it was his skill with a rifle that would buy him a few more hours.

Estefan sauntered over to her, his obsequious false deference already firmly in place on his face.

"Si, Madame B?" he said.

Her face was hard as she regarded him standing before her.

"I need you to take up a position at the edge of the woods, there." She pointed to a point on the monitor. "You see it?"

"Si, Madame B."

"Stay hidden but keep your eyes open for the big man and the women when they come. They should make it to the clearing in about ten minutes."

"You said I could have Princess Grace," Estefan said.

I swear I will kill this cretin before the night is over.

"I only want the big man taken out," Adele said between gritted teeth. "When they reach the clearing, you'll have less than a minute to line up the shot. Understood?"

The man nodded, then turned on his heel without another word. Adele watched him go to one of the SUVs and pull his rifle out of its scabbard from the back, before disappearing into the shadows of the trees. Giordano had been silent through the exchange. He too watched Estefan as the marksman got his rifle and left the area.

"You sure about this?" he asked idly.

"It's none of your business, Signore Giordano."

Adele turned back to the monitor and glared at the empty clearing while she waited.

"You know, Adele," Giordano said mildly, "I'm not sure the investors will appreciate one of the contestants being taken out of the game. Especially the only man. They might feel cheated."

"I don't care what they feel," she said bitterly, her eyes on the monitor. "Some things are more important than money."

48

As Luc drove along the Grande Corniche, Maggie strained to see in the darkness any alcove carved into limestone cliffs where they might turn off. She had no idea where the hostages might be or where Adele and Giordano were set up watching the game. As soon as they'd turned onto the Grande Corniche, he'd reduced his speed until Maggie thought they'd do better on foot.

"How do we find them?" Luc asked, his hands gripping the steering wheel as if for his very life.

Maggie imagined Adele and Giordano—like two hawks looking over their prey from their mountaintop aerie—watching the game and making sure no one escaped before time.

"The cameras," she said. "We look for cameras. And cameras need light so we—No! Don't take your eyes off the road!"

She shot out a hand to grab the wheel as the car swerved dangerously close to the edge of the road.

"*I* will look for them," she said firmly as Luc aimed the car to the middle of the road. Perspiration glistened on his forehead in the darkness.

"Okay," he said in a strained voice. "Just tell me where to go."

Maggie scanned both sides of the road. This section of the Grande Corniche was a narrow, winding road that rose up and down like an invisible ribbon as it hugged the rocky terrain. She imagined that the view in daylight was breathtaking, but she was glad at the moment not to see the heart-stopping sheer drops to the sea. It was hard to imagine how many accidents and sudden, terrible deaths this majestic setting had caused over the centuries.

She shook the thought from her brain.

Not helping.

She strained to catch any kind of glimpse of a hidden camera on the cliffs above them or on the few telephone poles along the road. But there was nothing. She assumed that most of what she was looking for would've been hidden at night anyway or camouflaged by the trees and shrubs.

This is hopeless.

"We need to park," she said.

"But we have no idea what section of the road they're on!" Luc said in frustration.

"And we won't find out by driving around," Maggie said. "Turn off at the next shoulder."

"Doesn't the map on your phone tell you where we can pull off?" he asked, wiping his face in agitation.

"Luc, calm down!" Maggie said. "Listen to me. We need to find where they are *on foot*. There! Up ahead! Pull off!"

The shoulder she was pointing at was narrow and sandwiched between the steep road and a forested hill. The clearing was bordered by weeds and bushes that swayed in the breeze. In the headlights they could see that a picnic table sat in the middle of it—a signal to travelers that this was the spot to pull off. Not only that, Maggie thought, but a picnic table meant there was a trail.

Luc carefully maneuvered the car off the road and turned off the engine. He stretched his hands out on the steering wheel as if attempting to steady his nerves. Maggie got out of the car and stood for a moment surveying the surroundings.

She could hear the sea but in front of her was what looked like an impenetrable woods.

"Are you sure about this?" Luc asked as he climbed out of the car.

Maggie's own frustration ramped up in her chest. The fact was she wasn't sure about anything. She was trying to make educated or logical guesses. But she was only too aware of what the stakes were if she was wrong. She was hoping against hope that they hadn't just pulled off the road miles away from the hostages. The night air was colder at this altitude and her arms prickled with goosebumps. No, she didn't know if this was right. But she knew driving around aimlessly wasn't right either.

"I'm as sure as I can be," she said. "Look up ahead. There's a sort of trail there."

She pointed in the darkness and then pulled out her cellphone and activated the flashlight. Even with nearly a full moon, they would need all the light they could not to fall off the steep trail.

Taking the lead, Maggie pushed through the fringe of brambles and bushes beyond the picnic table, quickly leaving the clearing behind. The night air felt oppressive as they made their way through the dense bush into the woods. Even at this distance from the Mediterranean, the sea breeze carried the scent of seaweed and fish to them.

The path they took was littered with thick roots and broken branches, making their progress slow and difficult. The wind in the trees sounded like an angry wail. The branches creaked and groaned overhead as if in pain. At one point, Maggie thought she heard dogs howling.

She thought about asking Luc if Adele would set dogs on the contestants but decided she didn't want to know. What difference would knowing make except to ratchet up Maggie's anxiety level another notch? She certainly wasn't going to do anything different from what she was already doing.

Maggie scanned the trees as they walked, looking for cameras installed on them. It made sense to her that Adele would position cameras at certain points along the playing field.

Someone like Adele would never leave it to chance or to other people reporting back on the progress of the game. Besides, if what Luc said was true, Adele also needed to control the outcome of the game.

How do you know when to unleash the dogs if you don't know how the contestants are faring?

No, cameras had to be here somewhere. In fact, Maggie was betting everything that they were.

If she was wrong, it meant she and Luc were wandering hopelessly through the dark countryside while many miles away Grace and Laurent battled for their lives.

49

Grace was so shaken she could barely walk.

Watching Rebecca fall to her death was a visual she would never forget. She knew the memory would haunt her forever. It was only marginally worse than seeing Rebecca's body sprawled broken on the ground twenty meters below them and then just turning and continuing to walk up the hill as if nothing had happened. Her heart hammered in her chest as her brain replayed the image of Rebecca falling.

Again and again and again.

Grace closed her eyes to blot out the image. She tried to focus on the ground directly below her, and on the people walking in front of her. She heard the sound of the pounding of her heart echoing in her ears, and imagined again and again the image of Rebecca's lifeless body. She stumbled on, her feet dragging with each step, acutely aware of her shallow breathing. Each step seemed heavier than the last.

She focused on the backs of Laurent and Joelle in front of her. But all she could think of was that moment when Rebecca vaulted over the edge of the cliff. And the scream and then the terrible sound as she hit the pavement below.

Grace knew she would hear that sound in her head for as long as she lived.

However long that is.

Laurent hadn't even gone back to see where Rebecca had fallen or to see the man with the wagon disappear.

Had he been sent to lure them? To distract them? To set up the fall?

Was this all a part of the game?

Grace found herself struggling to understand what had really happened. What was happening now. She stared at Laurent and Joelle, now even further ahead. Joelle had witnessed Rebecca jump from the embankment and fall to her death on the hard pavement. Now she just walked on.

Grace felt an overwhelming urge to sit down. She closed her eyes and realized with a start that she *was* sitting down.

When had she stopped?

"Grace."

She opened her eyes and saw Laurent kneeling in front of her. His eyes were clear as he took her hand. She was struck by how much damage had been done to his face. Broken, bloody, bruising.

How could I not have noticed before?

"Dear Laurent," she said, tears seeping out of her eyes as she reached to touch his battered face.

"Grace, no," he said, tugging on her hands. "On your feet, *chérie*."

"You're hurt," she said.

"I will heal," he said. "We can't stop."

"Why can't we? What's happening? Do you know?"

Joelle appeared from behind Laurent.

"Why are you making this so hard on all of us?" she asked sharply. "Don't you understand anything?"

"I understand a woman I spent the last two hours with is lying dead in the street!" Grace said shrilly. "I understand that!"

Laurent pulled her to her feet.

"We will deal with that later, *chérie*. Now you must move."

"Who is doing this to us, Laurent? Do you know?"

Laurent rubbed a hand across his face in weariness.

"He's lucky to be walking on his own steam," Joelle said. "And you want him to converse too? Why don't you help for a change instead of hinder?"

Grace turned to her. "Who are you again?"

"I'm somebody who understands how *teams* work," Joelle said archly. "Now move before you get us all killed—like Rebecca."

Grace began to walk behind them, her mind racing.

"So...so that was deliberate?" she asked. "It was a part of the game?"

"You catch on quick," Joelle said sarcastically. "There's a clearing up ahead."

"They will expect us to go there," Laurent said.

The three stopped walking.

"We could go around," Joelle said.

"How are we going to find the flags they left for us if we don't go where they intend us to go?" Grace asked.

Joelle turned to her in exasperation. But Laurent held up a hand to stop her from arguing.

"Grace is right," he said. "We can't hide from them. We need to play the game. Adele probably wants a quick kill. The longer we stay alive, the greater chance we have of making it through."

Grace took a breath and pushed past them both. She was embarrassed that Rebecca's death had affected her so badly and that Laurent had to take time to calm her. Joelle was right about that. He needed a teammate, not a millstone around his neck.

She entered the clearing first. It was illuminated and when she glanced back at Laurent, she was astonished once more to see the extent of his injuries. It looked as if his nose was broken and possibly his cheek. One eye was blackened, and he appeared to favor his right arm. And he was limping badly.

As she watched him enter the clearing, she watched him scan the area clearing uneasily. He didn't like being exposed under the lights.

Suddenly Grace felt a sickening stab in her stomach as a warning went off in her brain.

Something was wrong.

That was when she heard the noise.

∼

Adele held her breath as she watched the three figures enter the clearing. Her gaze went immediately to Laurent. She felt transfixed by the sight of him, oblivious to everything else around her.

Even as hurt as she knew he was, his six-foot-five frame moved with a grace that was mesmerizing. She watched him with her mouth slightly open. Suddenly, her skin pebbled uncomfortably and she felt a clot of fear form in her chest as the memory came back to her—as fast as an adder's strike. She felt his warm hands on her neck, the look in his eyes as they probed her own. They were so close that it could have been the prelude to a kiss. She had never felt so close to anyone, and she was sure Laurent never had. In that moment, with his hands on her naked neck, she'd felt an inexplicable rush of love.

Something she had never felt before.

Tears sprang to her eyes as she remembered it. She reached out and picked up the radio on the table in front of her and dialed Estefan's frequency without taking her eyes from the monitor, from the set of Laurent's shoulders, from the sure way he moved, or from his hands, large and capable.

"Are you in position?" she asked in a husky voice.

"Si, Madame."

"As soon as you're ready," she said, "take the shot."

50

The night air was heavy and humid, though Maggie found the sound of crickets and the occasional hoot of an owl oddly reassuring. She and Luc continued to trudge through the thick vegetation, their feet sinking into the damp ground with each step. Every now and then Maggie stopped to listen or strained to see even the faintest glimmer of light ahead, but she could only make out varying degrees of darkness as the moon reflected off the bushes and the trees.

Maggie watched her own shadow bobbing up and down on the ground as she walked. *The forest primeval*, she thought. She recalled the stories she used to read to Jemmy when he was little. Stories of creatures that lurked in the woods, their eyes glowing like embers in the dark.

They walked for what seemed like an hour, although Maggie's watch told her was only a few minutes, until suddenly she spotted a shaft of a light through the thickest part of the foliage. She felt a lightness in her chest as she hurried toward the light, stopping at the entrance of a small clearing to look around.

Sure enough, nestled high in the craggy rocks on the side of the cliff was a tiny camera pointing down at the trail they were on. Maggie felt the excitement pulse through her. Adele wouldn't bother setting up cameras along the entire Grande Corniche. This trail *had* to be where the game was being played! Were Adele and Giordano watching her and Luc even now? She stepped back into the shadows.

Had Laurent and Grace come this way? It was too dark to detect tracks or broken branches or footprints.

"You see the lights up above?" Maggie said to Luc as he came up behind her. "Check out the tiny camera right above. We're definitely on the right path."

Maggie wondered what would induce the hostages to take the lighted path as she and Luc were doing. Knowing Laurent, he definitely wouldn't take the path that had been marked out for him. So were she and Luc doing the right thing by taking it? She felt a flinch of indecision.

"Are we not going into the clearing?" Luc said.

"I don't know," Maggie said, her heart racing as she looked around. "This feels like a trap."

"*Everything* feels like a trap!" Luc said. "It's felt like a trap ever since we drove to Giordano's villa."

Maggie let out a long breath. He was right. How did one discern one level of anxiety from another? She'd been afraid when she went to the villa, and she was afraid now. How could she trust those emotions when they were so completely appropriate for the situation?

"What's our alternative?" Luc asked softly.

"None," she said, taking a step toward the light.

She felt Luc right behind her as they moved cautiously toward the center of the silent clearing. Maggie could already tell there were no people there. She watched the recording light blink on the camera.

Luc gently touched her arm and she paused.

"You know *we* are contestants now too, yes?" he said softly. "Whatever can kill the hostages can kill us too."

He was referring to the dogs they'd heard a few minutes earlier. Maggie didn't answer. There was nothing for it but to keep going. The light was brightest here in the clearing because of the camera lights, and now she could see a second camera on the other side of the clearing. Twenty feet above them was what looked like another tree-lined cliff and another road.

"Maggie!"

Luc made a choking sound and Maggie snapped her head around to see him standing at the edge of the clearing. Her eyes went to what it was he was seeing, and her heart jumped to her throat.

It was the crumpled form of a woman's body.

51

The enormous boar stepped out of the mist around the base of the cliff. The beast stood twenty feet from Grace, its putrid smell rolling off it in waves that made Grace's stomach lurch with nausea.

She had smelled him before she saw him.

Easily five feet long and several hundred pounds, it stared with single-minded malevolence. Black spots formed in Grace's vision as she stumbled backward and away from the creature. She looked in shocked disbelief as it lowered its head to charge.

A scream fought to escape her throat, but only a whimper slipped out as she watched in horror. In one motion, the beast surged forward, throwing clumps of dirt as it barreled towards her.

Grace stood frozen as every detail of its face—its bared teeth, its wet slimy snout—grew bigger as it raced towards her. She felt herself pulled to the side as the animal roared past her. Collapsing to her knees, she felt momentarily confused, before Joelle grabbed her arm and yanked her to her feet.

"Rocks!" Joelle screamed as she turned and let fly an

onslaught of rocks against the beast that now pawed the ground in front of Laurent.

Grace saw the blood pouring out of the animal's forehead where Laurent had smashed it with the heavy branch he held in his hands. Frantically, she turned and pried up boulders and rocks from the dirt before turning and flinging them at the animal along with Joelle.

The boar's dark eyes were wide with rage as it pawed the earth again before tossing its head and launching itself once more into a murderous lunge—this time straight at Laurent. Grace did scream then as Laurent's tree branch caught the beats across the face. The noise was heartrending as it squealed and then fell silent at Laurent's feet, the life draining from its eyes.

Grace felt her legs give out beneath her and sank to the ground next to the boar. It lay there, its legs bent at odd angles like a broken kite around a rigid spine. For one mad moment, she wanted to reach out and touch it.

"Grace?"

She looked up as Laurent came over to her, the broken tree limb still in his hand.

"Dear God in heaven," she whispered as bile burned in the back of her throat.

"She's hurt," Joelle said to Laurent.

Grace turned to ask who she was talking about and felt the pain in her ankle shoot up into her brain. She gasped at the sharp cramp. Laurent knelt down beside her.

"Let me see, *chérie*."

His hand was warm as he probed her already swollen ankle. Grace's eyes filled with tears at the pain and the gentle comfort she felt from his touch. For one insane moment she found herself feeling jealous of Maggie. Laurent regularly called Maggie *chérie*. She shook her head to clear her mind of the stomach-churning labyrinth of emotions she was feeling, one on top of the other. Ever since losing her ex-husband Windsor a second time, she'd been feeling more than a little lost.

"It's sprained," he said with a sigh. "Maybe worse."

"Well, now what?" Joelle said, nudging the carcass of the boar with her foot.

For the first time, Grace realized that the woman was barefooted.

"I'm sorry," Grace said, fighting tears.

The very idea that she was going to be the one who got them all killed was too much to bear.

"It's not your fault," Laurent said. "It's the way Adele plans for it to go. That's all."

"She hates you so much," Joelle said.

Well, she would, Grace reasoned. He tried to kill her. But of course Adele had hated Laurent before then. She'd hated him because he wouldn't let her love him. Joelle sat down next to Grace and startled her by picking up her hand.

"Let us take a rest, yes?" Joelle said, nodding at the dead beast. "We deserve it."

"You are all right, *chérie*?" Laurent asked Joelle, making Grace nearly laugh out loud.

If he was calling total strangers *chérie* maybe the endearment was merely an unconscious habit?

"I broke a nail, if you want to know," Joelle said with a shrug, making Laurent smile for the first time all night.

"We're not doing too good, are we?" Grace asked softly.

"We are doing fine," Laurent said firmly.

Grace wanted to laugh and wondered if perhaps she was dealing with a case of hysteria.

"Look," Joelle said. "I lied to your friend, Maggie. I told her I'd seen you. Both of you."

"Why would you do that?" Grace asked, aghast.

Laurent grunted and sat down next to Grace, saying nothing.

"I'm sorry. I hate myself, okay? It was just something we do, me and my partner."

Grace's eyes stung with tears. "What a horrible thing to do."

"I said I was sorry," Joelle said, nearly in tears herself. "I didn't realize."

"You didn't realize that Maggie was telling the truth? Or you didn't care?" Grace said heatedly.

"Grace," Laurent said. "It doesn't matter."

Grace bit her tongue to prevent herself from saying more. Just seconds ago, she'd been in the wrong and now it was Joelle who was. It felt good for someone else to be at fault. Not fair, maybe, but good.

"You have someone who will move earth and heaven to find you," Joelle said to Laurent, before turning to Grace. "You, too. You are both so lucky."

Grace reminded herself that she didn't know what Joelle's life was like. Maybe an abusive boyfriend made her lie to Maggie. Maybe she needed the money. Maybe she was just human and made mistakes.

"It's too dangerous for Maggie to be going around questioning people about us," Laurent said gruffly. "I wish I had one minute to have a word with her."

Grace laughed softly at the absurdity of it all. "Me, too, darling."

She turned to Joelle.

"Laurent's right," she said. "It doesn't matter. We've got bigger fish to fry."

Grace realized then that in her heart of hearts—no matter how bad things looked—she believed they would survive. How could she not? She looked around at their dark surroundings and heard the faint crash of waves on the distant shore below. She had to believe that they would make it home alive.

The image of Rebecca flailing in midair came viciously back to her. She swallowed hard.

Well, most of us, she thought grimly.

52

Adele stared at the monitor which showed the two women and Laurent slowly moving out of camera shot, leaving the body of the dead boar visible in the foreground.

"Now, aren't you glad I stopped you from killing him?" Giordano said to Adele.

The monitor screen glowed brightly under the inky night sky, casting an eerie greenish hue onto both their faces. Adele could smell the crackling bonfire the men had made along with the more pungent odors of cigars, beer, and the occasional whiff of marijuana smoke.

Giordano had pointed out to her that the boar had appeared mere seconds before Estefan was set to kill Laurent. To Adele's credit, she saw an opportunity when it presented itself and didn't hesitate to call off the shot. She knew when her emotions were getting in the way of her business sense.

She sat now, staring at the empty clearing, a feeling of stark disappointment fluttering about the edges of her gut, but also a feeling of arousal. Watching Laurent battle the beast—swinging the branch like a superhero bruised, battered, but never beaten—had been nearly as satisfying as anticipating his death. She couldn't help how she felt about him. It was complicated. And confusing. But she'd long ago stopped hating herself for feeling the things she felt.

She could hate him and love him at the same time. She could want him dead and also cheer for his victory over the boar. In fact, it was the sheer delicious incongruity of her feelings for him that told her they were real.

"And meanwhile the bets keep coming in," Giordano said as he poured himself more champagne. "Another fifty bets during the boar fight alone! I'm telling you, Madame Bontemps, we are going to walk away from these woods very rich people."

She turned to him. Her reluctant pause in Laurent's execution had given her time to take a breath and listen to the sense that Giordano was speaking—the online bets *were* coming in hundreds in an hour. This was definitely her chance to make big money. And to do that—being practical—she would need to let the game play out and not kill Laurent straight away.

"I'll have to leave the country," she said as they watched the monitor that now only showed the dead animal.

"*Si*, but you will leave a very rich woman."

"Some things are more important than money," she said, reaching for her own glass of champagne.

"Like revenge? Money is always the best revenge. And it's not like you think he will escape, do you?"

"No."

"No. He dies tonight no matter what. Be patient, *cara*. And it will all come to you as it should."

Adele stared at the screen remembering again how Laurent had looked, his shirt stretched across his back as he'd strained to hold off the charging beast, the way his hair fell, thick and wild around his head. The determination and concentration evident in every muscle.

Even the memory of it took her breath away.

Giordano got up to walk over to his group of men at the perimeter of the camp. Adele turned back to the screen, seeing the fight again in her mind.

Yes, she'd let him live. And then he'd saved himself from the boar—and of course the women—but she'd let him do it. Plus, if that idiot Estefan *had* killed him, it wouldn't have occurred to him to then shoot the boar to save the women. And if *that* hadn't happened, the game would be over. And the bets would stop coming in.

No, Giordano was right. It was better to let these things play out organically. And he was also right that in the end it would all be the same. Laurent wasn't going to see the morning. Perhaps she would have him strangled in front of her.

My eyes will be the last thing he sees in this world.

"Madame B?" Donato said to her.

"Yes, Donato." Adele felt a wave of irritation as her daydream was interrupted and found herself wondering why revenge and money no longer seemed to be enough. She banished the memory of Laurent to focus on the rest of the game.

"We have something on the other camera," he said.

Adele switched the channel to the other camera feed, wondering if it was possible for the three contestants to have made it to the next camera installation so soon.

"Not that camera, Madame B," Donato said. "The first one, where the woman jumped."

"What are you talking about?" Adele said in annoyance.

She'd already watched the video of the British tourist vault to her death. She'd see if Donato could create a *gif* out of it to amuse the next game's stakeholders. She switched the camera feed to the one on the first clearing, ready to berate Donato for wasting her time.

But as she stared at the screen, her breath caught in her throat. Her mind tumbled over on top of itself, thinking she was hallucinating. There was the tourist's body, as yet to be removed—and there, center screen, was something that made Adele want to shout out with sheer joy.

A thrill of pure ecstasy washed over her as she watched in near disbelief as none other than Maggie Dernier walked across the screen.

53

Luc and Maggie stood together looking down at the body of the woman before them.

Unlike in the city, where everything was dark the more removed one was from the city lights, here in the woods every detail around them was revealed in stark relief under the blazing camera lighting—especially a forlorn body in the middle of the forest.

Maggie moved closer to the body. The woman's dress was torn and her face was bruised and bloodied. It looked like she had been dressed for a night on the town. Maggie could see food stains and blood on the front of her dress. Her ankles were lacerated—probably by branches and brambles as she'd made her way through the woods in the dark. Her wrists were rubbed raw where she had been bound.

Maggie swallowed down her guilty relief that the body didn't belong to Grace or Laurent, then tried to resist the satisfaction she felt that this meant she and Luc were on the right trail.

"Do you know her?" Maggie asked.

Luc shook his head left and right. Especially under the

harsh lighting, Maggie could see the sick pallor beneath his tan. He wasn't used to seeing violent death. He breathed out slowly and turned to scan the woods as if looking for danger. A cricket chirped nearby. Something moved in the shadows.

"How do you think she died?" he asked.

Maggie looked at the ledge above them.

"I...I think she jumped or fell. But it does seem strange. I can't help but wonder if something happened to make her jump? Unless she just tripped?"

She looked around the clearing.

"There was some kind of vehicle here," she said, pointing to the tire tracks.

"Do you think that's the reason she died?"

Maggie frowned and looked up again at the ledge above them.

"I can't imagine she would've deliberately jumped," she said. "That makes no sense at all."

"Maybe the wagon was here when she fell?"

"Maybe."

"Surely whoever had the wagon would've called the authorities, right?"

Maggie ran her hands lightly down the woman's dress. There was no identification on her except for a small square of paper tucked into her neckline. It had the number four handwritten on it.

Contestant numero quatre.

"She was definitely a part of the game," Maggie said and then stood up, still looking above her. "The others must be near."

"Should we call out?"

"I don't know," Maggie uneasily.

Does this mean there are more contestants in the game than just the three we know about?

Maggie glanced at the two cameras and felt an uneasiness skittle across her bare arms.

"Let's keep moving," she said. "I don't like being out in the open like this."

"I am way ahead of you," Luc said, backing away from the body and turning in the direction of where another trail emerged from the clearing.

"We need to move faster now that we know we're on the right track," Maggie said, jogging up alongside him.

Luc hesitated and then walked to the far side of the clearing which hung over the side of another sheer drop.

"Why don't we think they took that road instead?" he asked, pointing at the lower road.

Maggie joined him at the edge and hesitated. He had a point.

"Because the woman fell from the trail above us," she said. "So it makes sense to think the rest of them—"

A rifle shot suddenly exploded in her ears.

"Run!" she screamed, swiveling away from the edge, and bolting for the opposite side of the clearing. She leapt over rocks and boulders in her path, feeling the twigs and fallen branches snap beneath her feet as she ran. Panicked, her breath was quickly ragged, her lungs nearly bursting until a painful stitch in her side forced her to stop. She turned to Luc behind her. But he wasn't there.

Suddenly, the realization of the sole gun shot came slamming into her.

No, no, no, no...

Off, in the distance, she heard a single howl reverberate through the trees. She turned, her heart pounding in her ears. She began to walk back down the trail toward the clearing. She stopped a few feet from the opening. The entire stretch of the clearing was visible and starkly illuminated from where she stood. She saw the woman's body where it had fallen from the upper trail. She also saw the spot where she had left Luc standing at the far edge of the clearing.

Maggie stood, frozen with indecision, her heart pounding as her eyes raked the area from side to side, her panic and disbelief escalating by the second.

Luc was nowhere to be seen.

54

The sound of the gunshot sliced through the air like a hatchet, instantly silencing the three hostages who halted and looked at each other with stark confusion on their faces. Laurent found himself holding his breath as if waiting for a second shot.

Had they fired and missed? Is there a sniper in the trees?

But no, the gunshot wasn't near. It was at least a half a mile away in the woods.

"Who are they shooting at?" Grace asked, her voice barely carrying over the pounding of Laurent's heart.

"I don't know," he replied. "But we can't stay here."

He slid his arm under Grace's shoulder. Any other time he would've just picked her up. But he was lucky to stay on his feet as it was.

The trio plunged into the woods, hurrying over downed branches and thick undergrowth. Laurent steered them past thickets of wild berries and vines in a seemingly impenetrable tangle of foliage, doing his best to keep them off anything remotely resembling a path.

Occasional wafts of fish and sea salt came to him from the nearby ocean. Overhead, limbs and branches whipped past, cracking and snapping at their heads and their backs. The temperature had cooled and the mist had begun to thicken. Laurent felt his feet press into the damp ground. With every step, his breath became labored and heavy,

"Laurent," Grace gasped from where she struggled next to him. "I have to rest."

"Not yet," Laurent said, heaving her up into his arms.

His arms trembled as he struggled to carry her without dropping her, careful to avoid the boulders and logs in his path. He could hear Joelle right behind him. He didn't have enough breath to encourage her.

Within moments, another clearing loomed ahead with another set of glaring camera lights.

Laurent hesitated and looked around. He couldn't go into the clearing. Somewhere in the distance—and not near far enough away—he heard the dogs baying. They were getting closer.

"Please, Laurent," Grace said.

"Not yet!" he panted, struggling over a last log in his path, his muscles screaming in protest at the effort it took to keep moving forward. Sweat streamed down his face, blurring his vision. Suddenly, his foot slipped on a slick patch of leaves, and he slammed into a tree. At the last second he tried to turn to spare Grace the full brunt of the impact.

The move torqued his knee, and he slammed to the ground, falling hard as Grace slipped out of his grip. His back thudded against the ground with a bone-numbing impact. The wetness of the leaves and grass seeped instantly into his shirt. For a moment, he just lay there, his breath hitching as if it had been knocked out of him, the strength to get up just out of reach.

Joelle shrieked in terror.

Her scream came on top of a deep-throated growl, low and vicious. Laurent turned his head in time to see the giant dog crouching in front of Joelle.

Its fangs were bared as it zeroed in on her.

55

Maggie's mind galloped in every direction at once. There was no way Luc could have survived being shot and then falling to the road below. With every fiber in her being she wanted to find him, to at least mark where his body had landed. But she didn't dare enter the clearing for fear of being shot herself. And as for the plummet to the road below, how would she even get down there?

Even if the sniper who shot Luc failed to shoot her, what good could she possibly do for poor Luc? If the shot hadn't killed him, the fall would have. What could she do for him out here in the middle of nowhere with no first aid?

It was true she'd practically forced him to come, but she couldn't become frozen with guilt. She still had to move forward to find Laurent and Grace. And Joelle. If only for Luc's sake, she needed to find Joelle too. Tears blurred her vision, and she pushed them back as best she could, silently castigating herself for bringing him here. It didn't help and she knew she wouldn't have done it any other way, but she also knew that, if it weren't for her, Luc would still be alive.

She said a silent prayer for him and pulled out her phone to call for an ambulance. Before she could put the call through, she froze and slowly turned toward the direction of where she heard the noise.

A vehicle was coming.

Was it someone she could flag down for help?

Or was it the person who shot Luc?

She decided she couldn't take the chance. She looked around for a hiding spot. If the people coming had dogs, a hiding spot anywhere around here would be a death trap.

Should she run?

She looked around her darkened surroundings, the sound of the vehicle growing ever closer.

Tick tock! Do something! Decide!

She backed into the recesses of a dark shadow and jammed her phone back into her pocket. Turning, she darted into the trees lining the clearing and raced through the woods. She could feel her breaths coming in shorter and shorter bursts, her heart beating wildly in her chest. The darkness of the night seemed to deepen with every step she took, the half-moon providing only a sliver of light.

The narrow cliff road wound ahead of her. She couldn't hear the vehicle any more but now she heard voices.

Her heart pounded as she slowly began to climb the nearest cliff face, keeping her body pressed against the rock and her movements small and controlled. If she could reach the upper road, she'd put significant distance between her and whoever was chasing her. She grabbed a small tree and hauled herself slowly to the top of the cliff road.

Instantly a spotlight exploded in her face, throwing the world around her in harsh relief. For one mad moment, she nearly turned and leapt back down the way she'd come.

Out of the blinding light came bodies rushing toward her. Rough hands grabbed her and dragged her from the edge. Maggie fought wildly, kicking and flailing desperately, but there were too many of them. One of them picked her up like a rag doll and flung her onto a patch of dirt and brambles away from the cliff's edge. She got shakily to her knees and saw a single vehicle parked, its engine running, its headlights pinioning her. The figures of three men morphed out of the shadows to face her.

One stepped forward and when he did, his face came into sharp focus in her memory. It was Giordano's man. It was the one she'd overheard complaining about the villa's guard dog.

He walked over to her and pulled out a handgun and put it to her forehead.

"Remember me, *cara*?" he said. "That boy you killed was my brother."

56

Laurent hit the dog a split second after it reached Joelle. He pulled back the animal's head but before he could break its neck, the dog twisted out of his grip and darted back into the woods. Laurent swung around to deal with the rest of the pack and saw them standing at the edge of the woods, growling, warning, and ready to attack.

Looking like a mix of Rottweilers and Doberman Pinschers, the dogs were back lit by the moonlight, making it look like the forest itself had come alive. In the half-light their blinking eyes appeared as yellow flashes. Laurent saw as their white teeth glinting in the moonlight. They moved together as a single unit as they prowled beside the clearing and looked for the right moment to attack.

They'll attack as soon as they find it..

The pack crept closer until he could smell their bristling fur and see their muscles tensed and ready to spring. The malevolent eyes of the lead dog locked onto Laurent.

"Grace!" Laurent shouted. "Throw me a branch! Check on Joelle!"

He faced the dogs and held his hands out to them. These

were not wild animals, they were trained attack dogs. He would not be able to trick them or reason with them. It was brute force or nothing. And he had less than nothing.

They'd been ordered to attack them. Nothing Laurent had —no branch or even a knife—would deter them. The one he'd tackled off Joelle had rejoined the pack so now there were five of them.

Laurent licked his lips. "Grace! Can you and Joelle get up a tree?"

But he knew Grace could barely walk, and he'd already noticed that the only trees in the area had smooth trunks with virtually no low limbs.

The leader of the pack stepped forward, its hackles sticking straight up, its gums pulled back in warning.

"I can't find a branch!" Grace shouted. "And Joelle is bleeding!"

Suddenly, the head dog made its move and leapt at Laurent. Laurent caught him at the shoulders. The force of the assault knocked him flat onto his back. He held the dog—its slathering muzzle and gnashing teeth inches from his face—at arms' length. Arms that were spasmodically shaking with the effort to hold the animal. Laurent couldn't hold him for long. He felt the other dogs moving around him, looking for a soft spot, a point of entry.

Grace screamed and then grunted loudly. The sound of a thump and a dog squealing came to Laurent as he squeezed his eyes tight and tried to hold the lead dog for just a few seconds more.

Suddenly a gunshot sounded. The dog Laurent held twisted out of his grip and ran after the pack who were already racing away. Laurent's arms collapsed beside him, his breath ragged and spent, his heart pounding in his chest.

"Break time!" he heard a cheerful voice say.

His brain could not decipher what was happening. He tried

to sit up. Instead, he turned his head and threw up. From where he lay, he saw the legs of two men and a woman come into the clearing.

"Napping already, darling?" Adele asked as she walked over to him. "That's not any way to win."

Laurent sat up slowly as Adele ordered her men to attend to Grace's injury. She walked over to Joelle and made a face.

"Ugh. This one needs a stitch," she called out. "Estefan, did you bring the first aid kit?"

"*Si*, Madame B," one of her men said and walked over to Joelle.

"Clean it first!" Grace said loudly.

Adele's laughter pierced the somber clearing.

"I think infection is the last thing you need to worry about tonight," Adele said, still chuckling, "But yes, all right, Estefan, clean it first."

She walked over to Grace where she was getting her ankle taped.

"Aren't you just a true princess?" Adele said sarcastically. "I don't suppose you remember me?"

"Sorry. I don't imagine we run in the same circles," Grace said. She was seated on a large boulder and one of the men was carefully taping her ankle.

Adele flinched at the insult but forced herself not to react. Everything in good time, she reminded herself. Just as Giordano had said. Let things develop organically. She'd have this hag's head on a pike before the night was over, but she'd do it in her own way and on *her* timeline.

She walked back over to Laurent and stood looking down on him. Laurent sat with his arms draped over his knees. He shook his head as if he were caught in a very bad dream.

"I see you've already lost one," Adele said to him. "I have to say that's a record to have one die so soon in the game.

Normally our players don't start dying within the first five minutes."

"You've had your revenge, Adele," Laurent said in a low voice. "Stop this madness."

"No can do, darling," she said. "I should show you all the online bets coming in. It's why I had to call off the dogs. I had no idea you would all be so intent on killing yourselves this soon. And that's not much of a game, is it? At least that's not what people betting on the game want to see."

It made some sense to Laurent now. Adele was keeping them alive because she was afraid the game would be over too soon. As long as she was still getting online bets, she had to keep them alive.

"Nice handling that boar, by the way," she said to Laurent. "Can you walk? We need to chat."

Laurent hauled himself to his feet. As soon as he did, both her men dropped what they were doing and pulled out their weapons.

"Oh, I don't think he'll try anything now, boys," Adele said to them, waving them away. "Not when he knows you'd execute the women immediately after he tried it."

The two men watched Laurent warily as he followed Adele to the edge of the clearing. As soon as they were face to face, she put a hand on his chest. Laurent forced himself not to recoil at her touch.

"So, you tried to kill me," she said and pulled the scarf from her neck.

Laurent didn't even glance at the bruises there.

"No apologies? Not even a fake attempt at contrition? You disappoint me, Laurent. I hope you know you don't have a chance in hell of surviving tonight."

"If you have something to say, Adele," he said wearily, "spit it out."

Her face hardened at his words.

"You are going to get these poor women killed, darling. If I hadn't come just now, the dogs would've ripped you apart and then your two girlfriends and there would've been nothing you could do about it."

"Have you got something to say?" he asked, his lip, split and bloodied was curled in disgust at having to be this close to her.

"I originally came to say that if you would only bend a bit you might save them."

She ran a hand down his chest. Laurent just stared at her.

"Only I've decided it's too late for that," she said, removing her hand. Cold hatred permeating her gaze as it drilled into him.

"As much as I might like it, I'm afraid that after what happened this afternoon, I could never trust you not to slit my throat some night after a romantic night of moonlight lovemaking." She touched the scarf around her neck.

"So, we'll have to do it a different way." She pulled out her phone and scrolled through it for a moment.

"Ready to see something interesting, darling?" she said with a smile. "Because I promise it'll be the best part of your night. It certainly was of mine."

She turned the phone around to show him a video with a caption indicating it was being live-streamed. At first, Laurent couldn't make out what he was seeing. And then his blood turned to ice.

It was a video of Maggie.

She was on her knees in the woods.

With a gun held to her head.

57

Maggie sat on a hard wooden chair off to the side of the campfire. Her wrists were bound in front of her. Her lip throbbed where the man who'd found her had hit her out of frustration when he was told he couldn't end her life right then—at least not without an order from his *jefe*, Signore Giordano.

As Maggie looked around the camp, she saw that Adele and Giordano's group consisted of no more than eight men. They stood talking amongst themselves, their eyes scanning the darkness for movement, guns at the ready to shoot anything that happened to wander past. The light from the flickering central campfire gave off a yellow hue, making the movements of the men appear robotic and erratic.

She recognized most of Giordano's men. And from the way they watched her, malevolent and predatory, they remembered her too. It seemed that, at least for now and for whatever reason, Giordano—or Adele—didn't plan on killing her just yet. There was relief in that, but the question, *why are they holding off?* made Maggie clench with dread.

Aside from the background chatter of the men, the camp

was strangely quiet. Suddenly, a shadow fell over her, and Maggie found herself staring up into the furious face of Vittoria Giordano himself. He glowered at her like an eagle eyeing its prey.

"So, we meet again, Madame Dernier. You're lucky Madame Bontemps wants you alive. My men are very upset with you."

"Did you ever have any intention of closing down the game?" Maggie asked.

"I thought about it," he said. "But I decided that continuing it was a better idea. By the way, the boy you killed was a favorite of mine."

"I left the dog alive," Maggie said with a shrug.

She could see the effect her words had on him and the struggle he was having to stop himself from hitting her. It made her realize just how powerful Adele must be that this big underworld honcho was pulling his punches—literally—for fear of defying Adele.

He turned away as Adele approached them.

"Here she is, Madame Bontemps," Giordano said, gesturing to where Maggie sat in the chair before them. "As requested. I cannot tell you how close your little pigeon came to becoming roast chicken tonight."

He turned to Adele who had just come into Maggie's sight.

"She killed one of my men back at the villa. My men want revenge."

"Well, I'm glad someone in your group has some self-restraint," Adele said as she stood in front of Maggie and looked down on her. "I have big plans for Madame Dernier and while I have no problem with one of your men doing the honors, *I* will choose the time."

"Long time no see, Adele," Maggie said. "You've aged."

She watched Adele's face tighten but quickly recover.

"At least I will make old bones," Adele said with a hard

smile. "Something you and your husband will not be able to claim. Or Princess Grace."

As Maggie stared at Adele, she tried to remember her from St-Buvard. But she'd rarely seen her in those days. Adele had been Laurent's business partner and Laurent's friend.

"I'd like to invite you to watch the proceedings with Signore Giordano and myself," Adele said. "I think I can promise some surprises and thrills."

Maggie said nothing.

"I've just come from talking to Laurent," Adele said, holding out her phone to show Maggie a photograph on it.

Maggie couldn't help looking. In the photo, Laurent's face was covered in blood. One eye was swollen nearly completely shut and his lip was split and bleeding. He held himself to one side as if favoring broken ribs—or worse. In the eye that was open, Maggie saw defiance and determination. Even so, tears sprang to her eyes to see how injured he was.

"You won't get away with any of this," she said, fighting back tears.

"Funny, that's just what he said to me. Especially when I told him you were joining us. I have to say, Maggie, that quite upset him. I'm wondering if I've ever seen him so upset."

The thought that Laurent knew she was in the hands of this monster filled Maggie with despair. Nothing weakened her husband like the thought of one of his loved ones hurt or in danger.

Knowing I'm here, she thought with dejection, *he must be to the breaking point.*

"You should know I've contacted the police," Maggie said, drawing herself up to make the bluff with whatever reserve of bravado she still had left, and hoping against hope that the threat might make Adele reconsider what she was doing.

"What a coincidence," Adele said with a smile. "Turns out, I called them too."

58

The forest was thick and impenetrable, its thick floor carpeted by fallen leaves and broken branches. Laurent stared at the path ahead and felt the wave of despair wash over him again as he began walking.

Adele's last words to him still rang in his brain:

"I wonder what you would do to stop me from killing her?"

Laurent didn't need to wonder. It was all he could think of as he trudged down the path. He could see that Grace, even limping, was forging ahead more resolutely now. Something had given her hope.

But then, she didn't hear what Adele said.

Should he continue to play the game? What did Adele want? Would he be willing to give her what she asked?

He would die for Maggie. Easily, without a second thought. But he was pretty sure Adele wasn't going to make things that easy.

∼

As she walked, the air smelled to Grace of pine and damp earth.. The wind seemed to carry with it the scents of decaying leaves along the forest floor. For some reason, all she could think of was the fact that they had survived so far against all odds. They'd lived through a boar attack and a pack of dogs. True, Adele had stopped the dog attack. But still, they lived!

Glancing at the moonlit path and the relentless gloom of the forest that encroached their trail, she felt her determination stiffen her shoulders. They were alive and moving forward. They could survive this night. She looked over at Laurent and was disconcerted to see he was the very picture of despair.

She felt her optimism waver a bit then. Why couldn't he just give the woman whatever it was she wanted? Clearly, she didn't want to kill Laurent. Maybe the dead woman that she and Laurent had found in the woods when their car stalled before they were kidnapped had been an accidental death? They never did learn the truth behind that. Perhaps there was a perfectly reasonable explanation for it!

Over the sounds of the breeze rustling through the leaves and the creaking of the branches overhead, Grace heard a faint sniffling. She turned to glance at Joelle who walked silently behind her, holding her injured forearm to her chest. Her head was down as if she was studying the ground instead of looking around being mindful of attacking animals.

"Are you okay?" Grace asked, slowing her pace to walk next to her.

Joelle wiped tears from her face. "It doesn't matter."

"I'd still like to know," Grace said, softening her voice.

She'd been hard on this young woman and she wasn't sure why. They were all in this together and they needed each other to survive.

"Does your arm hurt you?"

Joelle shook her head. "I barely feel it."

"Then what is it?"

Joelle stopped walking. Grace turned and waited. The woman took in a breath as if she was having trouble getting the words out.

"The guy who bandaged my arm said…"

Joelle stopped and took in another long breath. Grace felt the anxiety of what she might hear begin to creep up her spine.

"He said his buddy shot Luc," Joelle said.

Grace frowned. "Who's Luc?"

Joelle looked at her and then shook her head. "Never mind."

"No, he's obviously someone important to you."

"He and I were partners," Joelle said. "It was him and me who tried to sucker your friend Maggie." She glanced at Laurent who still walked ahead.

"I don't understand," Grace said. "He told you they shot your partner?"

Joelle nodded and sniffled again. She wiped away another tear. Grace tried to make sense of what she was saying.

"When? Tonight? Here?"

"Yes, here," Joelle said. "He said they shot him about an hour ago."

For a moment, Grace felt the woods begin to spin. "Was he alone?"

"I don't know," Joelle said. "All I know is Luc came after me. He was trying to find me."

Tears streamed down her face.

"I'm sorry, Joelle," Grace said encouragingly to her. "Come on, let's keep walking."

Joelle began to move forward again. She held her bandaged hand close to her chest, her head dipping in defeat.

"It's just that I didn't know him at all, you know?" she said sadly. "And now he's gone."

59

The campsite where Maggie sat wedged between Adele and Giordano—her hands still tied in front of her—was utilitarian but sufficient for the needs of the game's surveillance. There were no tents since presumably the game wouldn't last long enough to warrant them. The director-style chairs the three sat in were camouflaged under netting and branches, as were along the three SUVs parked on the perimeter of the clearing.

Before them, a single large monitor was perched on a sturdy metal tripod.

Maggie counted seven men including Adele's two thugs who roamed the clearing, laughing and talking in low voices. All carried rifles as they moved about the campsite.

Maggie felt a wave of dread wash over her as she watched how eagerly both Giordano and Adele stayed glued to the monitor looking for any sighting of Laurent and Grace and Joelle. She felt so helpless sitting here having to watch what terrible thing might unfold next—with no way to do anything about it.

As for her own situation, she was a hostage, but nobody was

going to be asked to ransom her. She hated herself for thinking she could outwit Adele and the whole Monaco police force. It wasn't just Laurent and Grace she'd risked for her hubris, but also Amélie. How could she have left the child knowing that something like this might happen? Adele wasn't just destroying three people tonight. She was destroying so many more.

As if she heard her name, Adele turned a cold, calculating gaze on Maggie.

"It won't be long now, Maggie," she said. "Then you'll see how it was always going to end this way."

Maggie suppressed a shudder and glanced again at the armed men behind her, rough mercenaries all from the looks of them. They laughed and joked as if this was some kind of boyish camping trip. But Maggie felt the menace that lurked beneath the surface of their comradery and casual conversations. Her very body was primed for the impending end to the game—the one that she was now powerless to stop. All she could do was watch it happen.

On the monitor before her was a split screen showing two different views of woods. Adele could switch among as many as five views from the different cameras installed on the trail. She'd cycled through them just a moment ago as she did regularly. All the cameras except one were currently shooting empty areas. Only one showed any movement, but it was shadowy and difficult to make out anything clearly.

The intensifying dread of what she was seeing on the screen compounded in Maggie's mind as she found herself squinting at the dim footage to try to discern what she was seeing. There were no lights on this field camera.

Even so, between moonlight and the coming dawn, she could just make out Laurent and Grace and Joelle standing on an overgrown path—hardly worthy of the name—and stopping to rest. Maggie's anxiety spiked as she realized that the three of them weren't behaving as if they knew they were being watched. They were just resting and talking. None of them had glanced up at the camera even once.

Maggie knew that even without the continuous camera lights there had to be a telltale red light blinking on the camera that would tell anyone who looked that the camera was recording.

Her hands turned clammy as she watched in growing horror.

Don't they realize we can see them?

60

Laurent paused on the trail. He didn't turn around, but he could tell Grace and Joelle had stopped behind him. His broken ribs ached with every step on the uneven terrain, like a kettle drum pounding into his sides.

The moon peeked out from behind a line of fir trees perched on yet another high ridge over ahead. The moonlight seemed to illuminate each blade of grass before him. It was quiet, except for the crickets. It reminded him of springtime at Domaine St-Buvard.

He had never been much interested in nature as a boy. Raised in Paris and then always living in cities as an adult, he'd had little connection with even the concept. But as a farmer for the last twenty-five years, his mind and body had become inextricably tuned into the seasons. The vineyard had become his place of refuge. Whether he was walking it to feel the solidity of the ground beneath his feet—ground which he *owned*—or whether he was showing his children how to love the hectare after hectare of fields as he did, he'd never felt the love of *terroir* until Domaine St-Buvard.

At the thought of it, his heart seemed to shudder in his

chest in sorrow. He was surprised he'd grown to have so much to lose. Given the way he'd grown up and how he'd made his living for so many years, it had never been an expectation of his that he would have land and a family he loved. Always before he'd lived on the cusp of ruin, failure, and death.

And now, he'd shocked fate and the universe by having been given it all—and proving himself deserving of it after all.

He smiled and a sharp ache in his jaw reminded him he'd likely fractured it. He'd been able to put that aside for a bit, at least until he stood still and allowed his reflections to possess him. His knee was also in bad shape. Twisted, maybe. He didn't think the patella was broken. He could walk on it. The bastards had mostly concentrated on his face.

Laurent didn't care about that. He'd had his nose broken more times than he'd had hot meals. A broken face he could live with. If he was allowed to.

He turned at the sound of Grace and Joelle finally walking up the trail. He didn't have a plan for their survival beyond putting one foot in front of the other. He only knew that moving forward was better than laying down in the woods and giving up.

He still didn't know if he would be given the chance to save Maggie. Knowing Adele, she would use Maggie to torture him.

And then kill them anyway.

His eyes scanned the darkened woods. Worse than any physical pain was the knowledge that Maggie was somewhere out here in Adele's clutches. Because the end result meant that Amélie was orphaned and abandoned once more. He hated that Maggie had left her, but if the roles had been reversed, he would surely have done the same thing.

"You didn't have to wait for us," Grace said as they reached him on the trail. "Joelle found out her partner was here looking for her and got killed."

Laurent glanced at Joelle. "When?"

"The guy said it happened about an hour ago," she said.

Laurent grimaced. That was probably the same time they captured Maggie. Suddenly, the hairs on the back of his neck stood up. Later, he would realize it had been the smell first that had alerted him more than anything else.

"Stand back!" he said before he knew what he was warning them about.

Directly across the trail from them the bushes began to shake and jump. Laurent grabbed Grace by the arm as if to push her down the path behind him when two large boars emerged from the bushes.

They stood suddenly still as if anchored to the ground. The very air around them seemed to change. All noise ceased, even the breeze in the trees fell silent. It was as if someone had snapped off the volume of the world.

Until a sudden gasp came from Joelle.

And then all hell broke loose.

61

Maggie watched the boars on the screen emerge from the bushes twenty feet from where Laurent and the others stood.

"Adele!" she shouted and pointed at the monitor.

Adele turned and groaned when she saw what was happening.

"I can't rescue them *again*," she said, her face twisted into a grimace. "People are going to ask for their money back."

Maggie closed her eyes in helpless horror of what was about to take place. But even without looking and with no volume on the monitor, in her mind she could hear the snorts of the boars, the sound of their hooves pawing the ground, and the screams.

"They're going to want to see some blood so let this be it," Giordano said. "But maybe you could send one of your guys down to take care of the boars after they kill one of them?"

Maggie knew she was being a coward. If this was Laurent or Grace's last moments on earth, she should witness it. She should watch and pray—not let them die alone with no one to see.

"Estefan!" Adele called. "Get your gun and get over here!"

Adele's words burned into Maggie's brain, and she opened her eyes, terror rippling through her as she focused again on the monitor. Estefan came over to his boss.

"Now listen to me," Adele said to him. "I need you to get down there and make sure the boars don't kill all of them. Do you hear me? You don't get to choose who lives. So, if Princess Grace gets gored, that's just the way the cards fall. Understand?"

"There's no way he'll get there in time!" Giordano said excitedly.

"He can at least prevent the stupid hogs from killing them all!" Adele shouted, angrily.

"Maybe this is a better way to end the game," Giordano said. "Everybody dies in one big blood bath." He turned to Estefan. "Let it play out," he said.

Adele jumped to her feet, her neck corded and tense.

"How dare you give my men orders!?" she screamed.

Maggie willed herself not to listen to the bickering as she watched the screen in nauseated horror. Estefan—the only chance Laurent and Grace had of surviving—stood silently waiting for the argument to be resolved.

Tears filled Maggie's eyes as she focused on the screen and the sight of her loved ones facing down the killing boars.

Maggie began to pray.

62

The wild boars reacted to Joelle's gasp as if it were a starter pistol. They began pawing the ground and snorting even more loudly, their eyes focused on the trio in front of them. They were covered in mud and dirt and blood.

"When I give the word," Laurent said in a low voice, "run."

The boars lowered their heads in unison and for one moment, made no noise whatsoever.

And then they charged.

They came, hard, their jaws snapping, swinging their massive heads straight at Laurent on the path.

"Run!" Laurent shouted.

The first one hit him head on, knocking him to the ground. He slid a full foot on his back as he grappled with the beast, digging his hands into its pelt. Somewhere in the background, he heard Joelle and Grace screaming.

The boar's face was near his, its rancid breath blasting out beside its razor-sharp tusks, when suddenly a series of rapid-fire shots rang out, sending a spray of leaves and twigs flying into the air.

Laurent felt the bullets hit the boar on top of him in quick, metronome-like succession. The beast squealed sharply and then went limp, falling heavily on Laurent's chest. The gunfire stopped abruptly. The silence was so immediate that Laurent thought he'd been killed too. Everything was still except for the whimpering sounds of the women standing behind him. Laurent struggled to push the dead weight of the animal off him and turned to see Joelle and Grace on the trail, their arms around each other, their eyes wide with shock.

Both boars lay dead on the ground.

Laurent got to his feet slowly, scanning the woods for another onslaught of gunshots. He struggled to see into the depths of the forest where the gunfire had come.

It has to be Adele. She's trying to prolong the game.

He felt a swell of anxiety as various scenarios flashed through his mind as he waited for the gunmen to reveal themselves. He hadn't seen automatic weapons with Adele's men. It didn't mean they didn't have them, but why use them now?

Unless it isn't Adele's men.

He could hear people approaching on foot. He positioned himself in front of Grace and Joelle and faced in the direction of the snapping of twigs and rustling in the surrounding brush. His palms were slick with sweat as he clenched his fists, bracing for the confrontation.

63

The sounds of the men grew closer as heavy footsteps rustled the leaves in the bushes, not bothering to hide their tread. The figures morphed out of the mist and the gloom wearing camouflage fatigues and carrying AK-47s. Laurent's stomach tensed. He didn't recognize any of them.

"Laurent?" Grace said tentatively.

Laurent held up a hand for silence. He wasn't sure how he was going to meet this new threat—his arms still quivered from his efforts to hold the boar back—but he would have to pull from whatever reserves he still had.

"Who are they?" Joelle asked, fear lacing her voice.

Dread flooded Laurent as he watched the gunmen break through the first berm of low shrubs across the clearing. And then his jaw dropped in astonishment.

Margaux Labelle came striding across the clearing toward him, an AK-47 over one shoulder and an army of two bringing up the rear. Laurent stared, speechless, as she marched up to him, her face creased with concern.

"You look like serious hell, Laurent," she said with a grimace.

Laurent took two steps and wrapped his arms around her, lifting her off the ground with a strength he'd thought impossible just moments before. Margaux made an abrupt squeaking sound when he put her down and he saw her blushing face.

"Margaux Labelle," he said. "I cannot believe it's you." He felt his chest fill with something he hadn't felt since this whole nightmare began—hope.

64

Maggie heard rapid gunfire coming from somewhere in the woods not too far from where they were sitting. She let out a gasp of disbelief as she snapped her attention back to the monitor and watched both boars fall.

"They shot the boars!" she shouted. "They killed them!"

Giordano jumped to his feet, knocking his chair over and cursing loudly.

"Who the hell is that?" he shouted, pointing at the screen.

Adele stared at the monitor with one hand over her mouth, her eyes wide with surprise and confusion. She looked at Giordano and then at Estefan who still stood beside her. He hadn't moved since she and Giordano had begun arguing.

All Maggie could think was *they're safe!* Her mind whirled with the possible reasons or explanations. Maybe hunters in the woods? Maybe French park rangers had shown up? But who would be roaming the woods at four in the morning?

With assault weapons?

"What is this all about, Adele?" Giordano demanded, standing with his hands on his hips, glaring at her. His men had come over to look at the monitor. They too, had heard the sounds of automatic weapons in the woods.

"Don't look at me, Vittorio," Adele said sharply. "You can see that both my men are here. This sounds like the work of *your* men."

"Don't be ridiculous!"

But Giordano looked around and Maggie saw him do a quick head count. He turned back to Adele who had turned back to the monitor.

"You're supposed to be in control of this," Giordano said. "You don't know who these guys are?"

Just then Maggie watched as three shadowy forms appeared onto the screen. Immediately, her body shot up straight in her chair and tears jumped to her eyes.

Margaux!

Hours ago, before leaving the car on the side of the road and in a desperate bid for backup, she had sent Margaux the link to share her location. After everything that had happened since then, she'd totally forgotten that Margaux was even a possibility for help.

Estefan stood by the monitor, his rifle in his hands, looking confused. They watched Laurent sweep Margaux off her feet in a bear hug.

"Who are they?" Giordano demanded.

"That's a very good question," Adele said, turning to Maggie. "Is this your doing? Well, it won't matter. Besides, I count only three."

Adele turned to Giordano. "Between my two and your five, we outnumber them. Plus, I have reinforcements showing up."

Giordano frowned.

"What do you mean *reinforcements*?" he asked, querulously. "May I remind you that I have enemies around here? You should have told me you'd invited more to the party."

"Relax, Vittorio," Adele said. "It's the Monaco police."

"*You called the police*?!" he asked angrily, half standing from his chair again and looking around at his men who had heard her and were behaving in agitated restlessness.

"Chill out," Adele said. "They're not coming in the capacity of defenders of law and order, I can assure you."

Giordano glanced furtively around at his surroundings before turning back to Adele. Maggie watched him rotate his neck on his shoulders as if trying to calm down. He gestured to his men and she watched them visibly relax and then return to their activities.

"You'd better be right," Giordano said gruffly. "The Monaco police are not my friends."

"Don't tell me you don't pay them?" Adele said. "Tisk tisk, Vittorio. *That* is money well spent, trust me. I'll introduce you when Detective Latour is here tonight."

Maggie flinched at the sound of Latour's name. It made a lot more sense now—his refusal to help, or even to listen to her, or follow up on any lead or evidence. He was in Adele's pocket.

She felt a cramp of revulsion at the thought of him, but quickly tried to shake it off in order to recapture her joy of just a few moments before. At least Laurent and Grace weren't alone. And now they had an armed escort.

But they still were not out of the woods. So to speak.

Not by a long shot.

65

The two men with Margaux smiled guardedly at Laurent as they passed him on the trail and continued to scan the surrounding area. Neither of the men gave a second glance to the dead boars but paused just long enough to share a word with Grace and Joelle who were intent on showering their gratitude on them.

"How in the hell did you know where we were?" Laurent asked Margaux.

"I didn't," Margaux said with a shrug. "I was following the location share that Maggie sent me—and along the way we ran into you having a wild boar problem."

Laurent leaned against a large boulder which helped to temporarily relieve the ache in his ribs. He could still hardly believe that the Aix detective was here.

"Are you okay?" she asked, narrowing her eyes at him. "I have to say, Laurent, you look terrible."

"Seeing you, *chérie*," he said with a grin. "I have never felt better in my life."

Margaux grinned and blushed again when Grace turned to her, her face suddenly serious.

"It won't be a cake walk," Grace warned. "Adele Bontemps is the team leader and she said she called in the Monaco police as reinforcements."

"I assume not in uniform," Margaux said, dryly.

Laurent glanced at Margaux's men who were scouting the perimeter of the clearing.

"Is this all you have?" he asked.

"They were enough to save your butt a few minutes ago," Margaux said defensively and then paused. "Any idea how many Adele has before reinforcements arrive?"

Laurent frowned. "We've only seen two. But there could be more."

"Okay," Margaux said as she turned and gestured to her men. "We'll need to recon first before we do anything else."

"Can you leave us a gun?" Laurent said. "The two boars you killed were a part of Adele upping the ante on the game to keep it interesting."

"*Le Jeu*, right?" Margaux said. "Maggie told me about it."

"You've seen Maggie?" Laurent asked, his eyebrows high in surprise.

"Yeah, that's a great story," Margaux said. "And I'll love telling you over a glass of wine someday."

She pulled a handgun from her holster and handed it to him.

"Adele has Maggie," Laurent said to Margaux.

Grace snapped her head around. "What?"

She looked from Laurent to Margaux.

"Laurent, no! Why didn't you tell me?"

"What could you have done?"

Except agonize over it like me.

"Well, *we'll* do something," Margaux said with determination. "We'll get her back."

"I think you might have lost the element of surprise," Joelle said solemnly.

Laurent turned to look where Joelle was staring and spotted the lone unlighted camera mounted on a tall pine across the clearing. He cursed when he saw it.

He'd been so focused on fighting off the boars and then reuniting with Margaux that he hadn't thought to look around to see if there were any cameras in the area. It was true that these cameras didn't have lights—the main reason why Laurent had missed them—but it meant that Adele knew Laurent and Grace and Joelle had been joined by three others.

"Don't worry about it," Margaux said. "Get into the woods and stay out of sight and wait for us."

"Be careful, Margaux," Laurent said as she prepared to leave.

She turned to him—to say something or just to give him a reassuring smile, Laurent would never know because at that moment, he felt a sudden prick like an electric shock on his lower leg. He jumped at the sensation and felt the sting vibrate all the way up to his groin.

"Laurent?" Margaux asked with a frown. "Are you okay?"

Laurent felt a pulse of dread as he instinctively looked at the ground by his feet.

Just in time to see the snake slither away.

66

As Adele and Giordano discussed various ways to dispatch the Grace, Laurent and the others, Maggie continued to stare at the monitor with desperation and hope warring in her heart. To see Laurent and Grace alive and seemingly in one piece was everything she could've hoped for. When Margaux came over to talk with Laurent, Maggie felt her heart go out to her.

If I survive this, you, lady, are my new best friend.

For the first time since she'd heard about *Le Jeu*, Maggie had real hope that they were all going to make it out of this alive. But, on the other hand, the hostage group still didn't seem to realize that they were being watched. And now with all the excitement of Margaux's coming to join them, they appeared more distracted than ever.

And that was not good.

Maggie watched as Margaux and her men seemed to be preparing to leave and Maggie felt her stomach tense up. Then she felt a veritable explosion of butterflies as she watched Margaux hand Laurent a gun.

"Oh, my, now that should ante up the odds a bit," Adele said with a laugh as she watched the monitor.

Maggie saw that both Adele and Giordano were again focused on the monitor. They'd seen Margaux give Laurent the gun.

"Not that it will do them any good," Adele said. "Oh! Look! They finally see us. Hello, *mes amis!* Smile at the camera!"

Maggie watched all the people visible on the TV screen look up into the camera lens.

"Looks like their new pals are leaving," Adele said as Margaux and her men began to depart. "I wonder where they're off to?"

She turned to Maggie and then glanced at Maggie's jacket pocket.

"Please tell me your apes searched her before they handcuffed her," she said to Giordano.

She reached into Maggie's pocket and pulled out her cellphone and then turned to look at Giordano.

"Are you kidding me?" she said wagging the phone at him. "I guess this means we should expect company soon."

"Well, if she's being tracked, turn it off!" Giordano said, his voice anxious for the first time all evening. He reached out for the phone.

"We're not here to hide, Vittorio," Adele said, moving the phone out of his reach. "Let them come. This way we don't have to go hunting them in the woods."

Maggie felt a jolt of anxiety as Giordano suddenly stood up to walk over to his men where he informed them that three gunmen with automatic weapons were coming. She watched the men scurry off to position themselves in ambush locations.

When she turned back to the monitor, she saw Laurent jerk his leg away from where he'd been standing. What had just happened? Margaux and Grace instantly ran over to him. With mounting dread, Maggie watched Margaux bend down to examine his leg.

"What's happening?" Adele asked as she turned her attention back to the monitor.

"I don't know," Maggie said.

And then the three of them on the screen began to look around on the ground.

"Oh, God," Maggie murmured.

"What? What is it?" Adele asked, genuinely confused.

"I think Laurent's been bitten by a snake."

Adele squinted at the monitor as Grace, Joelle and Margaux all seemed to be actively looking for something on the ground. Laurent wasn't looking. He was leaning against a large boulder. He wiped a hand across his face.

"He's been bitten!" Maggie said sharply. "Adele, you've got to do something!"

"He looks like he's just resting," Adele said.

"Did you or did you not unleash a bunch of poisonous snakes in the area?" Maggie asked shrilly.

Adele continued to watch the monitor as everyone on screen except Laurent seemed to be panicking and running around in an attempt to fix the problem.

"Crap," she said with a sigh as she sat back in her chair in resignation. "Well, you know what? I'm pretty sure after two boar charges and a rabid dog attack—not to mention a beating at the hands of my men that would've killed most men—" She turned to look at Maggie.

"I'm thinking that getting bitten by a snake might be the universe's way of telling us that this really is Laurent's time to die."

67

Margaux's earlier excitement at finding Laurent and the others quickly faded as she inspected the snake bite on Laurent's leg. Grace saw her men look at each other in dismay, the realization dawning on all of them that they were unprepared for this. They had rescued the group from the immediate threat of attacking wild boars, only to be presented with a new danger they could not hope to beat.

Grace and Joelle stood beside Laurent and wrung their hands. Margaux turned to her men.

"Each of you grab an arm," she said. "We'll take him to the hospital in Monte Carlo."

"Margaux," one of the men said, shaking his head. "It's a mile to the SUV under rough terrain and then another fifteen to the closest hospital. He'll never make it."

"Don't tell me that!" Margaux shouted. "Just do it!"

Grace realized that Margaux was breathing hard. In a minute she'd hyperventilate. As she watched the two men come up on either side of Laurent as if to lift him, Grace stepped between them and put a hand on Laurent's chest.

Already he was breathing shallowly and his eyes were

glazed. Grace turned to Margaux and saw the rabid determination in her face. Margaux just couldn't accept that she'd come all this way to save Laurent's life only to lose him now.

"Detective Labelle," Grace said to her. "This won't work."

"Get out of the way," Margaux said fiercely. "We need to get him to the vehicle."

"He won't make it to the hospital," Grace said.

"I won't listen to this defeatist talk!" Margaux snapped, her eyes on Laurent who appeared to be visibly fading.

"Listen, to me," Grace said, taking Margaux by the arm. Margaux made to twist away from her, but Grace held firm.

"When they were taping my ankle," Grace said, "I saw a vial of antivenom in the first aid kit. We don't have time to get him to a hospital. But you can get that medicine at wherever Adele is watching us from."

Margaux's eyes were still on Laurent, but Grace knew she was listening.

"You said you were on your way to find Maggie," Grace said. "So you know where she is?"

"I can track her," Margaux said. She turned to Grace. "We'll have to fight the group to get to the medicine."

"You were going to do that anyway," Grace said. "Find Maggie's location on your phone. Are they near?"

Forcing Margaux to look away from Laurent seemed to help break the spell of Margaux's focus on him. She looked at her phone screen.

"Less than a mile," she said.

She turned to the men who were now standing next to her awaiting their orders.

"Okay," she said. "It's fifteen minutes through the woods." She looked at Laurent. "It would be faster if he came with us to get the medicine."

"No," Grace said firmly. "You can't carry a two-hundred-pound man over hills and woods in less than thirty minutes. And he won't survive longer."

Her words seemed to echo in the air around them, freezing all of them by their hopelessness.

Thirty minutes to get there, subdue the mercenaries, get the medicine and get back here.

Impossible.

∼

Laurent listened to the muted arguing of the people around him as if it were background music with no specific words or melody. He watched their faces and saw the fear and panic in them but all he felt was calm. He knew the end was coming. There was no way they were going to beat the speed of the venom racing to his heart. He was going to die and leave both Grace and Maggie unprotected. He was going to leave this life in the worst possible way, knowing he left loved ones in danger.

As he watched Grace argue with Margaux, the emotions and intensity so painful on both their faces, he thought of his beautiful Mila, his optimistic and hopeful daughter, so lovely and perfect. And Jem, his firstborn, the one who changed him more than all the others because he made him a father. *My son.*

And of course Luc, his brother's child, and the only good thing Gerard ever did in his miserable life. Laurent felt his eyes sting with tears of failure when he thought of little Amélie who would be left alone in a cold hard world that wouldn't even try to understand her.

But for all of them, his biggest regret was to be unable to hold Maggie one more time. His one true love. The woman he was never supposed to know, let alone love. The woman so unlike him in so many ways. And the woman who made him the man he was.

He smiled faintly at the continuing sound of Grace's

passionate urgency. He prayed the world wouldn't lose her today. Not just for her children's sake, but because the world needed passion in it and dreams.

He wanted to tell them to stop fussing. What they wanted so desperately wasn't possible. He knew that. He accepted that. He leaned back and closed his eyes, feeling a peace begin creep over him and realized with a calm surprise that his work was done.

Not finished, maybe. But finally done.

∽

The world around Maggie seemed to swirl in a vortex of motion and sound. Things were happening too quickly but still not fast enough. The only thing that mattered was the drama playing out on the monitor in front of her right this minute. A drama she was powerless to alter or affect.

Her heart thundered in her chest, and she felt her palms dampen as she forced herself to close her eyes and pull hard from some deep hidden reserve for the strength for one last attempt with Adele. Maggie took in a deep breath and forced herself to let it out slowly. Then she opened her eyes.

"Adele," she said, forcing herself to sound calm, "you once cared for Laurent. He needs a hospital. Fast."

"Well, that's not happening," Adele said. "But if it *was* a snake bite, and I'm not convinced it was, we have antivenom medicine."

Hope swelled in Maggie's chest.

"Adele, please. I'm begging you," Maggie said. "You have to save him."

"I don't have to do anything!" Adele snapped, her eyes returning to the monitor as she watched Margaux and Grace hovering protectively over Laurent.

Maggie put her hands to her mouth and felt cold fingers of

dread trace down her spine. She had to believe that however much Adele hated Laurent, she wasn't ready for him to die. At the very least, whatever she had planned for him would now not take place if she allowed him to succumb to a snake bite.

"Donato," Adele said suddenly. "Go bring the big man in."

"What about the women?" Estefan said, hurrying over. "Let me go. I'll bring him in."

"Perhaps it would be good to wait to see if the women abandon the man as he begins to weaken?" Giordano said. "That might add a little something interesting to the stew."

"No," Adele said as she turned back to the screen where Grace was now ripping Laurent's pant leg away from the area of the bite. "He won't last that long. On second thought, Donato, forget bringing him here. Take the first aid kit and give the injection to him there."

"Si, Madame B."

Maggie gripped the arms of her chair tightly and she prayed harder than she ever had before. She wanted to scream at Adele's man *to hurry!*

"Oh, and Donato?" Adele said.

"Yes, Madame?"

"After you give him the shot, I need you to do one more thing for me."

Adele turned to Maggie with a smile.

"I need you to kill Princess Grace," she said.

68

Maggie jumped to her feet in horror.
"No!" she said to Adele. Her eyes went from Adele to Donato who simply nodded and turned away.

"Please, you can't!" Maggie screamed after him. "I'm begging you..."

Donato disappeared into the woods. Maggie ran two steps in his direction, but Estefan stepped into her path. Maggie pressed her hands to her mouth to keep from screaming. Her body began to shake.

They can't do this!

This was nothing less than an execution! She turned in frantic desperation to the monitor where she saw Grace kneeling by Laurent. Maggie was slammed with the terrible realization that she was powerless to do anything but watch her best friend die.

Adele turned her cold gaze on Maggie.

"Let's hear it, *chérie*," she said. "Make your best argument."

"Grace never did you any harm," Maggie said desperately,

knowing that Adele was baiting her but praying she might actually be sincere.

"Wrong!" Adele shouted. "She always acted as if she was better than me. Try again."

Maggie's mind raced but her brain was blank. All she could see were memories of Grace smiling and laughing. Brave, bold, beautiful Grace. She thought of Zouzou and poor little Philippe. The threat of what was coming was like a vise tightening around Maggie's chest. She struggled to breathe.

"Please! I'm begging you," she said, her eyes filling with tears.

"Oh, this is good," Adele said dispassionately, her tone belying her words. "It's almost as good as I'd imagined. It will kill me not to hear Laurent beg me to spare her too. I hate that there's no audio on these cameras."

Maggie pointed to the monitor.

"Laurent won't see you kill her! He'll be unconscious by the time your man gets there with the antivenom!"

Adele frowned and glanced at the monitor.

"Good point," she said. "I'll send Estefan to tell Donato to hold off shooting her until the medicine takes effect and Laurent can fully appreciate what's happening."

Maggie sank back into her chair. Had it just been moments ago when she thought things might actually work out?

"I won't do it!" Estefan said suddenly, his voice a mix of rage and desperation. "You promised me!"

Adele turned to look at him, her expression unreadable.

"I promised you nothing," she said coolly.

Estefan pointed to the radio.

"Call him now. Tell him not to kill the princess."

"Get a grip, you moron!" Adele said, quickly losing her temper.

"*You* need to get a grip of your own people, Adele," Giordano said rejoining them again. "I would never tolerate this kind of insubordination."

"I will go after Donato and tell him you changed your mind!" Estefan said hotly. "He will not kill the princess."

"You do, Estefan, and I'll kill you," Adele said. "In fact, I'll have Donato do it."

"He wouldn't do it. He hates you!"

Adele's face flinched at the assault.

"That's a lie," she said, but Maggie could tell Adele believed him. "But even if it's the truth, I don't care. He's just a hired gun."

"I'll tell him you said so. He won't work for you anymore."

"This is ridiculous," Giordano said. "We're leaving. You and your *reinforcements* can handle things from here. I'll send a man by tonight to pick up my winnings."

It was as if Adele wasn't hearing Giordano. Her face was flushed with fury.

"I don't think you're going to tell him anything, Estefan," she said as she reached under her chair.

But Estefan was ready for her. Without warning, he launched himself at Adele in her chair, sending her and her chair sprawling onto the ground. Maggie tried to leap out of the way but didn't make it before she and her chair also came crashing down. Dust filled the air as Adele and Estefan wrestled on the hard-packed earth beneath them. Maggie scrambled to get some distance from the melee when she heard a single gunshot.

She froze and turned to see that both Adele and Estefan had frozen too. Sweat was beaded on their foreheads, streaked with dirt and smeared with scratches. Adele lay underneath Estefan. The seconds seemed to tick by until slowly, and with a mighty groan, Adele pushed his body off her. He rolled into the dirt without a sound.

Maggie stared in horror when she saw the blood pouring

out of the single bullet hole in his chest. She turned to see Adele sitting up now, her face flushed, a long scratch down one cheek. She was holding a small pistol. And her eyes were locked on Maggie.

Maggie's heart pounded as Adele slowly aimed the gun at her.

69

Grace heard the gunshot, muffled and a long way away, just moments after watching Margaux and her men disappear into the mist of the surrounding woods. She had no idea what the gunshot meant or if it meant anything. She said a prayer the gunshot wasn't connected to Maggie but she could do nothing about it if it was.

She turned back to where Laurent sat leaning against a giant boulder. She needed to be philosophical about his chances. She would throw it to God and believe in her heart that whatever happened was what happened, and she would deal with it. But she was filled with a helpless fusion of cold dread.

When she moved back to Laurent she saw he was conscious but just barely. She knelt in front of him without a word and pulled his pant leg up to find the puncture site. Unfortunately, everything Grace knew about snake bites was what she'd learned from old black and white Westerns.

You cut the bite and suck out the venom and pray for a miracle.

The two tell-tale fang marks were indisputable. The serpent

had bitten him through his pant leg. A drop of blood gathered at the edge of one of the fang bites. Grace felt a shiver that promised never to stop if she didn't get a grip of herself. It wasn't that she didn't realize the fang marks would be there. But seeing them removed all doubt. Her chest felt weighted down with dread.

At least the bite was as far away from his heart as she could hope for. That was something.

"I need a knife!" she yelled to Joelle.

"Are you kidding?" Joelle yelled back. "If I had a knife, don't you think I would've mentioned it before now?"

Grace looked around in desperation for anything that might allow her to cut into the bite marks.

"Give up, *chérie*," Laurent said wearily. "It's done."

"Stop that!" Grace said, her nostrils flaring. "It's *not* done until we're all dead." She turned to shout at Joelle. "Joelle! The ravine we passed a few minutes ago...there was trash at the bottom. Go!"

Joelle jumped up and hurried back down the path. "On my way," she called.

"Wasting your time," Laurent said, his eyelids fluttering.

In her heart and in some deep recess of her brain, Grace knew he was right. There was no way Margaux could get back in time with the medicine. And all a broken bottle or a rusty nail would do would be to make sure Laurent died with a load of swarming bacteria in his blood. Tears splashed down her face.

"Don't talk like that," she said, crossly. "If I have to, I'll bite through it with my teeth."

"Rather...not," Laurent said as his head lolled to one side.

"Laurent?" she said, her panic deepening when he didn't respond. She considered waking him, but there was no point. At least this way, he was blessedly out of it. She heard a cracking of twigs. The noise was not coming from the direction

Joelle had gone. Instantly, Grace snapped her head around, her heart pounding.

She felt the surge of fear course through her as a man materialized from the line of bushes across the clearing. She recognized him as the same man who'd taped her ankle. He was also the one who'd given them all the talk about the game when he released them from the van.

She didn't immediately see a weapon on him, but his gaze wasn't kind or intelligent. He looked like the kind of man who followed orders because he was incapable of thinking for himself.

Which means he can't be reasoned with.

He stood at the edge of the clearing and scanned the area, his eyes resting on Laurent.

"Where is the other one?" he asked.

Grace saw the gun now in his waistband. She stepped in front of Laurent, her heart pounding wildly.

"She's gone to get help," she said.

The man walked over to her, his eyes drilling into her in a way she'd never experienced before in her life.

He looked at her as if he had found his prey.

70

Adele held the gun on Maggie.

"Are you really going to cheat Laurent out of the pleasure of seeing you kill me?" Maggie asked, surprised she could even get the words out.

"It got too complicated," Adele said, her face no longer sneering or even victorious, just weary.

She pulled the hammer back on the gun. In that moment, Maggie saw her children and Laurent and her parents. There was no escape route this time, and the cavalry wasn't going to come in the nick of time. As she closed her eyes in acceptance of what was to come, she was suddenly deafened by a barrage of bullets echoing throughout the campsite.

Adele jerked in shock at the sound and Maggie dove for cover under the nearest parked car as bullets began to rain down. The night sky seemed to literally light up with a flurry of bullets.

Margaux!

Praying Adele would have her hands full trying to stay alive, Maggie crawled from under the SUV to a nearby bush and watched the campsite erupt into chaos. Giordano hadn't quite made it out yet. He was knocking over camp tables and chairs in an effort to get to his car. Two of his guys lay motionless on the ground.

From what Maggie could tell, the attack was coming from the encroaching woods. Bullets whizzed through the air, striking trees around where the monitor was set up, sending chips of bark flying.

Screams pierced the air, along with the smell of gunpowder as Giordano's men shot blindly into the woods. Maggie saw Giordano struggle to open his car door and then crouch behind the open door, a handgun in his hand.

Margaux's group definitely seemed to have the upper hand. She had Giordano's men pinned down, although the three who were left had taken cover like Giordano and were trying to wait them out. Maggie wasn't sure how that was going to work out. At best it was a stalemate. Then she remembered that Adele's group was waiting for reinforcements.

They didn't have time to wait! Somehow she needed to end the stalemate before Detective Latour and his men showed up. But even more important than that, she needed to stop Adele's thug from killing Grace.

She glanced around the campsite. She was still handcuffed and hiding under a bush. Adele was somewhere nearby with a gun.

"Margaux!" Maggie called, knowing she was letting Adele and Giordano's men know her position but needing to risk it. "Adele sent someone back to kill Grace! You need to stop him!"

Maggie waited but Margaux didn't answer. Feeling a well of frustration and just seconds from breaking cover and running after Donato herself, Maggie saw movement in the trees and realized with a growing dread that she was seeing more men coming.

A veritable army of men.

She held her breath in an attempt to stifle the scream that

wanted to erupt. It was Latour's men. There had to be at least a dozen of them. The men came out of the woods dressed in paramilitary outfits. Maggie realized the sniper fire had stopped.

Had Margaux fled?

Maybe she went back to save Grace?

Maggie's heart sank as she watched Latour's army advance into the center of the campsite.

If she could make it out of the camp herself before Latour's men found her, she might make it to where Laurent and Grace were. She was sure she could tell the direction from all the shooting she'd heard earlier when Margaux and her men had killed the boars.

She crawled through the tall grass aiming for another set of bushes on the other side of the campsite when a man stepped out from behind a tree in front of her. Maggie recoiled sharply but he reached down and grabbed her by her jacket and dragged her to her feet. Maggie twisted in his grip to face him and then whitened. It was the same man who'd captured her before.

The man who'd been denied the satisfaction of killing her earlier.

He towered over her, a mirthless smile twisting onto his scarred face. At six and a half feet tall, he was a mountain of muscle and menace. His shaved head gleamed in the dim light, and a web of tattoos snaked down his neck and arms.

Maggie looked around in desperation. The balance had shifted. Margaux's snipers had gone quiet, probably left. She was on her own.

The man stared down at her, her hands still bound in front of her.

"Remember me?" he sneered.

He dragged her into the center of the campsite clearing where he flung her down onto the ground.

"No one to stop me now, American!" he said in a snarl as he pulled a semi-automatic pistol from his shoulder holster.

Maggie licked her lips. She could see Giordano straightening up from behind the door where he'd taken cover and looking around to check on his men. He didn't even glance in her direction. He had no intention of stopping this.

"Look," Maggie said desperately to the man. "I'm sorry about your brother."

The killer stepped closer to her and raised his gun.

"Apology not accepted," he said thickly.

Maggie closed her eyes, for the second time in a few minutes forcing herself not to think about what was happening. Her last moment, her last thoughts, were for Laurent and Amélie, Jem, Mila and Luc.

She heard the hammer click back on the assassin's gun.

"*Arrivederci*, baby," he said with a sneer.

71

The sound of the shot rang out like a thunderclap, obliterating all other sensation roiling in Maggie. She opened her eyes when she realized she hadn't been shot and gasped out loud and as a small fountain of blood suddenly appeared on the man's dirty t-shirt in front of her.

He looked at her in confusion, his large bald head bobbling on his shoulders, before falling to his knees. Maggie pushed herself shakily to her feet and looked around the clearing expecting to be shot by the same sniper any moment.

Giordano screamed in outrage.

"No, you idiot!" he shouted angrily. "He's one of ours! You've shot the wrong one!"

Latour's men, armed with rifles and handguns, fanned out across the campsite in twos and threes, jerking weapons away from the two remaining Giordano men and forcing them to their knees.

Detective Latour stepped out of the middle of the swarm of men. He too was dressed in camouflage, his face painted for night battle, and not a hint of police insignia to indicate his rank or true identity. He held his gun with both hands, still aimed at the man who now lay face down on the ground in front of Maggie, bleeding out. Latour surveyed the scene quickly, his eyes taking in the positions of Giordano's men and the weapons on the ground beside them as his men tied their hands. He pivoted slowly, his gun moving with him, past Maggie to where Giordano stood by his car.

"Put your hands in the air, Signore," Latour said to Giordano. "You're under arrest."

Maggie felt a surge of shock. Then immediately relief roared through her body like an out-of-control freight train. She looked frantically around the campsite and saw Margaux and her two men running to the SUVs to rummage in the piles of supplies inside them. Latour's men walked through the camp, weapons drawn, securing the site, holding Giordano and his men at gunpoint.

Suddenly, Maggie remembered Adele. She turned to look around the camp—half expecting the woman to still have a gun trained on her—but there was no sign of her.

Nor of the SUV she'd come in.

∼

Grace faced down the man who stood before her, his gun drawn on her. They'd all heard the firing of automatic rifles in the distance. The man showed no concern about the noise. Grace had to assume it was Margaux engaging the camp.

And this man wasn't worried about it.

"Calm down," he said coldly. "I've come with the antivenom."

The hope that his words brought warred immediately in Grace's brain with the strong belief that he meant them harm.

"I don't believe you," she said.

"It's the truth. Madame doesn't want the game to end yet."

Just then, out of the corner of her eye Grace saw Joelle

return. The young woman froze when she saw the man, and tension in the clearing ratcheted up to nearly unbearable levels.

"What's happening?" Joelle called out.

"He says he's brought antivenom," Grace said breathlessly and then addressed the man. "Let's see it then."

She took an involuntary step back as he jammed his gun into his waistband and pulled out a small plastic case which he waved at her.

"Do you want it or not?" he asked.

Grace nearly jumped at him in order to snatch the case away. Of course they would have seen on the camera that Laurent had been bitten. And Adele wouldn't want Laurent out of the game so soon! It made sense!

She watched him as he opened the case and pulled out a vial and a syringe. Her heart was pounding as he attempted to attach the syringe to the bottle. He cursed when the needle broke in his hands. Grace watched in horror, a terrible shudder rippling through her.

"Hold on, hold on," he said, tossing away the broken syringe. "I think there's another one in here."

Joelle stepped forward and held out her hand.

"Give it to me," she said. "I was a nurse."

The man didn't hesitate. He gave her the whole case and then turned to look at Grace while Joelle inserted the needle into the vial. She then quickly turned to Laurent and gave him the injection, Grace glanced at the man and saw he was staring at her. The look he gave her chilled her blood. In that moment she knew without a doubt that he was here to kill her.

Trying to stay calm, Grace looked back at Laurent. She saw that the gun Margaux had given him had fallen from his hand. It lay now in the dirt by his hip, partially hidden. But only partially. Her mind raced as she tried to think if she should run or try to grab for the gun on the ground. Just then the man reached for the gun in his waist band.

Time was up. She turned to see how far away the line of trees was. She would never make it before he shot her in the back. Suddenly the man's radio crackled. She watched him reach for his radio clipped to his shoulder.

At that moment Grace heard more gunfire in the distance. Was it Margaux's team? Were they being killed even now? Or doing the killing?

"Si, Madame B?" the man said into the radio. "I have given the big man the medicine."

He glanced at Grace.

"Do you see me, Donato?" Adele said over the radio.

Just then, Grace saw lights flashing in the dark overhead. Two headlights poised twenty meters on the upper road above them.

"I do, Madame," Donato said, glancing up.

"There's been a change of plans."

The radio static was worse as a cold rain began to fall. Grace had trouble understanding what Adele said. But to her ears, in spite of the rain and her exhaustion and mounting fear, it sounded as if she had said *Kill them all.*

72

Giordano and his men lay spread out on the ground as Latour's men systematically went to them one by one, frisked them, relieved them of any hidden weapons and then secured their hands behind their backs.

Maggie ran to Margaux who was coming out of one of the SUVs. Maggie knew she was looking for the antivenom.

"It's not there!" Maggie said to her breathlessly. "One of Adele's men took it to save Laurent."

"He did?"

Margaux rubbed the space between her eyes as if trying to make sense of that.

"Never mind about that," Maggie said. "He also went there to shoot Grace! We've got to get to them!"

Suddenly the sound of a lone gunshot came to them from somewhere in the woods. Maggie felt her stomach drop in horror.

"Now, don't panic," Margaux said. "It might not be her."

Maggie's legs buckled under her and she found herself sitting on the ground.

Please don't let it be Grace. Please don't let it be Grace.

"Come on, Maggie," Margaux said. "Get a grip."

"I know, I know," Maggie said. But dread and apprehension continued to build up inside her.

Margaux squatted in front of Maggie. "Get it together, okay?"

Maggie swallowed hard and tried to nod.

"Where's Adele Bontemps?" Margaux asked, looking around the camp.

Maggie glanced up to see that the monitor they'd been looking at just minutes before was knocked over and had gone dark, likely hit by a stray bullet.

"Gone," Maggie said.

Latour strode over to them.

"She won't have gone far," he said as Margaux cut the plastic ties on Maggie's hands.

"She'll try to head for the border," he said. "I've already alerted the Italians."

Maggie remembered there weren't really any restrictions on the borders anymore. Adele would have no trouble crossing. She looked at Latour but felt no residual recrimination toward him. She felt nothing. Not even gratefulness that he'd shown up in the end since it likely had been too late to save the ones she loved.

73

Grace had heard the message loud and clear.
Kill them all.
There could be no more subterfuge or mystery about why the man was here. Grace felt her fear turn to ice in her veins as she watched the man turn off his radio and raise his gun. She watched him as if she were watching a movie in slow motion. A movie she'd seen before and knew how it would end. She felt bizarrely at peace as she faced him.

He turned to stare at her, his eyes blank and unfocused, and then just for a moment, his gaze dropped to her breasts. Suddenly without thinking, Grace reached up and ripped open her blouse, exposing her lacy bra underneath.

He gaped at her, his gun sagging just a few inches as he stared in wonder at the sight of Princess Grace in her bra...which was why he didn't see Joelle on her knees swivel around and stab at him in the groin with the hypodermic needle.

He howled and jerked away from Joelle, at the same moment Grace launched herself onto his back and bit his ear.

He screamed and dropped the gun, raising his hands up to try to pull her off. While his arms were up, Joelle slammed the syringe again and again into his groin. Grace felt the man's legs give out as he crashed to the ground, howling like a demented animal.

"His gun!" Grace gasped. "Get his gun!"

She toppled off him as he rolled on the ground holding his groin in agony. Joelle snatched up the gun from the ground and put the barrel to his head.

"No!" Grace said. "Don't!"

Joelle hesitated and then jammed the gun barrel against the man's knee and pulled the trigger. The sound reverberated up the wall of stone to the cliff top road where it echoed in the dark night for several long seconds.

Donato's howls intensified and he continued to rock back and forth, now gripping his leg, which was gushing blood. Grace crawled over to where he had dropped the first aid kit and wrenched it open. Shaking, she found a tourniquet and a thick bandage and crawled back to him, slapping his hands away. She didn't think Joelle needed to shoot him but possibly the woman was afraid he could overpower them otherwise.

"Help me, Joelle," Grace said desperately, glancing at Laurent who had begun to rouse, the effects of the antivenom already working. "Give the gun to Laurent. He can cover us."

Joelle ran to Laurent and placed the gun in his hand.

"He can't even hold it!" Joelle said.

"Then come back here and point it at this guy," Grace said as she struggled to put pressure on the bleeding wound.

"But first, tie his hands," she said breathlessly as she pressed on the bullet wound.

Joelle put down the gun and rummaged in the first aid kit until she found a thick rubber tourniquet and quickly bound the groaning man's hands. Grace felt the perspiration pouring down her face. She heard the crackle of the radio and wondered if Adele had figured out what had happened. And if she would be sending someone else after this guy.

"Give me the radio," Laurent said softly, his voice barely carrying across the clearing.

Joelle snatched the attached radio off the thug's shoulder and ran over to where Laurent was now sitting up against the trunk of a tree. He held the gun that Margaux had given him. His face was a less chalky shade of gray. The antivenom was fast-acting.

Joelle glanced around the clearing for anything else deadly that might be crawling around and held the gun they'd taken off their assailant as if ready to shoot anything that moved. She glanced at Grace who was now sitting back on her heels, wiping the sweat from her brow with one hand.

Donato was securely bound, his hands tied in front of him. His face was pale and strained from the pain, and he winced with every movement he made. Sweat dotted his forehead and temples. Grace wanted to ask him if anyone else was coming. But she knew he'd only lie. She heard the crackle of the radio again and turned to see Laurent holding the communications piece to his mouth.

"*Essai radio*, Adele," he said into the radio.

"Donato?" Adele said. "What's happened? I only heard one gunshot."

"That's because Donato was the only one shot," Laurent said. "It's over, Adele. You're finished."

There was only static on the radio for several seconds before Grace glanced up and saw the car's headlights overhead where the woman sat. Slowly, Grace saw the headlights move. They were not backing up.

"Laurent!" she screamed.

The three of them looked up as the sound of the car's

engine revving came to them over the radio and in the distance. They watched in horror as the car plummeted over the ridge to the ravine twenty meters below.

74

Maggie led the way from the campsite even though Margaux was the one with the position locator on her phone. Maggie's urgency to find Grace and Laurent trumped her need not to see the terrible aftermath of that lone gunshot. If Grace had been killed, Maggie didn't deserve to be spared that. It was because she'd been too late and too ineffective in convincing the people who might have helped—

"Maggie, slow down!" Margaux said, panting behind her.

But Maggie couldn't stop. Now that she was determined to punish herself to the fullest extent that she knew she deserved, she needed to face it immediately.

"Do you have a gun I could use?" Maggie asked.

"Are you insane? No!"

Just then Margaux's phone rang. She shot out a hand and grabbed Maggie by the arm.

"Wait!" she said and then looked at her phone.

"*Allo?*" Margaux said suspiciously and then glanced at Maggie and her face relaxed into a near smile. "Yes, okay, okay fine. She is right here." She held the phone out to Maggie.

"*Chérie?*" Laurent's voice came across the line.

Maggie nearly screamed with relief and for a few moments was unable to speak.

"We are all fine, *chérie*," he said.

"But Grace—?"

"Grace, too."

"Oh, Lord in heaven!" Maggie said, so wrung out with relief and emotion that she sank to her knees in the dirt. "Oh, my dearest, I can't believe this!"

"Adele is dead," Laurent said.

"How?" Maggie asked.

"*Ce n'est rien*," Laurent said. "Did her police reinforcements show up?"

"Yes," Maggie said. "But it turns out they weren't *Adele's* men after all. They backed up Margaux and her men."

"Detective Labelle is a treasure," Laurent said. "I will owe her until I die."

"We all will," Maggie said, wiping tears from her eyes. "We're heading your way, darling. Sit tight."

Maggie handed Margaux's phone back to her.

"Adele is dead," Maggie said.

Margaux shrugged. "Oh, well," she said. "On the bright side, Detective Latour has enough collars tonight to make his career."

"Are you not astonished that he showed up to arrest Adele instead of backing her?" Maggie asked.

"Not really. It seems Adele took someone she didn't realize was connected to the detective."

Maggie stared at her for a moment until the penny dropped. "Joelle?"

Margaux nodded. "Right after he got the call from Adele telling him to come tonight, he got a call from his father telling him his sister had been taken."

"That reminds me, Margaux," Maggie said as she finally got

to her feet. "After we get Laurent and Grace, we need to find the man who was shot off the cliff. He's a friend of Joelle's and he was helping me."

Margaux looked at her in bewilderment and exhaustion.

"Seriously? Is it just you or does everyone you touch end up shot or thrown off a cliff?"

∾

Laurent watched the night sky soften into lavender and pink hues as dawn finally broke, slowly spilling golden light onto the deserted coastal highway below them. A new day was born, full of promise and beauty. To Laurent it felt like more than the birth of a new day. It felt like a new life unfolding around him.

Adele's thug lay groaning on the ground where Joelle and Grace had trussed him. Laurent glanced up at the camera and noticed that the red recording light was no longer on.

"How are you feeling?" Grace asked him from where she sat resting her ankle on an elevated rock.

"I'm good," he said, incredulous that he could say the words and mean them.

He'd literally been dying. And now he *was good*. He took in a long inhalation of the crisp country air into his lungs and felt the rush of his new reclaimed life fill his senses.

He heard the people coming through the woods long before they broke into the clearing. Maggie was first. She stood and looked around her, looking for him. She wore a sequined dress with sneakers, her hair pulled back in a ponytail. When she spotted him, their eyes met across the clearing. Then she ran across the space and flung herself into his arms, rocking him back on his heels, and nearly knocking him over in his still weakened state.

But he held onto her and felt her energy blossom inside him like a transferable strength that carried him past his weariness and pain. As he held her, he saw Margaux talking with Grace and Joelle and behind them came Margaux's loyal paramilitary duo.

Laurent pulled back to look at Maggie's face, knowing that when he did, she would see his as well. He watched the look of horror come over her and he shook his head.

"We are both alive," he said. "Nothing else matters."

He could tell she wanted to say more. But she merely nodded and gently leaned in to kiss him on the mouth.

"I will need to have a word with you about putting yourself in danger when you have responsibilities at home," he said into her hair, holding her tighter than he ever had before and so full of relief and joy he could barely breathe.

75

The sun had climbed steadily in the morning sky by the time the two ambulances came and loaded everybody up for their respective journeys to the hospitals in Monte Carlo and Nice. Maggie rode in the back of one with Laurent, Grace, Joelle and Margaux. Donato had his own ambulance and was being escorted to Monte Carlo by one of Latour's men.

It was while they were en route to Nice—Joelle for her dog bite, Grace for her ankle and Laurent for his snake bite—that Margaux got word from Latour that the British woman's body had been recovered and also Luc—alive.

Legrand had been found at the bottom of the cliff with a broken arm and leg. Several saplings had helped break his fall and he was nearly delirious by the time they found him. It turned out he'd not been shot after all but merely startled at the sound of the gun going off and had fallen off the cliff.

Margaux turned to Joelle.

"He's been life-flighted to Nice," she said. "You can see him there."

Joelle put a hand to her mouth, overwhelmed with

emotion, and Grace leaned over and gave her uninjured hand a squeeze. Joelle's eyes were brimming with tears.

"I don't deserve all that's happened to me," she said.

"Well, you certainly didn't deserve to be shackled, kidnapped and attacked by wild dogs," Grace pointed out.

Joelle glanced at Maggie and lowered her voice.

"You know what I mean," she said.

"Forget it, Joelle," Maggie said. "We're good."

"Really?"

Maggie slipped her hand into Laurent's where he lay with his eyes closed, resting.

"Are you kidding?" she said. "Laurent said you singlehandedly saved him on two separate occasions. I'm sorry all this happened to you but I'm glad as hell you were there with these two."

Joelle smiled gratefully at Maggie. Margaux frowned.

"So you're not going to press charges?" she asked disapprovingly. "You know she and her boyfriend both tried to steal from you."

Grace and Maggie both groaned.

"Ease up, Margaux," Maggie said. "People make mistakes."

Margaux harrumphed as if she didn't accept that answer for a single minute.

"What I want to know about is Detective Latour," Maggie said to Margaux. "Do you think he was in on it? At least in the beginning?"

"*Le Jeu?* Probably," Margaux said. "But when it became personal for him, he did what any brother would do."

"Thank goodness for us," Maggie said.

"What are you saying?" Margaux said, stiffening at Maggie's words. "Do you doubt that my men and I couldn't have done the job without him?"

"Surely, you're grateful for Latour's help?'

Margaux shrugged.

"It was a team effort," she said, before turning to Grace. "She sends me her share location and this over-the-top typical American text saying: *If I don't survive this, I need you to help raise a troubled girl who is Laurent's granddaughter. I'd prefer she didn't grow up to be a policewoman but that's your call.*"

Grace and Joelle laughed. And Maggie saw Laurent smile too although his eyes were still closed.

"Darling, you didn't," Grace said, wiping tears of laughter from her eyes.

"I thought it was quite restrained," Maggie said as she slipped her hand into Grace's. "I can't believe all that you've been through. I want to hear every minute of it."

"And you will, too," Grace said. "After I've had a shower, a manicure, and a weekend spa treatment."

They laughed.

"Oh! What about the antique secretary?" Grace asked suddenly. "Did it survive the push over the cliff? I have my heart set on seeing it at *Dormir*."

"Somebody stop the ambulance and throw this woman out," Laurent said with a growl to more general laughter.

Maggie smiled and looked at everyone—each to a degree battered or injured in some way—and she couldn't remember being happier or feeling more alive in her life. She pulled out her phone and texted Danielle.

<*Will call soon but Laurent & Grace are with me and ALL IS WELL*> She added a few heart emojis and then disconnected.

All *is* well, she thought happily. And what a miracle it was to be able to write those words.

76

The lavender-scented air was soft and warm as the sun set over the back garden of *Dormir*. Thick steaks and sausages sizzled on the grill, sending up mouthwatering aromas as Maggie surveyed the long wooden table that Amélie and Danielle had set for dinner. There was bread from the village *boulangerie*, a bowl of local olives, and a colorful salad made from the vegetables picked that morning from the *Dormir* garden.

Strings of lights flickered overhead on a wire as Maggie turned to watch Laurent man the grill with Philippe and Amélie by his side. Laurent was steadily recovering from his injuries, but Maggie knew he still had headaches. In the two weeks since they'd returned from Monaco, he kept a bottle of ibuprofen by his bedside now. He'd had a CAT scan at the hospital in Nice, but had refused all other tests. She would keep an eye on him.

Maggie knew that something more had happened during Laurent's ordeal although it was something he wasn't putting into words—at least not with her. Since they'd returned, Laurent had started inviting Maggie to join him in his nightly walks through the vineyard—his domain—and often urged her to accompany him on his shopping trips to the produce market in Aix with Amélie. There wasn't anything extraordinary about these changes, certainly nothing that Maggie could put her finger on, but in a way, she felt that Laurent was reaching out for an intimacy he'd taken for granted before and perhaps, for twenty-four really terrible hours, had imagined he'd never experience again.

She knew how he felt. Because she felt the same thing.

The sounds of the dogs barking dragged Maggie's attention from the pleasant pre-dinner scene before her. They'd brought their two dogs Fleur and Nougat from Domaine St-Buvard for the meal tonight; they were now romping around the garden with Philippe's dog Kip.

Philippe had been a little clingy during the first few days after Grace came home, but Maggie was happy to see that tonight he seemed to have shaken that off. When he wasn't parked at Laurent's elbow being his assistant cook he ran around the garden with the dogs and Amélie.

Maggie turned to go back in the house, waving to Margaux who had come for dinner tonight too. While Margaux tended to stay fairly close to Laurent most of the evening, Maggie believed that she and the detective had made real strides in their friendship. When Laurent wasn't around, Maggie was pretty sure Margaux would be open to going out for lunch or a drink with her.

Fairly sure anyway.

At some point after they'd gotten home, Margaux told Maggie what she had found out: It *was* Signore Tassoni who had indeed snuck out and disabled Laurent's car that fateful day. Adele had been following Laurent for months—once even coming back to Aix and following Grace where she overheard her plans to visit Italy with Laurent later in the month. Adele then went to Signore Tassoni, threatened his family unless he sabotaged the car, and sent her men to collect Laurent and Grace once they'd had car trouble.

Maggie never did find out if there were any further communications between Latour and Margaux or if she'd gotten into any trouble on her job for being involved in the off-the-books operation on Les Corniches that night.

Especially since there were four dead bodies at the end of it all.

Five if you counted the boy at the villa, although Margaux told her that no one had reported his death. Maggie wondered if the boy—and his brother shot in the back by Latour at the campsite—had family who were wondering what had happened to them. Or had the brothers been abandoned years before?

As for Vittorio Giordano, Latour seemed to think his arrest and conviction would hold, especially since there was an open warrant on him for embezzlement. One fewer mobster probably wouldn't make that much difference in the Monte Carlo crime scene, Maggie reasoned. But if one had to go down in flames, she was glad it was him. One of the first things she'd done when she got back home was to contact the local animal humane service to report that the dog Bruno was being mistreated.

She hoped they found him a new home with people who threw a ball for him and gave him cuddles.

And then of course, there was Adele.

Maggie knew Laurent blamed himself for not finding out where Adele had gone when she left St-Buvard twenty years ago. He held himself responsible for assuming Adele's acrimony for him was over when he knew that couldn't be the case unless she was dead.

Maggie hadn't known Adele all that well in her days at St-Buvard, but she did know that people who wrestled with mental illness often got worse, upending the lives of everyone around them. She couldn't find it in herself to forgive Adele for the terror she'd caused Maggie and her family. But she did have a glimmer of hope that someday she might be able to.

That was enough for now.

Danielle pulled the *tian* from the oven and settled it on the counter while she searched for a spatula to press down the vegetables on top. Maggie had seen her make this dish dozens of times, and watching her go through the motions now gave Maggie a deep sense of continuity.

"Mmm-mm," she said. "That smells so good."

"Amélie says it's her favorite now," Danielle commented.

Maggie was well aware that Amélie had refused to eat this dish the last time Danielle made it.

"She really has settled down," Maggie said as Danielle continued to press the veggies flat on the colorful *tian*. "What spell did you put on her?"

Danielle laughed.

"No magic, *chérie*. Amélie is just a child with emotions too big for her age."

Maggie had to admit that was a good way of putting it.

"Laurent has okayed our taking her to therapy in Aix," Maggie said.

"I'm sure that can't hurt."

"But seriously, how did you do it? I was sure she'd have burned *Dormir* to the ground by the time I got home."

Danielle laughed and put the *tian* on a tray which she then handed to Maggie to take outside.

"Well, we must keep trying, yes? In life as with anything, it is the only way."

Maggie had recently decided that nothing had tested her more than the past forty-eight hours had. And as hard as that experience had been, giving up had never been a serious option. Even when she knew how much she had to lose by leaving Amélie an orphan a second time, she couldn't have stopped trying to find Laurent and Grace.

As she walked outside in the twilight to the table with the *tian*, she gazed around the garden at the dear faces of each of the people who made up her family. Grace caught her eye and winked, reminding Maggie that her dear friend would always be able to read her. No matter the situation, no matter how far apart physically they were.

Maggie's glance fell on Amélie who was sitting in Laurent's lap at the outdoor table waiting for dinner to start, her dark head leaning against his shoulder, quiet and at peace for the first time all day. Maggie felt a rush of love as she realized how right Danielle was.

Life does test your determination, no matter how committed you think you are.

She put the vegetable dish down on the table, the summer torches flickering in the fading light and reflecting onto the faces of her loved ones.

But in the end, it's love that will guide you home.

LAURENT'S SOUPE AU PISTOU

Soupe au pistou is a classic Provençal soup that makes the most of the fresh summer vegetables and herbs from Laurent's garden at Domaine St-Buvard. This recipe serves eight.

Ingredients for the soup
    2 cups dry cannellini beans
    3 bay leaves
    6 TB olive oil
    6 leeks, white and light green parts only, peeled and diced
    4 tsp fresh thyme
    5 medium carrots, peeled and diced
    5 medium zucchini, diced
    2 cups green beans, tips removed and cut into 1-inch pieces
    8 cloves garlic, peeled and minced
    Sea salt and fresh-ground black pepper
    1 cup fresh or frozen green peas
    2 cups dried elbow or other small pasta

Ingredients for the pistou
    2 large cloves garlic

½ cup olive oil
1 big bunch fresh basil leaves (around 4 cups)
3 small tomatoes, peeled, seeded and dried
3 oz Parmesan cheese, grated
1 tsp sea salt

Soup Directions
1. Soak the beans overnight in cold water. Drain.
2. Heat the olive oil in a Dutch oven or large soup pot.
3. Sauté leeks until soft.
4. Add beans and 4 quarts/4 liters of water. Simmer until the beans are soft.
5. Add carrots, zucchini, green beans, potatoes, thyme, tomatoes, peas and garlic.
6. Simmer 1 hour, stirring from time to time, adding water as needed.
7. Add sea salt and fresh-ground pepper to taste.
8. Add pasta and simmer until pasta is soft. (The pasta will soak up water so replace water as needed.

Pistou Directions
(Make the pistou while the soup is cooking.)
1. Dice the tomatoes.
2. In a large mortar and pestle, pound the garlic and the salt into a paste.
2. Chop the basil leaves finely and pound them into the garlic until the mixture is relatively smooth.
3. While pounding, drizzle in the olive oil slowly, then pound in the tomatoes and cheese. Taste and add more salt if desired.

To serve: to each bowl of hot soup, add a generous portion of pistou to the center and swirl gently.

ABOUT THE AUTHOR

USA TODAY Bestselling Author Susan Kiernan-Lewis is the author of *The Maggie Newberry Mysteries,* the post-apocalyptic thriller series *The Irish End Games, The Mia Kazmaroff Mysteries, The Stranded in Provence Mysteries, The Claire Baskerville Mysteries,* and *The Savannah Time Travel Mysteries.* If you enjoyed *Murder in Monaco*, please leave a review on your purchase site.

Visit her website at www.susankiernanlewis.com or follow her at Author Susan Kiernan-Lewis on Facebook.

Printed in Great Britain
by Amazon